## Advance Praise for *The Daughter Who Got Away*

"Freedman is as skilled at capturing the nuances of religious practice as she is at sketching the wild and beautiful Canadian landscape. Though the novel details Israeli and New York locales, Freedman's writing shines most when she's honoring the setting where no one would expect to encounter complex discussions related to Jewish identity. Themes of change and continuity, acceptance and rejection are all handled with elegance. *The Daughter Who Got Away* is a moving and provocative encounter with various modes of religious being."

—*Foreword Reviews*

"For me, Leora Freedman's wonderful new book is a vivid and magical time capsule from an era and a place which are extremely dear to me: the Upper West Side of Manhattan, where my grandmother lived for much of the twentieth century. With artistic skill, Freedman manages to bring people like my grandmother and the society she inhabited back to life."

—**Chana Jenny Weisberg**
blogger at www.jewishMOM.com
and author of *Expecting Miracles* and *One Baby Step at a Time*

"In this compassionate family saga spanning generations and continents, Celia, an aging sophisticated New Yorker, sets out into the wilderness of British Columbia to retrieve her free-spirited daughter Sharon, who abandoned a privileged city life for a hut in the bush. With vivid imagery, Freedman brings the setting alive. The author reveals wisdom and sensitivity in capturing the contrasting worlds of Celia and Sharon as the two bond together and are enriched by the reunion. This is a rich and powerful work: lyrical, contemplative, and polished."

—**Lily Poritz Miller**
author of *In a Pale Blue Light* and *The Newcomers*

"*The Daughter Who Got Away* is an engrossing and accessible novel. Set in greatly varied environments and time frames, Leora Freedman's novel captures intergenerational ethos through the prism of family relationships and diverse cultural experience. A novel of ideas, *The Daughter Who Got Away* reflects the complexities of Jewish existence of our time in multi-layered stories and engaging characters. It is a work that stays with the reader and deserves a wide readership."

—**Frieda Forman**
editor and translator of *The Exile Book of Yiddish Women Writers* and *Found Treasures: Stories by Yiddish Women Writers*

"In this warm, insightful, and often funny novel, Leora Freedman plumbs the mystery of how—and to what extent—we can love one another across differences of culture, belief, affiliation, and even temperament. And in Celia and Sharon Rosenbloom, she has created two women who show us that it's never too late for growth, change, and mutual understanding."

—**Susan Olding**
author of *Pathologies: A Life in Essays*

"Leora Freedman paints a colorful collage of people, place and time: including the younger and older characters, the urban and wilderness settings, and the present and past generations. The Jewish flavor and nostalgia for Yiddishkeit are woven throughout *The Daughter Who Got Away*. Freedman demonstrates beautifully in this multilayered story that universal human themes such as aging and human connection are indeed shared by all people; thus our personal stories are linked to our collective history."

—**Liz Pearl**
editor of *Living Legacies: A Collection of Writing by Contemporary Canadian Jewish Women*

"This is a novel steeped in the details and nuances of life in Jewish communities, whether in the rural expanses of British Columbia or among the urban enclaves of Manhattan. It is bustling with scenes and conversations full of insight and generosity, holding up a mirror to the attempts we all make at forging connections between family members across the generations, even as we take our own deepest measure."

—**Linda Rui Feng**
author of *City of Marvel* and *Transformation: Chang'an and Narratives of Experience in Tang Dynasty China*

"Leora Freedman's novel *The Daughter Who Got Away* is a touching story of a mother and daughter who each undergo a spiritual transformation while coming to terms with their underlying differences. Set in two polar opposite Jewish communities (Upper West Side Manhattan and rural British Columbia), Freedman's novel explores the tension between assimilation and religious renewal. Populated with a diverse array of characters, the novel offers a glimpse into the ways in which Jewish life can flourish in disparate settings."

—**Sharon Hart-Green**
author of *Bridging the Divide: The Selected Poems of Hava Pinhas-Cohen*

"The marvel of Leora Freedman's splendid novel *The Daughter Who Got Away* is that the story gets so deeply inside both Celia, a widowed Jewish Manhattan mother, and Sharon, her wilderness-loving daughter. The rich voices of both the older and the younger woman fill a whole continent with the texture of their relationship. They evolve to a fascinating balance when the New Yorker comes to her daughter's outpost in British Columbia. Whether in a solitary Canadian cabin or a huge Central Park West apartment, whether with a sexy shepherd single dad and his ethereal daughter or a rabbi or the ghost of a deceased husband, a constellation of relationships unfolds, all in the midst of questions of Jewish life and how—and where—to live it. Misunderstandings abound, but this novel, exquisitely attuned to nature *and* to human nature, is about understanding. Freedman writes for mothers and daughters everywhere."

—**Molly Peacock**
author of *The Paper Garden*

# The *Daughter* Who Got Away

# The *Daughter* Who Got Away

## Leora Freedman

Yotzeret Publishing
St. Paul

This is a work of fiction. Names, incidents, and locales are the product of the author's imagination or are used fictitiously, and any resemblance to any actual persons, living or dead, or actual locations is entirely coincidental.

First edition.

THE DAUGHTER WHO GOT AWAY. Text copyright © 2016 by Leora Freedman. All rights reserved. Printed in the United States of America on acid-free paper. No part of this book may be reproduced, scanned, or distributed in any form whatsoever without written permission from the publisher except in the case of brief quotations embodied in critical articles or reviews. For information, address Yotzeret Publishing, PO Box 18662, Saint Paul, MN, 55118. http://yotzeretpublishing.com.

The tzaddi logo is a registered trademark of Yotzeret Publishing, Inc.

Cover photos:
"Tourist Cabin" copyright ©SNEHIT | Shutterstock.com
"Emerald Lake Café" copyright ©Jack Booth | Shutterstock.com

Grateful acknowledgment is made to the following for permission to reprint previously published material:

Jason Aronson: *The Judaic Tradition: Jewish Writings from Antiquity to the Modern Age* selected and translated by Nahum Glatzer. © 1987. Reprinted with permission of Rowman & Littlefield.

Behrman's Jewish Book House: *The New Haggadah* edited by Mordecai M. Kaplan, Eugene Kohn, and Ira Eisenstein. © 1944. Reprinted with permission of Behrman House.

While every effort has been made to provide accurate Internet addresses at the time of publication, neither the publisher nor the author assumes any responsibility for errors, or for changes that occur after publication. Further, the publisher does not have any control over and does not assume any responsibility for author or third-party websites or their content.

Publisher's Cataloging-in-Publication data

Names: Freedman, Leora, 1959- , author.
Title: The Daughter who got away / Leora Freedman.
Description: St. Paul [Minnesota] : Yotzeret Publishing, 2016.
Identifiers: ISBN 978-1-59287-140-7 (print) | LCCN 2016931119
Subjects: LCSH Women--Family relationships--Fiction. | Mothers and daughters--Fiction. | Generations--Fiction. | Jewish women--Fiction. | British Columbia--Fiction. | New York (N.Y.)--Fiction. | Jewish fiction. BISAC FICTION/Literary.
Classification: LCC PS3606.R44 D38 2016 | 813.6—dc23

To the memory of Florence B. Freedman

# I

## NEW YORK, 1990

Snow swirled around Celia as she hurried up 72$^{nd}$ Street, carrying four boxes with chocolate cake, lemon meringue pie, petit fours, and assorted fancy cookies for her guests that night. The light over Central Park was softening through the gray Hanukah clouds. Tonight was the first night, a candle in the darkness of all motherly worry. Hers was mainly about her younger daughter, Sharon, living alone in a tumbledown log cabin in British Columbia. Sharon had promised to be at home late this afternoon so Celia could phone her before the holiday. Walking, Celia glimpsed her own face reflected in a shop window. She looked like her own mother and father if they had both lived to the age of seventy in the same body. How she missed them still! It was they who'd begun inviting people for dinner on the "First Friday" of each month, and she carried on the tradition, though in an easier, more secular, after-dinner fashion. Her mother had chopped gefilte fish in the big wooden bowl; no matter how many guests her father collected on his way home Friday night, there was always miraculously enough food. She could make her next children's book out of that, painting the endless dishes and guests in bright swirls—another project! Celia lived for her projects, which took the edge off motherly worry, aging, and the loss ten years ago of her husband, Raymond.

Inside her apartment on Central Park West, she left the cake boxes on the front table next to the large, cast bronze sculpture of a racing charioteer. Draping her coat over his chariot, her mink hat perched on the head of one of his horses, she went quickly to her bedroom office in order to avoid Sophia, the maid. Celia was a retired professor of art education and an illustrator of children's books. For ten years now she had been writing a book called *Sonia Delaunay and a Vision of Art for Our Schools*. She had great admiration for Sonia's talent as a modernist painter and textile designer— why, Sonia had revolutionized the approach to color more than any of her male colleagues in Paris of the 20's! Celia's own existence stood for realism, pedagogy, inculcation. Yet she admired the side of life Delaunay had experienced: abstraction, experiments, a wild dress designed by the artist, worn while dancing at the Bal Bullier ballroom, a favorite haunt of Paris expatriates. Oh, Celia had loved to dance, how she had danced at New York parties, and on the sea-packed sand of Tel Aviv, her young limbs swinging in the moonlight!

She had never become computerized, she was too old, and so she rummaged through note cards to find material for her next chapter. Drawings, notes, and articles also covered her bed and filled eight boxes. These were piled behind a Chinese screen decorated with a dragon curled submissively around the legs of a serene maiden. In Celia's mind the maiden was the Goddess of Finished Projects, and the dragon was Time. If only children could be taught about beauty and harmony through the materials they held in their hands as they learned! If real art could be democratized like the computer! It was not too late; she sat at the small desk in her bedroom where she preferred to work and furiously typed a few paragraphs.

"Dr. Rosenbloom!" trilled Sophia. "Doc-tor-Ro-sen-bloom!"

Reluctantly Celia left her desk, went through the foyer containing bookshelves and her collection of hundreds of dolls from around the world, and walked to the end of the hallway. People had started treating her like a dotty old lady, so she'd decided they all must call her Dr. Rosenbloom—the doorman, the elevator man, even her own doctor—in deference to her PhD in art history and her continued validity as a human being. When Sophia came to work for her two months ago she thought they might as well begin that way, though Sophia was darling, really.

Sophia stood in the main foyer, an eighteenth-century silver Viennese hanukiah in one hand, a blackened polishing cloth in the other. She was too absent-minded to make a good maid. In Russia she had been a television newscaster, disbelieving, she said, every word that left her mouth. With her chin she indicated the stack of bakery boxes Celia had left on the table next to the charioteer. "Dr. Rosenbloom, I saw the cakes, and I remembered it is Hanukah *and* First Friday. I can arrange cakes for you before I go, on the plates, and then you won't have to. I am so sorry to interrupt your work on the book!" Sophia said *book* as if speaking of a holy object.

"Yes, you may arrange the cakes after you've finished with the hanukiot—I'll get down the platters." Sophia wanted nothing more than to interrupt her, poor thing; she hungered for culture, for conversation. It was more possible to live a cultured life in Moscow, less possible in America without money, specifically less possible in Brighton Beach, where Sophia lived with her daughter, who was in fourth grade. Also Sophia hungered for religion, including, though not restricted to, Judaism. She had asked for and listened to a lengthy explanation of the Bodhisattva which sat on the cabinet in Celia's living room, over the collection of Japanese ivories.

"Just don't think too hard about any of that silver," Celia joked.

"No! Never!" Sophia was often quite literal. But in Russia she had studied parapsychology, at peril to her life. She could bend silver spoons with her mind and heal with her hands. She held the Viennese hanukiah in her hands tenderly, fingers spread, as if it were the head of a person she was trying to heal. "It is one more candle for each night?" she asked. Celia nodded, thinking that she must find in her collection a small, inexpensive hanukiah to give to Sophia before she went home that afternoon.

"Thank you, Dr. Rosenbloom! You must think of us as people who have just come out of a prison!" Sophia's eyebrows, normally rather arched, went higher with fervor.

So Celia's mind, as she settled her body back into the comfortable chair in front of her bedroom desk and the window overlooking Central Park, was saying unhelpfully, Prison! Prison! She turned over a scrap of yellow paper on which she'd made research notes and saw printed directions to a hall on Long Island where they were holding the wedding reception for her friend Estelle's grandson. Next week he was marrying a non-Jewish girl, a wonderful choice in every other way, getting her PhD in linguistics. He's so shy, Estelle said, and she was the first girl he tripped over in graduate school. Nearly everyone was making these weak excuses now. Celia and her friends could not think of any real reasons half their grandchildren were marrying non-Jews; like Sharon's log cabin, this was an unexpected development.

The phone sitting on the side table rang. It was Estelle, who always called when Celia thought about her. They usually spoke at least once a day.

"Yedidja came home upset," said Estelle. Celia and Estelle had spent 1938 and 1939 studying Hebrew in Palestine: Celia returned with a broken heart but Estelle returned with her husband, Yedidja Abella. "He went to visit his grandfather's grave in Jaffa. So he found they've torn down the old gravestones and put up a big new monument to all the martyrs of '21. The problem is, there are two stones on this monument that are both for his grandfather. One has his name, Yosef Abella, and one says Habibi, 'dear one,' which is what his Arab neighbors called him."

"Oh, my."

"Yes, and so Yedidja went to the municipal archive and told them that Yosef Abella and Habibi are the same person, but this stupid woman said they are two separate people on the computer, and she refused to believe him. Now he just keeps saying, they've divided my grandfather. He told her it was a very great sin in Judaism, to divide a person. Anyway, I picked out an evening bag and shoes for the wedding. And they've all been waiting for some speech of approval from me, that I think it's wonderful he's marrying this girl, and I won't make that speech. They can make me feel too guilty to stay home, but they can't make me say I'm happy."

Celia thought how Estelle had never really been happy; she had a melancholic temperament, unlike Yedidja. Celia remembered him singing Ladino romances during the Arab riots, while piling up stones on the ground floor of his family's house in Jerusalem. There had always been this matter of his grandfather, Yosef Abella, one of the first Jews to settle in Jaffa in the 1880's, murdered in the riots of '21. Yosef was found lying in the street in front of his house, knife wounds in his front and back. Celia had seen the photograph, an old man with a long white beard, his mouth still open in his final cry. His children had climbed out the windows to hide in the candy factory next door. The Arabs yelled, you are a Muscobi, and Yosef cried, I am not from Moscow, I'm from here! Actually he was from Morocco, and before that Gibraltar. Not that his origins made any difference to the Arabs who murdered him that day. Afterwards everyone argued over whether his murderers were local Arabs or others from outside Jaffa. Did the same Arab friends who had called him Habibi, dear one, betray him during the riot and divide his body with their knives? Some said yes; Yedidja was not sure; his sister said yes, he knew them.

After hanging up, Celia sighed and did not return immediately to her work. Instead, she swiveled her chair to look at the Sonia Delaunay painting on the wall, its planes of color suggesting concentric circles of feeling, deeper and deeper to a still center, then out again into the world of shape and movement. *Brilliant*, she thought, as if she'd never seen the picture before. Were the murderers his neighbors or not? The story repeated, went round again, truth somewhere in the still center of history, unrevealed. This was the kind of thought she could tell Sharon, if she could put it into words when they spoke. She wished she could talk to her daughter in person; it was already two years since Sharon's last visit to New York.

Celia reached for part of a cream-cheese-and-olive sandwich sitting on a small Limoges plate, balanced on top of several folders relating to consulting work she was doing for the Board of Education, and took a bite. They'd have books created entirely by the students, their personal histories literally unfolding like one of the experimental books designed by Sonia Delaunay, decorated with designs derived from their mix of cultures. Could it be included in the curriculum this coming fall? She felt the dragon Time snapping at her legs. *Delicious*, she thought, as if she'd never eaten olives and cream cheese before. *I shouldn't have gotten fat.*

The phone rang again; it was her very dear friend, Bernard. "Hello, dear," she said. He always said she was voluptuous, that her body was the sign of a generous nature.

"Hello darling," replied Bernard. "What sort of day is it?"

"A bit distracted. Delaunay and distraction seem always to go together. Of course I'm glad you called, dear, how is your day?"

"Fine. I was on the phone with the Nigerians a good part of the morning, but the projects are coming along." Bernard was an expert in water resources and international relations; he ran his own consulting business. He was almost ninety and rarely missed a day of work, driven as he was by a great vision of an ordered world, with goods, energy, and opportunities flowing easily from one end of the globe to another, like well-managed water resources. "I won't keep you, darling, if you're working. I just wanted to know what time you expect me tonight."

"Maybe you could come around seven-thirty. Then I'm sure to be ready when people arrive."

"Ah, so you do appreciate me. Maybe you ought to have married me."

She thought of him, always in a nice suit with cufflinks, and those wonderful European manners. His face was delicately formed and seemed to smile even in repose; his brown eyes were alert—a creature poised equally for thought or action. Certainly she loved him.

"You'd be very tired of me by now if I had," Celia reminded him. "My desk is piled with papers, and on the papers are a bowl with dried-up breakfast cereal, a plate with a half-eaten sandwich, and three dirty tea cups. And the bedroom floor is littered with things I mostly can't mention."

Bernard was fastidiously neat. Eight years ago, two years after Celia's husband Raymond died, Bernard had proposed. When she'd objected on the grounds of her appalling personal habits, he said, you will live just as you've always lived, and I will arrange everything; I'll clean up after you. She replied, and I'll hate you for it. So they didn't marry, though they saw each other every day and often traveled together. It was not as it might have appeared, since Celia did not approve of sexual relations outside of marriage. She wasn't a prude, she just felt that way.

After she and Bernard hung up, she looked at the small statue of a galloping female centaur on her desk. She picked up the centaur's front legs, which held down a pile of papers, and pulled out another scribbled research note. The centaur pranced, her little bare breasts pointing straight ahead.

Each day, Bernard's goodness enveloped Celia, making her old mane stand up and her hide glow while her hooves trotted along confidently. His own mother had been a white witch, expert at performing spells against the evil eye. Sonia Delaunay was the western European version of spiritual counselor, perhaps, democratizing the harmony of the soul.

Ah Sonia, she thought, you weren't the first Jew to have the big vision, permeating every clip-clop of the hoof on the long, long road. You were adorable in your patchwork dress, you deserve another book written about you. She typed several more paragraphs, consulting Delaunay's lecture at the Sorbonne, interweaving it with stuff about the nature of perception, going, going. Then she heard the maid calling to her that she'd be leaving soon. Celia got up to give her the hanukiah.

Sophia was overwhelmed by the gift. "Thank you, you are an angel. When we first came we didn't have money, so the landlord threw us out on the street with our suitcases. He was Jewish! And I said, these are the Jews? But you are not like that, *you* are a Jew."

Celia was moved by this assertion. She walked with Sophia to the door, where she opened the three deadbolts and then went out to wait with her for the elevator man. After stepping into the elevator, Sophia kept smiling and waving to Celia through the gilded mesh inner door right up until the man shut the outer door, which was made of dark polished wood. Once Celia was back inside the apartment alone, the three deadbolts relocked, she counted how many hours remained before she was supposed to call Sharon: two and a half.

On Sharon's last visit to New York she'd arrived on this very night, the eve of Hanukah. They'd sat together in the breakfast nook off the kitchen, which had a view of the whitened rooftops clambering out into the murky sky. Sharon looked so uncomfortable in New York; her clothes were all dark and simple, and slightly out of date. She'd been mourning the loss of Thunder, her Cree boyfriend. Celia often thought she should have realized Sharon's difference from other people earlier. Or perhaps she did, but she'd thought it meant Sharon would distinguish herself in New York.

"He became so jealous," Sharon told her. "It wasn't rational."

Celia stirred sugar into her tea with one of the small silver spoons her mother had brought over from Russia. She'd liked Thunder, but she wanted her daughter to marry a Jew. Thunder had struck her as charming, charismatic, and very damaged by that sexual abuse business with the priests. "Were you in love?"

Sharon smiled and lifted her cup to her lips; she drank her tea strong and plain. "That's a good question. But I'm not so sure it's part of the contemporary idiom, if you don't mind my saying so. Everything is always shifting, you're never quite sure what all those nice, loaded old words mean. I *was* very taken with him."

Celia looked at their two reflections in the double glass doors leading to the terrace: the slender young woman, curved like a young fruit tree, the heavy old woman with a large brooch resting on her breast. This piece of jewelry was actually a tiny abstract canvas painted by David—a former student and her closest friend next to Bernard—which she'd had set into a small silver frame. Yes, Celia wore the badge of art on her breast: She'd illustrated over two dozen books. Her other badges—photographs of her older daughter Anna with her husband and their children, of her son Marc with his wife and children, and of Sharon—hung framed above the breakfast nook table. She'd earned all her badges. She remembered leaving the house to teach, her briefcase in one hand and the kitchen garbage in the other, looking down at her feet and noticing that she wore two different shoes.

Celia felt she was getting too old not to speak her mind; she felt freedom rising in her old breast beneath the energetic strokes on David's little painting. "In my opinion," she said to Sharon, "it's good you didn't settle for that. You can afford to wait until love appears. I think it will."

Sharon just grimaced, as if the idea of love really wasn't all that appealing to her.

Celia then told Sharon what she'd never told any of her children: how her own young heart was broken by Yunis, her boyfriend during the years she spent in Palestine. Of course

Yunis was Jewish and his name was actually Yonatan, but he was known by his Arabic nickname. He was handsome, intelligent, extremely charming, and mean. "It's amazing to think that if I'd settled for that, I might not have met your father in New York the following year," she told Sharon. "I would have missed meeting the love of my life."

Sharon said, "Wow," shaking her head. "You've always been very romantic."

At that moment, Celia realized she sounded old-fashioned. Sharon was resistant to falling apart if some man didn't love her, but she was also, in some curious way, shielded from love itself.

It wasn't exactly traditional to do so, but Celia worked that evening until just an hour before her First Friday and Hanukah guests were due to arrive. Sharon was expecting her to call ten minutes from now. Celia changed into a dark knit dress and the Navajo squash blossom necklace she and Raymond had collected on a trip west in the forties. She quickly applied some lipstick and then sat down at her desk again, reaching for the telephone. The snow had stopped and the city had sharpened her appearance for night, the lights across Central Park glimmering like the jewels of a woman who enjoyed being the center of attention. She dialed the number that would ring in the log cabin in British Columbia where Sharon was living. Alive and well, Celia hoped, always at the moment she dialed seeing someone creeping up behind Sharon in the woods, grabbing her axe, blood on the snow—her baby!

Sharon answered on the second ring. "Happy Hanukah."

"Happy Hanukah, dear," Celia replied. "Did you get my package?"

"Yes, yes. I've got my candles; I got all the stuff you sent, thanks."

"I'm so glad you're celebrating Hanukah!"

"Look, the Maccabees lived in the hills. Somebody has to do it."

Well, she sounded like herself. There was still plenty to worry about, though. When Sharon had said she was quitting the law firm in Vancouver and moving out to the interior to work as a legal aid lawyer, Celia could still picture her daughter's life in East Coast terms, something like a small town practice in Vermont; the son of a friend of hers had done that. But last spring, when Sharon cut her work week to three days and moved into the mountains two and a half hours' drive away from the town, into three hundred and sixty acres of what she called the bush—and she admitted the cabin was half gone—Celia began to worry. Her strategy was not to object directly because that might drive Sharon further away. Instead, she tried to hang on to the parts of her daughter that she could still understand, while gently voicing her concerns, like what about social life out in the bush. Above all, Celia feared the dark forest of estrangement from a child, in which so many families lost their way.

"What are *you* doing for the holiday?" she asked her daughter now.

"Sitting in front of the fire. I was just out for two hours splitting wood. It was terrific. It's so quiet, there's about three feet of snow on the ground, and all I could hear was the axe hitting the wood over and over, and then this sharp sound ringing through the trees when the round finally splits. It's very elemental. When you don't hear human voices you realize that everything has a voice—the axe, the trees, the snow, and they're all sort of reverberating all the time. That sounds crazy, right? You're sitting in the middle of New York."

"The Maccabees lived in caves, didn't they?" Celia mused. "There must have been a lot of echoes."

Sharon laughed. "Celia, I miss you. What are you doing for the holiday?" This was another of Sharon's strangenesses which Celia had learned to accept: Sharon insisted that they relate as adults, which to her meant calling her mother by her first name.

"I'm having First Friday here tonight. Marc and Maxine are coming, and Anna and Ronnie and the children are driving up." Anna had three children and taught special education; she did not restore log cabins or take Indian lovers or do any of the other things her sister did, but the two of them were close, Celia knew, always writing to each other. Marc, despite being a psychologist, couldn't understand Sharon. He said he had unresolved issues around her.

"I've been thinking, maybe you could come out here and visit me," Sharon suggested. "It's been a long time. I think if you came, you'd understand the attraction of this place."

Celia's heart filled with relief: Of course the love was still there, even if they didn't understand each other. But at the same time, she saw a small plane with herself in it, green-faced, bumping through dark clouds over frozen mountain peaks. "Out there?" she asked. Of course she'd visited Sharon in Vancouver, but she had no idea what means one employed to go further. The Interior, they called it. She thought that sounded ominous, like *Heart of Darkness*.

"I don't mean in winter. You could come in the spring. There's a nice little motel about ten minutes down the highway."

"There's a motel? I had no idea!" Celia laughed. That didn't sound too much like a heart of darkness. There would be a bed, and eggs served on a thick white country plate in the morning. They discussed flights—on normal airlines, after all—the small store also ten minutes down the highway, and the wild lupines that purpled the meadows in spring.

"There are so many things I'd love to show you." Sharon's voice was more intimate now, projecting the silence that surrounded her, those black woods lit by the moon glowing on the crystal crust of snow. "When you're out here, you see that the world is in a constant state of new creation and death. The hardest thing is learning how to perpetuate evolution and become truly human."

Celia wished her daughter would just get married—she was thirty-nine, after all!—and then have a baby. Break right into the cycle of new creation, Sharon, and perpetuate—what, after all, does it really mean to be human? Her daughter frightened her, actually. Sharon would want to show her mother sheer cliffs and rock faces; Celia's old veined legs weren't up to this. "I'm not young any more, dear. It's been a long time since I walked up a mountain."

"We'll go slow. The mountain will wait for you."

AFTER CANDLE LIGHTING, Celia presided over her long table full of guests drinking coffee and tea. The bright petit fours were arranged on Celia's mother's Russian silver tray, brought over on the boat nearly one hundred years ago. Several conversations were going on at once.

"You can look down, even from this apartment, and see them selling crack on that corner," Estelle was complaining to Celia's son Marc.

"—but in his new book, he seems to be growing up," said her daughter Anna to Marc's wife, Maxine.

"It's a multimedia performance based on the interaction between my woodcuts and her dancing," her friend David told Bernard.

"—but he was called *both* Yosef *and* Habibi," Yedidja explained to Anna's husband Ronnie, who nodded with his eyebrows raised. "They have divided my grandfather into two people!"

"—you see, the rabbis used the miracle story to teach about Hanukah as a spiritual victory," Bernard informed David's girlfriend Patricia. "But these days most people don't believe in miracles, so we say the candles symbolize the triumph of the human spirit over tyranny."

"I still believe in miracles," Marc said loudly to Bernard, who was sitting at the opposite end of the long table. In the center, amidst all the cakes, sat two plump white porcelain doves a client had given to Raymond. Celia always felt they were listening to the conversation. Marc continued, "When everyone in my department agrees on something, it's a miracle. When I find a paper I'm looking for on my desk after searching for a week, that's a miracle." There was laughter.

"Your desk must bear a certain resemblance to your mother's," said Bernard, placing his hand over Celia's on the table. Her heart leaped like one of the little flames they'd lit hours ago. Sometimes, oddly, loving Bernard made her feel closer to Raymond's spirit, hovering over the table which looked much as it always had. She'd never baked Raymond a thing and he never minded.

"Yes, we're very right-brain in our family," commented Marc.

"We also have a tendency toward miracles," Celia began. The room got quieter. Her guests knew that she did not offer them homemade gefilte fish chopped in a big wooden bowl, but she *would* offer them well-seasoned stories. She considered that the duty of a hostess, something she'd learned in her parents' home.

"We had an ancestor who was a tzaddik, a type of saint," she continued. "He wasn't the showy sort of tzaddik, with a court and a following, but a simple sort of person, an artisan, perhaps. And he lived in a town called Konotop, which means 'the-place-where-horses-sink,' because the main street of this town had the reputation of being so muddy when it rained that horses could hardly walk through. One very rainy afternoon, it was time for our ancestor to go and pray in the synagogue. However, he had no shoes to wear that day because he'd given them to some poor soul who needed them more than he did. So he had to walk to the synagogue in his white woolen stockings, through Konotop. And the miracle was this: When he arrived, there was no mud on his feet at all. His stockings were as white as when he'd left his house." Celia paused, thinking of Sharon alone in the woods, facing a landscape harsh as the steppes. She saw her daughter walking barefoot beneath the huge Canadian pine trees, the snow not chilling her feet at all; then Sharon flew across the crust of snow, buoyed by angels.

"That's marvelous," said Maxine.

"He must have been an extraordinary personality," said Bernard. "I imagine that's a type of repeating folk tale, told about each great man through the generations."

"I like it because it's not about anything flashy," Celia remarked. "Just a nice, homey, unpretentious little miracle."

AFTER THE OTHER GUESTS had gone home, Bernard and Celia sat close together in the most intimate corner of the living room, where two sofas converged next to a large stone sculpture of a man leaning over to speak to a boy who stood at his knee.

"I'm thinking of going out to visit Sharon in the spring," she confided.

Bernard, his arm resting along the back of the sofa behind her, as Raymond's had often done while they were courting a half-century ago, sat up straighter in his perfectly tailored suit. "To the northern forest?"

"Yes, though of course, in British Columbia it's considered the southern forest."

He didn't look amused. "Celia, it's not that I haven't perfect confidence in your survival skills, and your resilience, your abilities. I'm simply concerned that it's a very remote location. Where's the nearest doctor?"

"I think there's one around." She understood his concern; she'd posed the same question to Sharon last year. The doctor seemed to be closer at times, further at other times. She didn't quite understand it herself. But much as she feared these things, when she thought of the warm note in Sharon's voice when she invited her, she wanted to go on this trip.

"Are there proper roads?" Without waiting for an answer, Bernard continued, "That area was a magnet during the gold rush, wasn't it? Wouldn't there still be some pretty rough characters around?"

"Darling, I'm not setting out for the North Pole with some dogs and a sled. There's a highway and a little motel with a café. Sharon will be there, and she's not a rough character." As she said that, she felt a tremor of fear. She'd seen her daughter only a few times in the ten years since she'd left New York, and not at all since she'd gone into the Interior. Sharon was now a person who talked about mixing cement in a wheelbarrow and chinking a log cabin, with her degrees from Swarthmore and Yale!

"I didn't say *she* was rough, I meant the area in general. If I were you, darling, I'd find out exactly how far this place is from the nearest town."

She already knew: two hours on a winding road, three in bad weather. "Quite possibly it's not as far as we think. I suppose it depends on what you call a town."

That sounded wrong, and she hated to win Bernard's disapproval. It made her feel their souls begin to separate, as when Raymond had left her for the other world. Even now, Raymond often surfaced in her dreams, sitting at a heavy wooden desk with his papers spread out. In this other world he worked with full energy, without the overburdening responsibility for his family, for prisoners in Russia, for the many people who came to him for help, which had curved his shoulders in life. Funny that her image now, of Sharon, was so similar to Raymond in the other world. She imagined her daughter sitting alone in the log cabin, working at her computer in a small circle of light. Around her were the eternity of mountains and rivers and roads that separated one soul from another.

THE NEXT MORNING, Celia loaded the dishwasher with last night's teacups and cake plates. It whirred in the kitchen with a sound suggesting order and calm in the universe, while she sat in the breakfast nook writing letters—her usual Saturday morning occupation. In two hours she was to have lunch with some cousins from Raymond's side. The phone rang. It was Marc. They talked about how nice First Friday and Hanukah had been. Celia said it was altogether a rather miraculous holiday evening. She had even spoken to Sharon, she said, and was thinking of making a trip out to see her in the spring. This would be very good, as none of them had seen Sharon for two years.

"I want to see her," Celia told him. "And I really want to know what her life out there is like."

"Does she have a guest room in her shack in the wilderness?" Marc sounded incredulous.

She explained about the existence of the highway, the café, and the motel, none of which they'd suspected. She didn't mention the reverberating voices in the striking axe, the trees and the snow. "And it will be spring. It'll be warm, and she says there are beautiful wild lupines."

"Warm probably means you don't need a balaclava, just your winter coat."

Celia laughed, but uneasily.

"Do you really think you can depend on her?"

"What? She's always been very dependable."

"I'm not so sure," said her son. "How do you know she won't suddenly decide she needs to hop in her four-wheel-drive and head for some distant mountains to clear her head, just when she's supposed to be meeting you?"

"I don't think she would," Celia said, but weakly because something about the way he said it made it sound possible. "She said she'd meet me at the airport in Calgary and then we'd drive west through the Rockies. There's a particular glacier she wants to show me."

"A glacier?" He paused. "Can't Bernard go with you?"

"It's not really his sort of trip." Actually, Bernard had suggested going along, but she wanted to spend a couple of weeks alone with her daughter.

"Well, there's a special warning device I've seen advertised. It makes a very loud sound that would scare off bears or let people know you were in trouble. Maybe I'll get you one before you go," Marc suggested.

She thought he was hard on his sister. Marc said once that he'd become super-responsible, super-conventional, just because Sharon was so irresponsible and unconventional. Celia thought he exaggerated, but she couldn't help worrying after they'd hung up. The letter sat unfinished as she pictured Sharon, possessed by some strange compulsion, driving off in her truck and leaving her elderly mother standing alone on the edge of a glacier, at the mercy of bears, demented gold-seekers, and slowly creeping ice.

Then Estelle called. "You have to think of your physical condition. We're not young anymore," she objected, when Celia mentioned the trip to British Columbia. "Are you up to walking long distances? And you'll have to wear tough jeans."

"Jeans!" Celia had scarcely ever worn pants and certainly not jeans, much less tough ones. "I'm beginning to wonder if I'm really up to this. No one else seems to think so."

"Well, it's your decision. We weren't exactly comfortable in Palestine either, if you recall."

"I remember I had no long underwear and I was freezing."

"You see! Celia, will she treat you nicely?"

"Of course she will. She's my daughter, and she's a nice person!"

"I know, I know, but sometimes people get so wrapped up in themselves."

"Stella, I really feel I must go. My daughter is getting away."

## II

About six weeks later, Celia received a letter from Sharon.

*I've made quite a good trail to the north part of the property, and I often ski up there in the afternoon on the days I don't go to the office. It's funny that the deer and rabbits and even the mice will all use a trail I've made instead of making their own. I often go up there to see this tree I love. It's a thick old larch, about thirty feet high. You can see it was badly damaged in a forest fire—the whole middle section of its trunk is an enormous black crater. The wounded bark is now worn into smooth black ripples, very eerie-looking. But above that the tree is clean, growing big curved limbs, and very wide at the top. Did you know that larches are deciduous? They look like evergreens but in the autumn the needles turn yellow and fall off. So if I scrape aside the snow a bit with my ski, I see piles of yellow needles on the ground. In spring the larches get little purple cones. I named this tree The Survivor Tree.*

Celia hadn't known that Sharon still felt so wounded by the breakup with Thunder. Learning this was like suddenly coming upon the larch tree itself, in Central Park perhaps, its beautiful spreading branches just starting to bud, its black center gaping. Oh Sharon, she thought. My little purple cone.

# III

## GREENVILLE, BRITISH COLUMBIA

In the first blue light of a Monday morning, Sharon noticed a great horned owl sitting on the hood of her truck. She could make out the strange hulking shape, the two pointed ears. On Mondays she worked at Legal Aid in town, so she'd woken up early to put some documents through the computer. The owl was facing straight ahead, like a giant hood ornament. It was warm in the cabin as she'd fired up the wood stove earlier, and she wiped some condensation off the window to see the bird more clearly. Her old boyfriend Al Thunder used to say that an owl is a sign of coming change.

She didn't want to think about Thunder, whom she'd heard on the CBC last night, being interviewed about the priests who'd sexually abused aboriginal children like himself. She got up quickly from her swivel chair, which rolled backwards on the plank floor she'd refinished. Since she was already wearing a skirt and stockings, all she had to do was put the documents in her briefcase. Then she pulled on her coat and opened the weathered wood door that had been salvaged from the collapsed barn.

She stepped outside, walking carefully in her town shoes; then she closed the door softly so as not to disturb the owl. The air was freezing, and a red streak of dawn showed down the field, through the trees on the other side of the creek. She walked closer to the truck, and the owl turned its head to look at her. Now she could see its brown and white speckled feathers, its white chest, and its strong feet curled around the underside of the truck's hood. She drew in a deep breath of cold air and felt stauncher than she had for a while. Then, softly, she unlocked the truck door and put her briefcase on the seat. The bird, on the opposite side of the wide hood, still hadn't moved.

"Owl, I have to go to work."

The owl stared. It did not look like it would ever move, and something in her rejoiced at the thought of driving down the highway with her staunch-owl hood ornament.

"I have a client coming at nine," she told the owl.

Still the bird stayed. As Sharon watched it, she felt her body getting round, softly feathered, her cold feet in town shoes clawing a hold on the earth.

"You'll have to fly off," she informed it. "This truck moves fast; you won't like it."

Then the owl lifted its wings and, after a small disdainful flap, swooped off the truck hood and back into the woods. Sharon watched it swinging gracefully through the small spaces between the trees, which seemed almost magically to widen to accommodate the huge wingspan.

She started up the truck and bounced down the poorly graded road. The sun had risen like a huge gold star above the neighbors' farmhouse in the distance. It was very early spring. She noticed that the circles around the trees where the snow melted first were now so wide they were almost touching.

AFTER WORK THAT DAY, she drove to the Jewish Community Center. Like the Legal Aid office and much else in town, it looked like a small shopping mall. HAPPY PURIM! read the billboard in front. MEGILLAH READING, COSTUME PARTY 6:30 P.M. TONIGHT. For two years she'd been reading the center's billboard, which looked like the billboards on all the churches out here in the Bible Belt, constantly advertising SPAGHETTI SUPPER and lectures like DOES MEANING EXIST?

Oddly, she'd been to the Native Friendship Centers in Vancouver and here in Greenville; she'd danced at a dozen pow-wows, but she'd never been to a Jewish place anywhere in the province. Thunder claimed he had a Jewish grandfather, though to most other people he said he was pure Cree. Together, they'd never done anything Jewish. Sharon simply assumed she wouldn't have much in common with the Jews here in the same way she assumed that most of her New York or even Vancouver friends would never—no matter what they promised—come out to her cabin in the bush.

Her costume, taken from her office wall, was a small, modern Kwakiutl bear mask given to her by an old woman, the daughter of a Kwakiutl chief, whom she and Thunder had first met at a native lawyers' conference in Vancouver. Disguised as Bear, Sharon walked across the dark parking lot. She opened the door of the community center into a bunch of teenagers and the blast of a dozen pop songs, mixing with each other into electronic mud.

When it subsided she asked, "Is this the entertainment?"

A kid answered, "No, it's instead of a grogger."

A tall man with a pair of moose antlers tied to his head came out of the sanctuary, where she could hear they were chanting the megillah. On his feet he wore a pair of mukluks. "The teenagers are blotting out Haman in their own way," he explained. "That's a very interesting mask—do we know you?"

"I'm Bear."

"Bear. I see. Do you have another name, Bear?"

A roar of groggers, stamping and shouting came from the sanctuary, and the teenagers flipped on their boom boxes. A small Queen Esther emerged and tugged at the hand of the man in moose antlers. He waved and smiled apologetically. "Talk to you later, Bear!"

"We could hitch down to Friendly Burger," suggested a teenage boy with a huge music machine under one arm. He was dark, handsome, and wore no costume.

"What about Purim?" asked Dr. Bear, anthropologist taking a survey from behind her mask. She could see not much had changed since she was a teenager.

"I'd rather go to Friendly Burger," the dark-eyed boy told her.

"You're not a kid, are you?" asked a girl wearing a leather headband that may or may not have been a costume.

"No!" shouted Bear, over another blast of noise.

"I never go there because their fries aren't kosher," said a lovely girl with the face of Queen Esther, number one beauty of the kingdoms of Persia and Medea. Her blond hair was braided and twirled into a shining crown on her head, with a few golden ringlets spiraling to her bare white shoulders. She wore a black strapless evening gown—of some vintage, Sharon guessed. "They use beef tallow."

Sharon turned her eye-holes on the girl. "Do you keep kosher?"

The girl looked at Bear with eyes dark blue as a mountain lake. "Yes. I'm also the only one who wants to be here." She was, in fact, the only teenager discernibly in costume, besides the boy wearing a rock-climbing outfit and a rope with carabiners slung over one shoulder, who'd read part of the megillah. He explained that he was the rabbi's son and couldn't even consider going to Friendly Burger.

During the next outburst of noise, Bear lumbered into the sanctuary and sat in one of the new-looking pews of light wood. The man in moose antlers was now up on the bimah reading the megillah, his hand aloft to silence the children, who wore Halloween costumes and rubber monster faces, whirling their groggers and screaming. Next to Moose was, presumably, Rabbi, in a big curved cowboy hat and a leather jacket with fringes. The rabbi took his turn reading, then, in a winding cantillation that pierced the din. He was about six and a half feet tall with dark, fine features, and the notes he sang had a Middle-Eastern wail at their tips. Bear leaned forward in her seat. When he read "Haman" and the room exploded, he pounded the podium and shouted, "This noise is the indestructibility of the Jewish people!" The congregation ignored him; they were laughing and eating little chocolates from baskets passed around. A very pregnant woman sitting in front of Sharon turned and offered her a basket of caramels, which she refused, and then a man offered her brandy in a little cup, which she tossed back through the bear's mouth hole. The man laughed and clapped.

"Excuse me," said another man sitting next to her. "Why are they making all this noise?" He had more serious eyes than most people, and she detected an Alberta accent.

*What?* thought Bear. *You prairie farm Jews don't know about Purim?* "Well," she hastened to explain before the next burst, "whenever they read the name of Haman, the enemy of the Jews—" She was interrupted by the sight of the very pregnant woman, who had risen and made her way to the aisle. The woman sat down heavily on the edge of the pew and breathed deeply with her eyes closed. She wore a long embroidered Bedouin gown, and every inch of her skin looked swollen. Her head was tilted back as if toward the sun.

"I think that woman is going to have her baby very soon," remarked Sharon's neighbor, speaking with the slow cadence of a country man to whom birth and death, heat and cold, darkness and light are the primary stuff of everyday life and also the most deeply interesting things he knows.

There was tumult, then, a carnival of woman-going-into-labor. Cowboys and fairies and a giant deck of cards tried to help her walk to the door, but she had another contraction before they got even halfway. Then she couldn't walk and was carried by six or seven men while Moose, who was apparently a physician, shouted to them, "Bring her to the library and call an ambulance—I'll get my emergency kit from the car!"

The rabbi seemed to be reciting a blessing, loping down the aisle on long legs; he then shouted to someone about some blankets in the day care. From the hall there was a long wavering cry, then the sound of doors shutting. Children stood around in their costumes, looking surprised and giggling. Since all the adults were distracted, the boys vaulted over the pews and the girls threw candies at them.

"Excuse me," said the man next to Sharon again, "but I may as well introduce myself. Jacob Wakeman." He held out a hand to the bear.

She pulled off her mask and wiped her sweaty face. The lights dazzled her; it was strange to have peripheral vision again. "I'm Sharon Rosenbloom," she said, and they shook hands. The pretty Queen Esther had appeared in the doorway. She was talking to the rabbi's son who wore the rock-climbing outfit, her strapless-clad, kosher-fed body curving gracefully toward him. She looked over at them and waved.

"That's my daughter," said Jacob, waving back. "Otherwise known as Queen Esther."

"She looks quite capable of ruling Persia and Medea and a whole lot of other things," said Sharon. Jacob looked at her with his daughter's deep aristocratic-blue eyes, and then he suddenly laughed. He seemed both tense and enthusiastic, throwing himself into his laugh. She felt curious abut him, though that was as far as she let the feeling go, not wanting to feel the hunger for a man.

"—and *she* gave birth in their Jacuzzi!" someone was saying.

"My daughter-in-law went into shock after they botched her episiotomy," another woman's voice said. "By mistake the doctor cut into—"

"—broke my tailbone—"

"—and in this town in Mexico," a young woman with a ponytail was saying, "they'd never heard of natural childbirth, so I was the doctor's demonstration piece. All along she said, 'Now you see, the patient is controlling her breathing, the patient is sitting up in a comfortable position'—but I thought I'd die when she said, 'The patient will now get up and *walk* to the delivery room.' I felt like I couldn't let her down—"

There was a chorus of female groans.

Then an older woman appeared in the doorway of the sanctuary. "There's coffee and cake if anyone wants it! Rabbi Bernstein says we'll have refreshments first and then resume the megillah. Circumstances permitting, of course," she added with a stiff smile. Sharon noticed that all the older women had absolutely no sense of humor about the unexpected birth. She wondered if they really feared for the mother's life or if it was just a remnant of the tradition of not acknowledging the coming baby until they knew all was well. "Coffee!" said the woman again.

Jacob's daughter beckoned him to the door, and he invited Sharon to come and meet her. The rabbi's son had disappeared. "The kids all went to Friendly Burger," said Queen Esther. "All of them whose parents said they could, and some whose parents didn't say."

"This is my daughter Keturah," Jacob said.

"I'm Sharon Rosenbloom."

"Oh yes, the bear," said Keturah. She nodded toward the closed library door. The doctor, without his antlers, had darted out for some boiling water and a sheet of plastic; then he banged the door shut again. "Dad, maybe you could help."

"I don't think they need me. They've got at least two or three doctors here. Plus Rabbi Bernstein for the spiritual angle."

The rabbi, in his cowboy hat, was swaying back and forth in front of the closed door, reciting in Hebrew from a miniature book. "Psalms are the protective language of God," he said, glancing up at them. He resumed in English. "'By day the sun will not strike you, nor the moon by night . . .'" A young man wearing a yachting club sweatshirt stood nearby listening, half smiling, but everyone else ignored the rabbi.

"We have prune, poppy seed, *and* apricot," said a female voice from the kitchen. Then the rabbi paused in his prayers. The dishes stopped clinking, and for a moment there was a crack in the palpable noise of Purim and the shock of the birth, a slender, widening silence. For a second no one spoke.

Then from inside the library came a long scream, followed by shuffling and voices. Several minutes passed before they heard the faint cry of the baby. Then they heard yipping, howling laughter. Sharon thought the mother sounded like a coyote in the hills.

"Unbelievable," said Rabbi Bernstein. "She's laughing like Purim." He held up a long finger. "It's the only holiday that will remain with us after the Messiah comes."

"All these children here," fretted one of the coffee-and-cake ladies, peeping out of the kitchen with a cake server in one hand. One of the mothers had gathered the younger children into a circle and was trying to read a story, but the kids kept jumping up and racing around.

The library door opened slightly and out slipped a young woman whose large, bright green eyes shone. She went to the rabbi and they held each other. "Tanyale," he said; it was his wife, no doubt.

"It was unbelievable." Her voice was shocked, reverent. "It was the same exact way Elise herself was born when her parents were escaping, trying to get out of Hungary. The baby was born just the way she was, with the cord around her neck. She was blue. Mike did CPR." Tanya wiped her eyes.

"Thank God!" said the rabbi, the young man in the yachting club sweatshirt, and the cake lady all at the same time.

"And Elise's *mother* was also born with the cord around *her* neck," Tanya added. She and her husband looked at each other and nodded, as if agreeing that God would be given big points for revealing His hand in the birth of Elise's baby.

"Well, these things run in families I guess," said a man who stood, stirring sugar into a plastic cup of coffee.

"Do you have children?" Jacob asked Sharon. When she said no, and that she wasn't married, he indicated Keturah, who had wandered off to the refreshment table. "That was her mother's evening dress. She died almost ten years ago."

"I'm sorry," Sharon murmured. She found herself looking at Jacob's hands. He worked with them, she could see; there was that faint shadow of wear that made the patterns of the palm more visible. Looking for something to say, she commented, "This rabbi and his wife really believe in God—I've never seen anything like it. I mean in our generation."

"I have faith too," Jacob said easily. "Whenever I'm out in a cold barn in the middle of the night delivering a kid or a lamb, and I have to do a caesarean or something, I'm certainly glad to think of the Almighty guiding my hand."

Sharon became aware of her breath, the way she was when the freezing air of the mountain valley was in her nostrils, the smell of pine and manure. "So you don't live in town."

"No, I have a sheep and goat farm on the Boundary River. It's not too far from here." He laughed. "A large distance of the mind, perhaps."

She smiled. "Yes." She didn't tell him that she lived in the same valley and that they were probably neighbors. He seemed to assume she lived in town. Keturah returned, holding a poppy seed hamantaschen in one hand. She ate it delicately, her square white child-looking teeth biting the dark jam. Sharon thought vaguely that Jacob and his daughter looked unlike any Jews she'd ever seen. Their blond curls framed rather round faces, and the cadence of their speech was so purely Canadian-interior. Well, who knew? "One summer," Sharon told them, "I was a shepherdess on a kibbutz."

"So you've been to Israel!" Jacob said, as if this were a magnificent accomplishment.

"I want to go to Israel *very* much," said Keturah. "My dearest wish is to start an orphanage there. Do you think it would be possible?" She looked at Sharon, her mouth a serious rosebud swallowing Haman's hat, almost supplicating, as if Sharon had the keys to the future orphanage in her pocket.

A siren sounded far away, then closer, in the parking lot. The big double doors were flung open and white-suited paramedics appeared. They carried Elise and her baby out of the library on a stretcher. The mother was pale and smiling a little, the baby wrapped up in what looked like somebody's ski jacket. "They'll be fine!" said Dr. Moose-antlers, and other people cried, "Mazal tov!" Elise's husband and two older children followed the stretcher down the front steps and climbed after the paramedics into the ambulance. Its interior spilled yellow light into the darkness.

"I watched the whole thing!" said Elise's daughter to the costumed people who'd followed them outside and were crowding the front steps of the community center.

"I didn't look," said her brother, whose face was painted purple and green, with gold glitter around the eyes. "Well, maybe I looked once."

"—no place for children!" exclaimed one of the coffee-and-cake ladies.

Sharon and Jacob looked at each other and laughed. He had the eyes of an intelligent animal, knowledgeable but with no real guile. His body looked hard and supple. For an involuntary second Sharon imagined him grappling with her in a dark barn, pressing her against a sweet block of hay. He seemed to possess some wisdom and some permanent wound, both won in struggles with angels of his God in freezing barns at night, the blood of newborn kids on his hands.

"I have to go now. Nice to meet you," she said abruptly to this farmer and his daughter, whose lipstick, Sharon now noticed, had smeared across her upper lip. A moment later she exited into the night behind the now-faint siren, bear mask in hand, her face feeling unusually exposed in the cold. A Purim spiel: Attorney Rosenbloom Beds the Jewish

Shepherd. Driving home fast over the pass, she was glad to be well ahead of them.

MUD SEASON ARRIVED a few weeks later. At its height one day Sharon's truck was roaring in four-wheel-drive over the road that led into her land and was shared with the neighboring farm. As she approached the farmyard, the sheep and goats and a few cows looked glued down in a mixture of mud and manure. She saw her neighbor, Charlotte Hammond, waving to her, and braked as Charlotte, in a green parka and black rubber boots to her knees, stepped toward the big wooden gate. Sharon opened the side window and watched some kids suckling, up to their knee joints in mud. The wind was still cold, and there were small patches of snow left in the shady areas of the forest, where each twig and pine cone had melted a space around itself.

"Hello!" said Sharon as Charlotte approached.

"Would you like to come in and have some tea, make like neighbors?" Charlotte invited her.

Inside Charlotte's living room, Sharon sat in a wing chair upholstered with a design of cherries and leaves. Through the doorway she could see Charlotte pouring water into the teapot and setting cookies out on a plate. "How is your place coming along?" Charlotte asked. "Are you comfortable?"

"Yes, I was quite warm all winter. The logs are good insulation."

"I'm glad to hear that. We haven't seen you at all; you're a real hermit." Charlotte set the tea tray down on a table between Sharon's wing chair and another. She was about fifty, thin, with bangs over large tired eyes. Yet there was curiosity in her eyes as well, and her movements, as she poured the tea and stirred sugar, seemed reluctant but energetic. It was as if she were saying, well, here are the roles we have to play, newcomer and old-time farm family, so let's get on with it. Sharon knew she had lost her husband, and that her son and his family lived in a house about a quarter-mile away. The Hammond's farm was more than six hundred acres.

"Well, I've had a fairly heavy case load this year," Sharon said.

Charlotte looked surprised. "Oh, yes. Well, I suppose at Legal Aid you have no shortage of clients." This was perfectly true, yet she made it sound like a liability.

"Your fireplace is lovely," Sharon said quickly. It was built of large stones, the browns, grays, and cream of the surrounding hills. Directly in front of the fireplace was a sunken area, also lined with the stones, where comfortable chairs were arranged in a semi-circle. On the wall above the mantle hung the antlered heads of a moose and a buck deer. What Sharon couldn't stop looking at, though, was a bear skin which lay stretched across the middle of the sunken stone floor. It was a complete cinnamon bear, spread flat with its head still on, and the plain spring light coming through the windows made its fur go a cool gold color. The mouth was open in a growl. Sharon looked at the expression with interest, having so recently been a bear herself.

"My grandfather shot that bear in 1920, when he first came to homestead in this valley."

"Really?"

"Yes. They had a long standoff. He met the bear when he was walking up on the west ridge one day. The bear was coming up the path and Grandpa was coming down toward it. They both stopped, and neither of them would move. Grandpa didn't want to go off the trail because it was getting dark and he didn't know these hills very well at that time. So he said to the bear, 'Bear, I'm going forward and you're going back.' Then he waited, and the bear thought about it for a while. Finally the bear took a step back. So Grandpa took a step forward. Then he said again, 'Bear, I'm going forward and you're going back,' and waited. And the bear took another step back, and Grandpa took another step forward. They kept on that way until Grandpa had advanced a considerable distance forward. Finally, the bear turned and ran off in another direction."

"But he shot it?"

"That was later. It must have followed his trail down here, and it kept going after their food cache. It even broke a window in the log cabin, so he had to shoot it." Charlotte indicated the plate of cookies on the tea tray. "These are Easter bunny biscuits," she said. "I always start making them early, with five grandchildren."

Sharon smiled knowingly, as if she were quite familiar with Easter bunnies and grandchildren. She picked up a bunny biscuit and bit off one ear. "They're very good," she said. Charlotte nodded once, bending her head deeply in almost mocking thanks. She was utterly gracious, attentive and pleasant, and at the same time conveyed a weary desire to be rid of Sharon, the world, Easter bunnies, everything.

"The farm looks wonderful," Sharon added. "I see you're building another pen." She ate the other ear.

"For the sheep. But the wool market is very bad right now. The whole world economy seems sick."

"That's true."

Charlotte sipped tea from a china cup with orange and blue flowers. All the china on the tea tray was beautifully mismatched, a riot of painted designs. "The fellow on the other side of our hill is doing very well, though. Do you know the Wakemans?"

Jacob and Keturah! "No, I don't think so."

"Well, he came out here a few years ago from somewhere on the prairies and bought that farm. He raises exotic breeds, and I would say he's tripled his number of animals in the last few years. He's the most successful . . . farmer in the valley." She smiled and added, "He thinks he's the biblical Abraham with his flocks."

Sharon bristled. "How do you know he thinks that?" she asked as sweetly as she could.

"He'll tell you so himself. He tells everyone that he's a Jew, although he's about as Jewish as I am. One of their ancestors was a peddler and was fussy about his food—but I don't think that automatically makes anyone a Jew. He has a lovely daughter who's in my grade ten class, and he's filled her head with all this made-up Jewish ancestry, of which she's very proud. Of course, I'm only her science teacher, but in my opinion she could be learning something a little more to the point."

Sharon, who was not afraid to live alone in the cabin surrounded by four feet of snow, felt a bit afraid of her neighbor. She had not intended to live in the countryside as a Marrano—usually she dropped 'I'm Jewish' casually into a conversation, as western Canadians did not recognize even the most blatantly Jewish names—but Charlotte's tone made her hesitate. "Well, it probably makes her feel special."

"I'm not saying she isn't special!" Charlotte sat up straight in her wing chair as if Keturah were here, arguing her Jewish ancestry. "She's very gifted, she could do anything. When I see a girl like that I think of myself at that age."

"Yourself?"

Charlotte laughed with charming mockery. She held an uneaten bunny biscuit in her bony hand and gestured with it. "I was a young girl from a small town up north, and I was going to be a veterinarian or a scientist—I was going to be like Rachel Carson!" The bunny hopped into the air. "There's just so much time in life we don't realize we have."

"I always think there's less time than we realize," said Sharon.

"Oh, no. No. And there's her father, running after all the Jews up in Greenville. If they knew who he really was they'd send him packing."

"Maybe, maybe not." Sharon observed again the bear's open mouth revealing its sharp teeth. Its dark claws were curled on Charlotte's stone floor. Sharon had the urge to lie down on the bear's cinnamon fur and enjoy the reversal of danger changed into softness, death into luxury.

# IV

## NEW YORK

Bernard looked so wonderfully energetic in his houndstooth jacket, bending over the wires of the public address system that Celia hooked up every Passover for her seder. It was hard to believe he'd be ninety-two next month. He and Celia's brother Yale were running wires along the living room floor and up behind the cabinet where Celia displayed her collection of historic *haggadot*. This included a facsimile of the famous medieval Bird's Head haggadah in which Moses, Miriam, and the Children of Israel were portrayed with human bodies topped by feathered birds' heads and beaks; no one really knew why, though scholars argued about it. They brought the wires behind her ivory Buddha who sat, idol-like with serenely pursed lips, surveying the white-clothed tables and long-stemmed silver wine cups. Then the wires traveled out the door to the dining room, where the table was extended to its full length with smaller tables added on at the end. Eighty-six catered kosher meals of chicken, tzimmes and green beans were expected at nine p.m. Yale stayed in the living room, while Bernard stationed himself in the dining room and Celia checked the sound in the library, where more tables crowded the space between her book-lined walls. A crackle and a whoosh went over the public address system.

"Testing," said Yale's voice from the living room. "Hello, hello. 'Once we were slaves unto Pharaoh in Egypt.'"

"Can't hear you in here!" called Bernard from the dining room.

"It needs to be louder," said Celia from the doorway of the library. "*Avadim hayinu, ha-yi-nu,*" she sang tunelessly, as always. We were slaves, we were. She could see Bernard fiddling with a black wire draped on a corner of her mother's portrait. The large seder was her parents' tradition which she and Raymond, and now she alone with Bernard, carried on. The guests always included gentiles who'd never been to a seder before, and years ago there were many Jewish refugees.

"'But the Lord, our God, brought us forth with a strong hand and an outstretched arm!'" Yale's voice boomed through the living-room microphone into all three rooms simultaneously.

"It's working!" said Celia.

"Has the slavery in Egypt been proven?" Bernard challenged Yale through the dining room microphone.

"Well, they haven't found any archaeological evidence," Celia announced through the library microphone. Then the three of them met in the foyer, still carrying on their amplified conversation. "But of course it's questionable whether people living as desert nomads would've left any traces of their existence."

"They haven't found Moses' sandals?" quipped Yale.

"The desert preserves things very well," Bernard objected. "I won't believe the story until they find something."

"He's always been sort of a goy," Celia told her brother, indicating Bernard, who stood very straight and smiling, handsome in his hounds-tooth.

"I'm not a goy, I was raised in a good Jewish home," said Bernard. "My mother was a white witch. I was an especially beautiful baby, so she rubbed me with salt to protect me from the Evil Eye. I know a lot about Jewish tradition."

"He knows the traditions," Yale intoned into his microphone. He blew some dust off the top of it. "'Let all who are hungry, enter and partake.' We say that in Aramaic so no one will understand and take us up on it."

"Really?" asked Bernard, interested, as if Yale had begun a serious interpretive discussion. Only the immediate family could tell when Celia's brother was joking.

"That is not true. Aramaic was the *lingua franca* of the Middle East, and anyone who recited that could end up with eighty-five guests, like me," said Celia. She turned to Bernard. "Sophia made chopped liver from my mother's recipe. I just have to spread it on some of those little matzah crackers."

In the kitchen, he helped her take down the silver trays and arrange the chopped liver on matzah, which was the same every year and expected by her guests. He used the spreading knife as dexterously as if he'd been doing nothing but serving her mother's chopped liver all his life. When she tried, it came out all lumpy.

"My mother would have said you were too thin," she told him. "Of course, she was fat herself, and I'm very much like her."

"Then I'm sure she was wonderful in every way," he said gallantly. "Including being fat." He followed her as she went into the pantry for more matzah crackers, putting his arm around her waist as she reached into the cabinet. She felt very free and happy for a moment. It seemed as if, on this night of liberation and rebirth, their hair might turn black, their wrinkles smooth out, and their unfinished projects miraculously complete themselves. She put down the crackers and she and Bernard did a little dance together in the pantry, stepping in perfect harmony toward the unknown points that still lay ahead of them both.

IT WAS A RITUAL: Once a year, on the eve of Passover, Celia unbolted all three locks on her heavy apartment door and propped it open with the doorstop, while the elevator man, turning his old-fashioned wooden wheel, brought up the car again and again full of guests. Tonight she stood near the open door greeting people in her Indonesian dress, batikked with a design of bright spring flowers. Estelle and Yedidja arrived, followed by Bea and Burt Moore-Owen, two Unitarian ministers who were like members of the extended family; and then Celia's daughter Anna with her husband Ronnie and their three children; and Celia's son Marc, his wife Maxine, and their three children. The oldest of Marc's children, Claire, had also brought along a strangely-attired boyfriend. Celia kissed them all, except the boyfriend, John MacDermott, with whom she shook hands.

"Most people call me Mac." He had a charming smile but wore a jacket that looked like he'd bought it at the Sally Ann, with huge pointed lapels that reminded one of tailfins on a car. "Except my mother, who calls me Johnny."

"It's nice to meet you," Celia said, with a little flat quaver in her voice, probably undetectable to anyone who didn't know how much she liked to see Jews marry other Jews. Claire, her favorite grandchild and the one blessed with artistic talent, was standing next to this Mac wearing a pair of tight leather pants. From her belt buckle hung a tiny padlock, dangling over her pubic area.

"Should I call you Mrs. Rosenbloom? Or Grandma Celia?" Mac asked. Apparently he was one of those people who imagine that a sweet smile will make others overlook any degree of impudence. Celia was reminded of Yunis, the boyfriend who'd caused her a great deal of misery when she was Claire's age. She wondered if Mac had the key to that padlock in the pocket of his tailfin coat.

"You may call me Dr. Rosenbloom," she said, equally sweetly.

"Grandma, I brought vegetarian chopped liver!" Anna's daughter Rachel, who was fourteen, presented Celia with a plastic tub of whatever it was, mushrooms, walnuts, and some other things, she said.

"Wonderful!" exclaimed Celia. "We'll put it out on a special tray." In between greeting relatives from the Island she saw only on seder night, colleagues from the college, teachers she'd taught or taught with ten, twenty, thirty, forty years ago, she described to Rachel where to look in the pantry for the Delft tray with white swans swimming into the green distance.

Briefly her mind served up a memory of Rachel only a year ago, reciting a blessing from a large Hebrew school textbook over the Creole chicken Ronnie had cooked, using a recipe given to him by a co-worker. Celia was visiting that weekend and she wouldn't eat chicken with bacon. Neither would Anna or Rachel's brother Bruce. But Rachel insisted on reciting a Hebrew blessing before she and Ronnie ate it. Now Rachel was a militant vegetarian who wouldn't even eat Celia's kosher chicken and wouldn't eat off plates that had once held meat—so she was either strictly kosher or had rendered the whole question of kashrut irrelevant. Celia's grandchildren changed so rapidly, it was hard to keep up. Though she tried, they disoriented her.

Now Claire, for instance, smiling and giving Celia an affectionate hug, was unaware of how the tiny lock dangling over her pubic area disconcerted her grandmother.

"I'm so glad to see you, dear," Celia told her. Claire had been away at the University of Michigan since the winter break. "I'm so pleased about your prize." She turned to the company standing around them. "I'm a bragging grandmother, so I'll tell you that Claire has just won first prize in a photography contest sponsored by a gallery—what is the name of the gallery, dear?"

"Heresies." Claire smiled and tossed her long golden hair off her shoulders.

"Mazal tov!" cried various guests.

"Of what is this a photograph?" asked Yedidja.

"It's a complex image," Claire began.

"Of me," said Mac.

*Oh!* Celia thought. She'd seen the photograph on the exhibit invitation, but she hadn't known it was Mac in that odd pose, half naked except for the skin of some animal. It did have a certain drama, she had to admit; it was graphically strong, all those shards of glass reflecting like glittering arrows around him. Yet the intimation of unleashed sexual fantasy shocked Celia.

"—so we found this old cougar skin in a gun shop," Claire was enthusing to her cousins and Celia's Unitarian friends, "and the guy traded it for a video camera Mac had that wasn't working—Mac's a film student—"

"You used a real animal skin?" Rachel objected. She'd brought out her vegetarian chopped liver on the swan tray.

"A person would never guess this was mushrooms and walnuts," said Ephraim Alexander, the principal emeritus of the high school where Celia had taught forty-five years ago. "It tastes exactly like actual flesh." He grinned wickedly in Rachel's direction. In Celia's time Ephraim had given—for no extra pay—an intensive after-school Great Books course for the students, who were poor, mostly Jewish, and ambitious.

"The poor cougar, it was probably shot while it was attacking someone's cow before you were even born," said Rachel's younger brother Bruce. "Man, this family is full of neurotics. Especially in the female department."

"Shut up, Bruce," said Rachel.

"The lighting almost killed me." Claire had learned a new, dramatic way of speaking. "I wanted certain pieces of the broken glass to become prisms around him and some fragments to remain in shadow so you can see they're only ordinary glass. I had so many wires—I almost burned down my apartment."

"The judges said I look like a young prince in a degenerated palace," Mac told Celia's seder guests. "They said, 'the artist creates an aura of sumptuousness and danger.'"

Celia noticed that Marc and Maxine looked proud of their daughter, and Anna and Ronnie looked interested. But the older people—Yedidja, Ephraim, herself—were obviously puzzled, and Bernard looked as if he were trying to understand someone speaking one of the many languages of which he knew only a smattering.

"They said it evokes the danger women feel in a relationship with a man." Claire laughed. "I mean, sure, but it's also about the enjoyment of danger, and the male attraction to the cougar skin in the gun shop and the female need to place him exactly in the center of that, wrap him up in it, just to see what the results will be—it's like acting out—"

"Acting up!" Mac broke in.

Marc went on smiling proudly. He himself had dated an African-American girl while he was doing his PhD field work on gangs in east New York. Celia and Raymond talked him out of marrying her by pointing out what a hard time the children would have. Nowadays it wasn't the children who had a hard time, only their grandparents. It upset Celia's certainty of her own being flowing on, as one is certain that a river continues after one has crossed it. To look upon the Exodus as if you yourself went up out of Egypt—but to whom would you retell the story? Celia had trouble even understanding her grandchildren when they spoke; they talked so fast it hardly sounded like English.

Yedidja, Estelle, Yale and his family, Celia, and Bernard sat at the long leaders' table in the living room, the windows overlooking Central Park behind them. The sun was setting in a red haze, and the tables looked lovely, decorated with flowers and seder plates with their wheel of symbolic foods. Celia thought of Sharon, the one close family member still alive but celebrating Pesach elsewhere, in her cabin in the woods. When Celia called earlier this afternoon to wish her a happy holiday, Sharon said she'd invited an old Holocaust survivor she'd met in town, an artist who painted houses for a living, and his wife, to join her for a seder in the cabin.

"'Once, while Moses was tending Jethro's flock...'" read Yale, "'a young kid ran away. Moses ran after it until the kid came to a pool of water, where it stopped to drink. When Moses reached the spot, he said, "I did not know it was because of thirst that you ran away. You must be weary." So he carried the kid on his shoulder.'"

In Sharon's most recent letter she'd written, *there's a plant called kinnikinnik that keeps growing, its leaves bright green, under the snow all winter.* Celia's eyes filled with tears. Oh Sharon, why under all that snow, my kid?

Yedidja looked out at Celia's guests from under his serious bushy eyebrows. "To be kind to animals has always been a very important idea in the minds of the Jewish people," he said into his microphone. He was a veterinarian. He returned to the animal theme, embroidering it, whenever the seder allowed. The Torah tells us, he said, that Aaron's rod, cast down before Pharaoh, turned into a serpent and ate the rods-turned-into serpents of the Egyptian sorcerers. Perhaps modern people were a bit skeptical about all this. "But even my own mother," Yedidja told them, "had the skill of charming a very large snake. It happened in the old days in Jerusalem, when I was a boy. In those days everyone lived in a quarter, where the houses were built around a courtyard in the center. One day, a woman of our quarter was hanging clothing to dry outside in the courtyard. Suddenly, this woman saw that a large snake had found his way into our quarter. I remember it had the design of a Palestinian viper, which is a very poisonous snake. It was lying in the courtyard, and it had frightened the woman so that she was standing like a stone—she couldn't move. And then all the other women and the children, and I and my brothers and sisters, were looking out of our windows at the snake. Everybody was greatly alarmed.

"But my mother was very brave. She went out into the courtyard where the snake was, and she sang to it. When she was young, my mother had the most beautiful singing voice of any girl in Palestine. She sang the romances of the Spanish Jews, which she knew from her childhood in Sofia, Bulgaria. These sad and beautiful songs about love she sang one after another to that snake, and he stayed curled up where he was in our courtyard and let both women go back inside. So it is very likely that our ancestor Aaron also knew how to charm a snake in the court of the Pharaoh."

"What was the outcome, of the snake in the courtyard?" asked Celia's son Marc, smiling. He was a sociologist and had once done a study of human responses to emergencies.

Yedidja looked startled, absorbed in the vision of his snake-charming mother. "Someone went to get help, and then they took away the snake."

"What did they do? Did they kill it?" asked Rachel. She was sitting up straight in her chair at a table a little distance away.

"Yes," Yedidja admitted.

"Jews have *not* always been kind to animals," Rachel announced calmly, with great aplomb. Celia felt uneasy but also rather proud of her.

There were murmurs of objection from Celia's seder guests.

"It's true!" said Rachel. She picked up the broiled beet Sophia the maid had cooked specially for her, which was dripping red juice and looked far bloodier than the usual shank bones placed on all the other tables to symbolize the biblical sacrifice. "This stands for the killing of animals! And what about kashrut?"

The murmurs turned into an uproar. "It *is* humane!" someone shouted. "It was advanced for its time!" said Bernard. "It still is!" someone else cried out.

"What are you talking about in there?" boomed a voice from one of the other rooms through the speaker. "Remember, we have forty pages until the meal!"

"Wait a minute," called the deep voice of Celia's friend Burt Moore-Owen, the Unitarian minister, who didn't need a microphone to be heard everywhere. "This is a very interesting topic. Can't we have a rational discussion about it?"

"I don't *want* any blood on my door post!" Rachel shouted at Burt.

"She's quite a firebrand, isn't she?" Bernard leaned over and said into Celia's ear. He was grinning. "Maybe she'll go into politics."

"I don't mind if she goes into politics, but she'll have to learn some tact," Celia replied. There were often moments like this with her grandchildren. They seemed to her at once refreshingly blunt, wonderfully loving, cruel and unrefined. "She's going too far."

"Maybe we're just old," Bernard suggested.

But Celia felt her seder was ruptured, her father and mother's old world hospitality that she tried so hard to recreate, the symbolic—though to Rachel nothing seemed symbolic—retelling of the ancient story, all oozing the blood of innocent lambs. Why was this granddaughter, product of two caring parents and an excellent education, striking a blow against Celia's seder like Moses in his rage against the Egyptian overseer?

"Omit all future references to animals," Yale instructed Yedidja, "or we'll never get to eat our chicken tonight."

Yedidja sang, charming the fractious guests into a state where the will to argue slept and the soul woke up. His voice was all Jerusalem copper plates, dust, charmed snakes, and sage from the hills, a voice sweet as the bags of little apricots Celia and Estelle used to buy at the market. He sang in Hebrew, "'What aileth thee, O sea, that thou fleest? Thou Jordan that thou turnest backward? Ye mountains that ye skip like rams? Ye hills like young sheep?'"

"Magic is the subversion of logic," said Claire's boyfriend Mac during a pause in the singing. Celia looked to her right and saw Mac lifting the roasted egg from the hammered Bedouin plate she'd placed on their table. The egg had been cooked with the shank bones and was spattered brown with meat juice. "It has a very slow vibration," she heard him say, "like something you might dig out of the ground that was centuries old. It's so *heavy*."

"It's hard boiled," said Maxine.

Then Mac held the egg against the center of Claire's forehead. "Look at it through your third eye."

Claire closed her eyes. "This is cool. I'm up high, floating in a round dome of sky. I see rounds, eggs, and worlds. Now

I'm looking down at the earth and I see the crowd in the courtyard. I see the priest dashing blood against the base of the altar. I smell blood in the hot sun. It's so hot, the egg is burning me, Mac."

"I won't ask what you two are doing," said Bruce.

"Magic exposes nature," said Mac. "Like sex."

"'My beloved is mine,'" sang Yedidja, "'And I am his who browses among the lilies. When the day blows gently and the shadows flee . . .'"

EVENTUALLY THE CATERERS served the meal, and Celia and Bernard moved over to the table where Celia's old friend, Sol Rudnick, was sitting. "I'm amazed at how you go on creating historic events," Sol remarked to Celia.

"It's nice of you to say that. I always think I'm in Tolstoy's version of history—the continuous motion of small events," she replied. They talked about her book on Sonia Delaunay and Sol's memoir of Greenwich Village in the 1930's; then they discussed their families and bragged about their respective grandchildren.

"And how's Sharon?"

Celia knew Sharon was Sol's favorite of all her children. "She's fine, she's still working at Legal Aid."

"Still out in the middle of nowhere? And what about Thunder?"

Celia shook her head. "They broke up."

Sol sighed and ate a forkful of sweet tzimmes. "She's not likely to meet many eligible bachelors out there in the rain forest, is she?"

"It's dry there." Celia was chewing her chicken. "They don't get much rain."

"It's not really so uninhabited," said Ronnie. "Didn't you say there's a small Jewish community somewhere?" He looked at Anna. "Maybe there's a place where she can tie a string around—of course it wouldn't be a rabbi's grave. Maybe an Indian chief's."

Anna smiled. "We heard the strangest story the other night. My friend's sister went on a Jewish singles tour of Egypt and Israel—she's thirty-four and not married yet. So, while she was eating in this Yemenite restaurant in Tel Aviv, she met an old woman who told her that if she went to the grave of a certain rabbi who's buried in the upper Galilee and wrapped a red string around the tomb, she'd be married within one year. She had a lot of trouble getting to this place, but finally she hired a taxi that was driven by a young Arab man from one of the villages nearby. He was very nice; he drove her up there and waited while she and another girl wrapped red strings around the grave. He was very interested in the whole thing. Afterwards, on the way back, he asked my friend's sister to marry him."

"Now that's a fast-acting charm," said Sol.

"Was he serious?" asked Rachel.

Anna nodded. "He was. He felt it was predestined. And she liked him. But she couldn't imagine living in his house in that village with all his relatives around."

"They need better water and sewage in those villages," Bernard remarked. "A few good pipes would greatly enhance the security of the state."

"Would she have been safe living there, if she'd married him?" inquired Rachel. None of the adults got around to answering her question. The caterers were busy serving trays of Passover cakes and cookies, and Celia noticed Claire and Mac leaving the room together. As Claire walked, her hips swayed in the leather pants and the tiny lock jiggled. Celia could glimpse some of the younger children out in the foyer cranking up the antique music box that stood taller than any of them and had *Musik* written across the front in large gold script. It was playing "There's a Long, Long, Road A-Winding." Bernard opened a package of Passover candies shaped like little colored watermelons and offered them first to Celia. She smiled at him and chose a yellow one.

"This has been a wonderful meal," said Sol. "You did a great job, Celia."

"I didn't cook a thing, that's why."

"Remember the carrots?" he asked.

"How could I forget them?" She'd met Sol while she was a student; she and four of her friends had pooled their allowances and rented an apartment in Greenwich Village. They lived in the apartment only during the day, between classes, and no one but Celia even told her parents about it. Celia was cooking carrots for Sol's lunch one day when she got the idea that became her master's thesis: Sol ate very burnt carrots for lunch that day.

"I always burned things, even after I was married," she said. "My father used to say, 'Celia, you can worship your husband without bringing him burnt offerings.'"

"But those burnt carrots smelled so good that the landlord knocked on the door and complimented your cooking," Sol continued the story. "He said, 'What a *beriah*!' That's a good housewife."

Rachel grinned. "What did you guys really *do* in that apartment?"

"We sat in front of a big smoky fireplace and studied or talked," Celia told her. "I'd go out and collect firewood in this voluminous coat I had—I'd stow the wood under the lining of the coat. There were lots of wonderful artists and writers in the building because the landlord gave them apartments without charging them rent. He just enjoyed their company, and so did we. The apartment itself was a bit strange because the toilet and bathtub were right in the kitchen. We called the place 'The Dive,' but we really weren't wild. For us, just having our own place was an adventure."

Rachel nodded knowingly. "Adventures were smaller back then."

Celia felt vaguely troubled by that remark. When Yedidja signaled to her that the meal should end soon, she excused herself from the table in order to get the *afikomen* presents. There were twenty-two children at the seder, from her own college-age grandchild down to a few babies, and Celia had bought and wrapped an afikomen present for each of them.

The gifts were in her bedroom in the large market basket she and Raymond had collected years ago in Peru. She made her way among the tables, greeting late arrivals, kissing old friends and family. No, it seemed to her that adventures were actually larger back then. When she was young, people simply had a lower adventure threshold: They didn't have to go all the way to British Columbia or take up with Mac the Knife. She kept moving toward the door, thrilled to be the hostess of such a marvelous seder, stopping to talk to her guests every few feet.

"When do you leave for the boonies?" someone asked.

"She's going to British Columbia—to visit Sharon!"

"What, you're leaving civilization, Celia?" asked one of Raymond's cousins.

"Celia!" called Yedidja. A-fi-ko-men, he said with his lips.

She called back, "It's as hard for me to get out of my living room as it was for the Children of Israel to leave Egypt! No comparison to Pharaoh intended," she added to her guests.

THE CHILDREN HAD BEEN PLAYING in her bedroom, which was supposed to be off limits. Years ago she and Raymond had bought twin beds which raised one's head or legs at the push of a button, and both beds were now contorted into roller coasters. On Celia's pillow lay a plastic candy-machine watch, and some of the papers on Delaunay which she'd pushed to the side of the bed before going to sleep last night had slipped to the floor. When she bent down to pick them up she saw the afikomen, half a square of matzah wrapped in a linen napkin, which the children had apparently hidden under her bed. From behind the closed door to her bathroom came a noise like a squelched giggle.

Straightening up, she listened, and again she heard the giggle, followed by a splash and the sound of her whirlpool going on. There was no reason for guests to use her bathroom—there were three others—and she had always impressed on the children that the whirlpool was not a toy.

"That's niiice!" she heard Claire's voice quite clearly. There was a deeper male response that she couldn't make out. Then she heard Claire gasp, "Mac!" There was more splashing. Then wordless gasps.

Celia stood frozen, her heart racing, which was bad for her blood pressure. There was a male groan—oh, it was vulgar, unbearable! She felt actual fear, listening to this and to the ominous silence that followed, filled only by the whirr of the machine.

Then Mac sang, "Up a lazy ri-ver, the Ri-ver Ni-le—"

Feeling ready to cry, Celia went around behind her Chinese screen with the Goddess of Finished Projects and picked up the large Peruvian basket filled with afikomen presents, furious that inside were a bottle of Dead Sea bath salts for Claire and a package of two writing pens for Mac. Her eye fell for a moment on the framed photograph of Sonia Delaunay on the wall near her desk, in which Delaunay, posing in her Paris studio, was wearing a skirt she'd designed in a bold geometry that matched the design on the large canvas she was in the act of painting. Sonia sat sideways on a high stool, her body draped in art: The artist, her art, and the artist's body all one. *They* would see Delaunay as quaint, naïve, Celia thought bitterly. They seemed completely unaware of her presence in the bedroom.

She retrieved the afikomen, so the children wouldn't surprise the happy couple floating down the Nile. She would announce that the afikomen was now hidden in the living room. Tucking the magical dessert, amulet of amulets, into a corner of the huge basket, she left the room with her heart still dangerously pounding. She might even need her heart medication, and it was in that very bathroom! As she walked down the hallway back toward the seder, her fury rose even higher. She would have liked to just rap Mac on the knuckles, as the angel rapped Pharaoh's knuckles every time he tried to touch Sarai.

With a sensation of unreality that she seldom felt in her own home, Celia returned to her living room, where people were eating sponge cake and colored candy watermelons. The tables were strewn with teacups and crumpled napkins stained with wine drops—the regretted blood of the Egyptians. Quickly she hid the afikomen behind the tripledecked ivory sailing ship from Japan, and returned to the table, slipping the basket of presents under the tablecloth. She was trembling all over.

Bernard smiled at her, resting his arm along the back of her chair. "Apropos of Anna's story, I remember my mother saying that if you eat a piece of the afikomen, you'll be married within a year."

She smiled. "I'll have to risk it." She understood the young Arab man's feeling of predestination, as she'd had it with Bernard. Once, soon after Bernard's wife died, Celia had paid him a call, partly to drop off some papers Raymond had prepared for him. He was alone in his large apartment which was filled with the sculptures his wife had begun to make in her later years. There was a lovely dark stone image of Bernard's head resting on a pedestal in the elegant living room. She remembered the odd sensation of Bernard's face looking at her from two directions at once as they talked. She'd had a little flash, a premonition that he would one day assume great importance in her life. Soon after that, Raymond died, and she remembered the moment guiltily.

Now, feeling the warmth of Bernard's arm, she tried to recapture her earlier, pre-Pharaoh-in-her-bathtub happiness. Turning to Anna, she said, "Well your friend's sister may have been proposed to by an Arab, but I was sold to an Arab as his wife."

"I know," said Anna, "Uncle Yale sold you."

"This I don't recall," her friend Ephraim said.

"Well, we were staying at the inn at Rosh Pina, and Yale and this young Arab man had become friendly. The Arab expressed great interest in buying me, and one evening they wrote out the entire contract. I was valuable because I was blond, so he had to pay thirty camels for me, even though I didn't know how to cook a single eggplant dish."

"Don't forget, I also convinced him that you were to be his favorite wife, no matter how many other wives he took," said Yale from the next table. People at the tables all around had turned their chairs to listen. "I looked out for your interests."

"I remember, dear. Being the favorite meant that I stayed at home and didn't go out to work. Also, I was allowed to go to the movies."

"That's a good thing," said Burt Moore-Owen. "Did you sign this document, Celia?"

"No, only the men signed."

"Of course," the daughter of one of Raymond's cousins called from two tables over. She too had brought a non-Jewish boyfriend to the seder. "You see, even in your generation you married non-Jews!" There was a roar of laughter, and someone said, "Touché!"

But Celia felt chilled, even while remembering the thick heat of that long-ago summer, the romance of the vast dark Hula Valley at night. It was only a joke! she wanted to say. *We* had a sense of proportion!

Several shouting children approached her table. "Grandma! We found it!" exclaimed Claire's youngest brother, triumphantly waving the half section of matzah in the linen napkin. He was excited, his face flushed, and he was followed by a pack of children. He glanced around at the adults, grinning. "What's this nice little afikomen worth to you?"

"I have a gift for each child, and for some not-really-children too," said Celia, pulling her Peruvian basket from under the table. The grandfather clock in the hall was already striking eleven, so she hurried to distribute her gifts.

THAT NIGHT SHE DREAMED she was riding a horse along with all the other women, hundreds of hooves pounding over the dry path. The women wore long robes and masses of gold and silver jewelry that jangled like a great tambourine as they galloped. As they rode, a wall of water rose up on either side of them, brilliant green and blue like the painting of the Red Sea parting Celia once did for a children's book. The women on horseback were pursuing the men, who were on foot ahead of them, and all the women together were shouting, "Horse and rider He has hurled into the sea!" Celia knew that Raymond was ahead of her, that Bernard was also ahead of her, and for a moment she was confused, thinking, how can they both be alive right now and I pursuing both of them at once? Yet she was, galloping on her horse amid the clangor of gold and silver, shouting with the rest, "Horse and rider He has hurled into the sea!" Then suddenly she noticed that the walls of water were slowly turning red; veins of dark blood were flowing through the translucent swells of the sea on either side of them. Someone was saying into her ears, "I'm sorry, I'm so sorry," and Mac was singing, "Up a lazy river, the River Nile . . ."

She awoke from the dream feeling torpid, and she reached for the ringing telephone as if she were fighting her way through the thick humid air of Egypt. The clock said eight. "Hello?" Her voice broke a little.

It was Bernard's daughter June, calling to tell her that Bernard had died last night. "I called him this morning around seven. I always call before work, and there was no answer. So I—went—" June was crying.

After the first shock, Celia started crying too. "When—?" was all she could say.

"It must have been not long after we left him last night. We drove him home after the seder, and we talked about how wonderful your seders always are. I'm calling from his apartment. He's still wearing the same suit he wore to your place last night; he's sitting in the chair by his bed. I think he must have been feeling quite content."

After assuring June she'd come right over, Celia got out of bed. She was scarcely aware of what she was doing, stumbling down the hallway to the front foyer. Still wearing her nightgown, she buttoned herself into her long dark mink coat, put on boots and her mink hat, and went down to have the doorman hail a cab.

IN THE WEEK FOLLOWING Bernard's funeral, Celia decided to organize her life. She bought a new date book and wrote in it the names of everyone she was meeting, working, lunching, dining, or going to theater with in the coming month and was surprised by how many names there were. She sorted through the piles of papers and drawings that were stacked on her desk and her bed. Everything went into color-coded folders and was rearranged according to a new system. Among the papers and drawings she found letters from grandchildren, pictures of people's babies, hard candies, crumbs from food she'd eaten while working, pens that didn't work, and coins from several different countries. She threw out bags and bags of stuff in between meeting people for lunch, dinner, work, and theater.

Then one day, returning from the stationer's with a new package of brightly-colored file folders for all the Delaunay papers, she realized she had done no work at all since Bernard died. She had spent days organizing herself but still couldn't find things easily. She sat down on her bed, pushing aside a pile of folders, and wept. She realized that in Bernard's absence she was trying to become him.

"I'm in a bad state of mind," she told Estelle on the telephone. "I thought I'd gotten used to living alone after Raymond died, but I really haven't been alone at all. I saw Bernard every day, and I talked to him on the phone at least three times a day. I suppose it's a bit ridiculous for a woman my age to have been so involved with that side of life."

"You always were," remarked Estelle. "I never had that high an opinion of romance, myself."

Celia awoke in the middle of the night not so much feeling, but remembering very clearly, the physical pain she'd suffered after Raymond died. It had felt as though a sharp palette knife were painting her hands with the shape and texture of pure pain.

## V

On Holocaust Day, Celia felt obliged to attend the performance of "The Little Ghetto that Everyone Forgot," even though she didn't feel like going out that evening. After all, she was chair of the program committee that had selected Evan Wolf—traveling puppeteer, consummate textile artist and one-man theatrical wonder—to perform this show which critics raved about. She arrived late at the museum; the lights had already dimmed in the auditorium. The silhouetted heads of men and women, and the smaller bobbing heads of children, were all turned toward the brightly lit puppet stage, waiting for the dramatization of the story of the Bialystok Ghetto.

The puppet stage set was a perfect miniature recreation of a shabby room in the ghetto, with walls of peeling painted cardboard and a tiny replica of a wooden eating table. It suggested the room a family once lived in, celebrating Shabbat and holidays, now askew, the cycle broken, crowded with chairs and extra beds on the floor. The members of *Hechalutz*, a Zionist pioneer movement, were living here now, and a young man named Mordecai Tannenbaum had been sent from the Vilna Ghetto to organize resistance. It was February, 1943. The comrades had two choices: a counter-attack against the Nazis or escape to the woods. It was a question of honor and how they'd be judged by history. Above all, the comrades feared history.

The puppet that was Mordecai began to speak: "I'm glad that at least we're in a good mood. Unfortunately, the meeting won't be very happy; this meeting is historic or tragic, as you prefer, but certainly sad. The few people sitting here are the last *chalutzim* in Poland. We are entirely surrounded by the dead."

*Perfect!* Celia thought. Mordecai's face was a masterpiece: Through her opera glasses she could see the deep shadows under his eyes made up of hundreds of tiny stitches of brown thread. Slight sags in the fine material used for his face showed the weakening of the once-muscular man training to drain the swamps of Palestine.

"Only one thing remains for us," said another pioneer named Hershl. His black button eyes burned in the stage lights. "To organize collective resistance in the ghetto, at any cost . . . to write a proud chapter of Jewish Bialystok and our movement into history . . . Our duty is clear: with the first Jew to be deported, we must begin our counter-action . . ."

For one moment Hershl ceased being a puppet and became his own transcendent image, fluid in the stream of white light directed at him. Celia cried behind her opera glasses. Wiping her eyes with an embroidered handkerchief given to her by Bernard, she looked at the silhouettes of children's heads against the lower part of the stage, little noses upturned. To recreate the Shoah out of the materials of childhood—puppets, storytelling, and diorama—was to infuse the very notion of childhood with the nightmare of history. It was to declare that real childhood, the clean slate, the innocent dream, was impossible. She would like to discuss that with this Mr. Wolf crouched under the stage.

"Comrades!" exclaimed the puppet named Sarah. "If we are concerned about honor, we have long since lost it. In most of the Jewish communities the murdering was carried out smoothly, without counter-action. It is better to remain living than to kill five Germans . . ."

Then Comrade Zipporah spoke. She was painfully thin, with yarn braids wrapped around her head. In Wolf's stitching of her worn blouse with a tear in one sleeve, in his impersonation of her voice, he seemed to capture her soul. "It's hard to choose the manner of your own death. There's a kind of argument going on inside me between life and death. It's not important for me whether I or somebody else will remain alive . . . I don't mean we should hold onto life for its own sake, but for continued work, for extending the chain that was not broken even in the darkest days."

Oh Zipporah-Bird, riding the terrible altitude of vision! Zipporah, Hershl, Mordecai, and Sarah must remain alive, not for their own sakes but for the pioneering that transcended them all. And Celia had wanted to return to Palestine, but Raymond, having come from Russia to America when young, had not wanted another immigrant experience, so they stayed in New York. With the handkerchief from Bernard she wiped her eyes, and at that moment she realized she had the right to remain alive and to continue her work. The puppet show ended amid loud applause—she and the committee had chosen well, he was very talented—and the *chalutzim* took their tiny bows. Then the top half of Mr. Wolf appeared on stage, with Mordecai on one hand, Zipporah on the other. He bowed, smiling, and the audience clapped. Like his puppets, he was young, handsome, and rather wild-looking.

In the lobby afterwards they all drank little cups of orange juice and complimented him. He was thin, intense, and modest; he said he was on a ten-state tour and would be in Philadelphia tomorrow night.

"Your performance was absolutely wonderful," Celia told Mr. Wolf. "Do you have a personal connection to Bialystok?"

"My mother survived Bialystok," he said, "and two years in the forest."

She nodded. "I thought there might be something like that. You conveyed such a powerful feeling."

"Amazing!" said several people in a row, interrupting them to shake Mr. Wolf's hand.

"Marvelous!"

"I couldn't stop crying," said a woman with a pink lace handkerchief sticking out of the pocket of her coat.

"Do you really sew and knit everything yourself?"

"Were your ancestors sailors?"

"More likely they were tailors," quipped someone else.

Gradually the crowd thinned and people drifted away, but Celia still stood next to Evan Wolf, attracted by his warmth, his dark hands that were so deft with needle and thread. He was about forty-five; he taught theater design, but he looked more like a Gypsy performer than a professor.

"Was your father also a survivor?"

"Yes." He hesitated. "But I never knew him; I don't even know his name. My mother met him in a Displaced Persons camp in Sweden. While she was pregnant with me, he just suddenly took off, and she never heard from him again. He may have gotten word that his previous family was alive, I don't know."

"Yes, that's quite possible."

"I don't usually tell people that right away."

"I'm very interested."

"I used to tell people that my father was a Gypsy; I almost believed it myself for a while. I decided I would travel from town to town someday, performing. Theater has always seemed to me like a tool for survival. You know, three years ago my wife and I had just separated, and then my mother died. I felt very alone, so I started looking up Bialystok survivors, here and in Israel. I met this one old lady on a kibbutz; I let her talk for almost eight hours straight. She told me that she survived nine transports and hid for months in the forest—it was like all the conversations I'd never had with my mother. One time she was saved by a Polish family she knew just slightly before the war. She arrived on their doorstep carrying nothing but a little book of psalms. She says it was her faith that saved her. I've tried *so* hard to understand her experience of faith! Every time I think I've got it, the understanding just evaporates. Celia, I can't believe I'm talking to you like this, as if I've known you forever."

By this time Celia felt that Evan Wolf was the most charming and interesting young man she'd met in many years. She wanted just to go on watching his dark Gypsy eyes as he told her about himself. In those eyes—and quite innocently of course—she saw for the first time since Bernard died that there might still be some pleasure left in life. She was about to invite him for coffee at a nearby café, or better yet up to her apartment for dinner that evening, if he had no other plans, when they were approached by a young woman who looked equally excited by Evan's presence.

"Excuse me, I'm sorry to interrupt you," she said. "I just wanted to introduce myself—my name is Jessica Horn."

"Jessica Horn!" said Evan Wolf. "Of 'The Magic Carpet Ride to Mother's Land?'"

"Yes." She laughed. She had shiny black hair and lively round eyes.

He turned to Celia. "This is Jessica Horn, she's a puppeteer. She just won an award for her show. I was reading about it. How great to meet you," he said to Jessica, and the two of them started talking excitedly about several festivals last summer, the new shows they were each working on, and the material Evan had used for Zipporah's dress. They talked on and on, and Celia suddenly realized that she was old, they were young, and she was in the way, or would be very soon.

"Excuse me, I just want to say good-bye," she said. "I enjoyed meeting you very much, Evan. Good luck to you both."

"Celia, I loved talking to you," said Evan. "It was fantastic to meet you. I feel like you're my long-lost aunt."

"Let me give you my number and my address, for the next time you're in New York." She wrote them on a piece of paper she found in her purse, which she then discovered was the reverse side of the directions to the cemetery where they'd buried Bernard last week. She apologized, feeling awkward, and as the two young people watched, she drew a scribble across the little cemetery map that had an X marking the entrance.

CELIA PICTURED HERSELF living in British Columbia, in the country motel down the highway from Sharon's land. Through her window she'd see mountains and tall evergreens as she worked in strange surroundings like an expatriate—even if it *was* only Canada. The idea was consoling. All her friends said that going to the British Columbia forest for two weeks was as good as putting her life on the line. She phoned Sharon and said she wanted to come as soon as possible.

"And I'd like to stay for a month, if that doesn't interfere with your plans," she told her daughter.

"Well, no," said Sharon, obviously surprised. "Sure, come for a month if you like."

"Maybe I'll even buy a pair of blue jeans. I want to get out into the real bush."

There was a long silence, and then her daughter said, "Sure. We'll go walking in the woods. Is everything all right there?"

"Bernard died, on seder night." She described his peaceful death, and Sharon said she was sorry. Celia noted again the strange tone in which her children acknowledged this news. They seemed embarrassed that their mother had placed such high value on a romantic attachment with a man in his nineties, even though they'd all been fond of Bernard.

"Yes, dear," Celia continued. "So I think the best thing for me is to do something completely new. I can't concentrate here anyhow. I think it would improve my spirits to take them out of New York and put them down in a remote place."

Certain that she was about to do something daring and dangerous, she made all her travel arrangements in less than a week.

Estelle shrieked when she heard the news. "A whole month! You'll go crazy!"

"Sharon says that in the woods you become more of what you really are," Celia explained. "And I need to become that right now."

She packed books, drawing materials, and her research papers. *What would I bring to a desert island?* she wondered. *To me?* Then she took the framed photograph of Sonia Delaunay and her cat off the wall, wrapped it up in a warm sweater, and put that in the suitcase too.

# VI

## BANFF, ALBERTA

On a sunny morning in late April, Sharon was waiting at the Calgary airport for Celia's plane to land. Sitting across from her were some Ukrainian families, the older women wearing bright babushkas and carrying shopping bags full of food. The families were eating sandwiches and little cakes and drinking orange soda. They were fortified for any length of wait; the very act of waiting seemed intrinsic to them. Each time a group of passengers deplaned, at least one Ukrainian family would hurry from their seats, exclaiming and crying, to embrace the travelers.

No one from Sharon's family, immediate or extended, had yet made this trip to the interior to visit her; Celia was the pioneer. The woman in the seat next to Sharon, who wore a purple babushka with red, yellow, and orange flowers, opened a shopping bag and gave little triangular pastries to two young boys, who took them and ran off to watch planes through the big plate glass window. You can only really do the family thing by instinct, Sharon thought. Once you have arrived at the point of thinking about it, you've cut your chances. The woman sitting next to her reminded her of New York, childhood, of Estelle and Yedidja, and her parents' big seders. Instinctively she reached out and took the triangular pastry she was being urged to accept. It looked and was delicious, and she said so.

The woman beamed. "It is a Ukrainian cake," she explained, making a diffident gesture with her head and hand.

"Wonderful," Sharon replied. Half her own ancestors were Jews from Ukraine, but recently there had been trouble between the Ukrainian and Jewish communities on account of some elderly Ukrainian Nazis living peacefully in Winnipeg, so once again she played Marrano.

"You are waiting for someone?" asked the Ukrainian woman, who, Sharon calculated, was probably not old enough to have been more than a teenage girl during the war.

Sharon nodded, brushing flakes of pastry off her jeans. "My mother."

"Oh, your mother! She lives here with you?"

"No, no, she's coming in from New York."

The woman's face expressed great sympathy. "That's hard," she said. "You have no one to talk to, no one to watch the children."

\* \* \*

THE FLIGHT FROM TORONTO to Calgary passed quickly and pleasantly, thanks to Celia's adorable seat-mate, Mitzi, who was the art teacher at the Calgary Talmud Torah. She had read Celia's children's books to her own children and was thrilled to meet, as she said, "the real Celia Rosenbloom."

As they flew at a lower altitude over the western prairie, half an hour from Calgary, Mitzi poured non-dairy creamer into a cup of coffee and asked, "Where exactly does your daughter live? Is it just north or just south of Greenville?"

"Well, actually it's about two hours south of Greenville, on the Boundary River."

"But that's a *very* desolate area!"

"Well, she says there are some small stores—"

"But why does she want to live there? Why not just live in Greenville?" Mitzi's eyes were bright with curiosity and maternal outrage. Celia suspected that none of Mitzi's children had yet strayed from the straight and narrow path.

"Well, she's the daughter who got away," Celia explained.

"Got away! Out there with nothing but bears and lumberjacks, I'll say she got away. She must be a little bit—different, is she?"

Celia looked out the window at a carpet of clouds. "Well, it's natural to try to make your children into the type of people *you* are. But once in a while a child wiggles out through the cracks in the edifice. It shows that there *are* cracks, and I'm not so sure that's a bad thing. We did bring them up to be independent-minded. I was brought up that way myself. When I was twelve, I told my father I didn't want to go to Hebrew School anymore because I was an atheist."

"And what did *he* say?"

"Well, he said that was all right, as long as I continued to study Hebrew. He had all the books by Robert Ingersoll, the famous atheist, and he let me read them. But then one day a friend of my parents was visiting. I remember he sat down next to me on the front steps and said, 'I hear you're an atheist.' When I said I was, he said, 'Well, I'm one too.' Then he thumped the step and said, 'Does this step exist?' He pointed to a chestnut tree in the middle of the yard and asked, 'Does that tree exist?' Well, I decided that if anyone so stupid was an atheist, I wasn't going to be one anymore."

Mitzi laughed. "You're saying it's just a phase. Your daughter is a bit old for phases, though. I'm sure she's a very interesting person. She must be," she added kindly.

But the conversation reawakened Celia's fears; her heart pounded as they flew in low over a lovely geometric abstraction of brown and yellow fields. Hidden in the palm of her hand was a pill in case of heart trouble. She gave Mitzi her address in New York, hoping that Mitzi would have disappeared into the crowd at the terminal by the time Celia discovered that she was stranded, alone, her daughter having escaped again. She knew it was ridiculous to think this way, but Mark's warning about Sharon's unreliability kept nagging at her. A strong wind made the plane bump and strain, and Celia's heart did likewise.

But walking up the ramp, she spotted Sharon instantly, looking much as she had the last time she visited New York two years ago. She wore jeans and cowboy boots and, Celia noticed as they hugged each other, a lined suede jacket that seemed warm and appropriate for the season.

Celia felt emotional with relief. "I'm so glad to see you, dear! I was so worried you might've been . . . delayed." She laughed and cried at the same time.

Sharon smiled; she didn't cry easily like Celia did on both happy and sad occasions. "It's fine. I got to Calgary yesterday afternoon. I left plenty of time, and it's not a difficult drive."

"Never mind. It's just that the imagination of disaster gets keener somehow with age." Celia was tangled in her own words, a thing that rarely happened to her. She felt out of her element already. The very air in the airport felt different: It moved around her head and body in wide western currents, smelling of grain and earth.

She waited with the luggage out in front of the terminal while Sharon went to get the truck, and in a few moments her daughter reappeared behind the wheel of an enormous red pickup truck with a little white house stuck onto the back. Celia was wondering how she would ever manage to hoist her many pounds on her bad knees into this truck, and already suspecting that perhaps she oughtn't to have come. It would be too rough, and the jeans Estelle made her buy were still in her suitcase. Then Sharon hopped out, opened the door on the passenger side, and pulled out a little wooden step.

"I made this for you to use getting in and out of the truck!" she announced, with a look that reminded her mother of when she was three and had built a tower of blocks. The step was made of thick varnished wood. Celia stepped onto it and it didn't move, and then she climbed easily into the truck—even in her skirt!— and sat down, feeling nimble and western. The seat covers were in a Navajo-type design, and a beaded necklace swung from the rear view mirror. They drove around town in the pickup and then ate perogies at a restaurant. Calgary looked very nice, very civilized—oil money, Sharon said. The bed in the motel room Sharon had reserved for Celia had soft flowered sheets like the bedding in an old farmhouse. On them she fell asleep easily for the first time since Bernard had left the earth.

\* \* \*

SHARON SLEPT OUTSIDE in her camper in the motel parking lot. In the morning, after breakfast, they started their drive into the foothills. Sharon wanted to show Celia the big white ice in the mountains; she wanted her mother to love this landscape as much as she did. The truck gained altitude easily, even carrying the little camper that always made Sharon feel safe—if she ever got stuck anywhere she had all the essentials. It struck her again how New Yorkish Celia appeared, wearing a knit suit jacket and matching skirt, and a blouse with a droopy tie. She had bought the *Calgary Herald* in town and was reading an article headlined "Israel Honors War Dead" as they drove along.

"I have to call my friend Emma in Jerusalem. This is the most difficult time of year for her."

"You can phone her later from Banff." Sharon had heard the story many times, how Emma was in her apartment eating lunch with her two grandchildren while her daughter and son-in-law were doing errands downtown. She and the children heard the sound of the explosion that killed their parents. The victims' body parts had to be pulled off the branches of nearby trees. Eventually, Emma sent the grandchildren to Long Island, where they were adopted by her son and his wife, but she herself stayed on in Jerusalem.

"She's like a plant growing out of a stone. Stubborn." Celia deftly folded the paper into quarters to read the inside pages, as if she were commuting on the subway. They were climbing into the high foothills now; the truck rounded a turn and there was a view of a big valley of evergreens and rock outcroppings descending to a river. The air was cool and heavy with moisture. Celia kept looking up from the *Calgary Herald*. "You know, I don't think I've ever driven through such a remote place. It's lovely."

Sharon glanced at her mother and noticed that Celia's mouth was puckered in a very sad expression. "Well, this is actually quite a well traveled road," she assured her. Something seemed to be frightening Celia. Sharon didn't know whether it was the thought of death in general or the fear of something sinister she imagined emerging from the bush. Celia was always more emotional than other people, so Sharon wasn't sure how distressed her mother really felt. She saw a sign for a rest area and decided that it might calm Celia if they stopped for tea.

They got out of the truck at the picnic site, which was on the curve of a steep switchback, with a view up the wide valley toward a few snowy peaks in the distance. The entire world seemed made of mountains, the earth heaving her curves into the cool wet atmosphere. I'm still young, Sharon thought suddenly and with joy. She turned on the propane valve and then went inside the camper to start the water for tea. Through the little window she could see Celia standing and looking into the distance. Sharon had a strange feeling that Celia could now see further into life, or into something beyond life, as if Bernard's departure had opened a passageway to another dimension of existence. After a while she slid the window open and called, "Celia! Tea's ready!"

Celia came, and Sharon helped her up the folding metal steps into the camper.

Sharon had put out rice crackers baked with tamari for herself and chocolate-covered graham crackers for Celia. Celia ate lots of both of them, and she drank the black tea which Sharon had made as weak and American-seeming as possible.

"We used to eat these at camp." Celia held her red enamel camping mug as if it were Limoges, and sipped. She seemed to have recovered her spirits a bit. "We also used to raid the kitchen late at night and make mayonnaise, onion, and peanut butter sandwiches. Then we'd eat cookies topped with butter and whipped cream." She laughed. Sharon smiled but said "ugh." Then Celia's chin puckered again. "Roberta died last year, did I tell you?"

"No, I don't think you mentioned it." Sharon thought eating like that would kill anyone. Looking at her heavy mother, she thought of how many times she'd seen Celia eat a whole plate of little smoked fish with their heads still on, along with a whole little block of cream cheese. Actually, if Sharon didn't know better she would have been tempted to eat like an old-time Jew, too. Both Marc and Anna tended toward overweight. She felt anxious about the cholesterol level of her family.

"She'd retired to Florida. She didn't see well anymore, and she was hit by a car while she was crossing the street."

"I'm sorry." Not cholesterol, then. Which one was Roberta? Yes, the one who'd been a secretary at the United Nations. She never married, so she used to bring Anna, Marc, and Sharon the little woven baskets, dolls, and carved toy animals that representatives from all over the world gave to her. Celia had so many friends; there were always so many people at the apartment when Sharon was growing up that she could never keep them all straight. In New York she'd often felt misplaced in her own home, knowing that her parents expected her to have emerged from the womb as a socially adept extrovert—something she would never be.

A powerful wind blew through the valley, sweeping a cold scent of evergreen in through the camper window. Celia buttoned her New York jacket. "We're at quite a high altitude already, aren't we?" she asked, and again her mouth seemed to tremble. The deaths of Bernard, of Roberta and other friends, even of Emma's daughter and son-in-law so long ago in the heart of Jerusalem, seemed to be whirling around her and shaking her back and forth like a big old tree in the wind.

\* \* \*

AS THEY TRAVELED ON, the mountains loomed, each one singular and fierce, coming one after another like life's challenges. They were different from other mountains Celia had seen, the Alps with rounded peaks and charming pubs spaced along their paths. These Canadian mountains were sharper, like jagged arrowheads piercing the gray spring sky. She couldn't see any pubs. If Sharon tossed her out by the side of the road where the snowdrifts were still six feet high, how long would she last? She told herself she was being absurd—what about the little wooden step and the soft flowered sheets last night?—but she was in a state. The endless views into the wilderness, the sweeps of gnarled evergreens and snow reminded her of death, or rather, of the comfortless habitation of those left behind in life.

Banff was cold, and it existed solely for the purpose of catering to visitors to the mountains, the glaciers, and the hundreds of miles of desolation. Yet Celia was soothed by vegetable soup with marvelous croutons in the restaurant and the streets with fancy shops.

"I'd like to get you something—is there anything you'd like to have?" she asked her daughter.

Sharon shrugged. "Not really. I have everything I need."

But Sharon had so little; she discarded things and people instead of accumulating them, as would have been natural at her age. They were passing a shop that sold mountain clothing, and Celia was struck by the beauty of a soft green wool scarf in the window and the fact that Sharon's delicate throat was bare, so she insisted on buying it for her. Then she bought lots more gifts for other people in New York. Returning to the truck laden with packages, she felt that perhaps, after all, she was not going to die alone, poor, and with only a few cans left in the pantry—a thought that haunted her lately.

After checking in to the motel in Banff, which was also very comfortable, and stopping at an ice cream parlor where they shared a concoction called an Athabasca Freeze, they drove to Lake Louise. If Celia had not been told it was a lake, she would never have known. Even in spring it was covered in thick gray ice, and the sheer rock cliffs rising around it were topped with variegated layers of snow that melded with piles of low-hanging clouds. Their red truck was the only vehicle in the parking lot, and the old Canadian Pacific Railway hotel was shut, its Tudor façade lifeless. Sharon took two pictures of Celia standing on the silent paths, where Celia imagined the ghosts of elegant journeys past, Victorian ladies and gentlemen strolling along the lakeside in summer while servants unpacked their trunks.

The sun dropped behind the cliffs, and blue shadows lay across the snow. "Stand right there, at the end of the path." Sharon waved Celia toward the giant cliffs that closed in around the darkening lake, while she herself backed away toward the parking lot, stopping occasionally to peer through the viewfinder of her camera.

"All right," Celia called, watching her daughter back away. She tried to think cheerfully of this trip evolving into a collage, a piece of folk art that she would hang in the breakfast room. Celia Rosenbloom: Explorer of the North.

"Can't you take it from there?" Celia called again, ashamed of her suspicion of the daughter behind the viewfinder.

Sharon jogged back a few more steps toward the parking lot and Celia suddenly became absolutely convinced that she was going to hop into the truck and drive away, leaving her mother marooned on the edge of the frozen lake. Celia would be alone in the most elemental landscape she had ever seen, where everything was the brutal remnant of a past geologic age—clay pulled up by the sharp fingernails of the Creator. Her own life would be obliterated as casually as a trickle of melting snow.

Sharon clicked the shutter and called triumphantly, "I got in the whole mountain behind you!"

Celia burst into tears.

\* \* \*

SEVERAL YEARS EARLIER, using pitons and a rope, Sharon and Thunder had ascended the slope of the Athabasca Glacier, up into the ice fields. It was like discovering a new country, a great plain of pure ice circled by peaks. They walked for several days across the plain, the sun making a powerful white light around them. It was the best time she'd ever had with Thunder, in a place with no one else around.

"We pitched our tent on the ice and went to sleep," she was telling Celia the next morning as they drove to the Athabasca Glacier, one of the wonders of the park which she'd been looking forward to showing her mother. She'd already reassured Celia, who really seemed not quite herself, that tourists took only a little walk on the lowest part of the glacier's downward flow and that it would be quite safe, especially since she'd booked two spaces for them on a guided tour led by expert climbers. Sharon wanted Celia to experience the magnificence of the glacier, even for a short time and in a touristy way. "And in the middle of the night," she continued her story, "I woke up and felt like a giant hand was shaking my shoulder. I was so sleepy I thought it might be Thunder. But it turned out to be the paw of a grizzly bear."

"You never told me about this!" Her mother looked as horrified as if it had just happened. Celia rummaged in her purse and brought out the sizeable container she carried these days, full of different kinds of pills. At a glance Sharon could see white tablets, oval green pills, and some large red capsules. Celia selected a green one and swallowed it without water. "How did you get him out of there?"

"We shouted at first, and he let go of my shoulder, fortunately. I still have a scar. Then Thunder sang Indian songs really loudly and the bear went away."

"You were lucky," said Celia, frowning.

Of course one didn't tell one's mother these things. Sharon was warming too enthusiastically to Celia's presence; it wasn't often, living the small town life, that she had a conversation with another reflective human being. She was surprised to discover how starved she was for intimate talk.

When they arrived at the foot of the glacier for the tour, a group of people were busy lacing up hiking boots supplied by the tour company and pulling hats and scarves from cardboard boxes, because, as their guide said, "It may be spring down here but it'll feel like Christmas up on that ice." Almost immediately Celia befriended an older couple from Pittsburgh. They were visiting their son, who lived in Calgary and loved mountain climbing; the son told Sharon he hoped to bag three new peaks this summer.

They ascended the packed slope of the glacier. "The glacier appears stationary," said the guide, turning to face the group. He wore a battered ski hat that said Whistler, except the W was half gone. "But actually it's slowly receding." He had them all line up and hold on to a rope as they moved past some large crevasses.

"My courage is slowly receding." Celia held the rope in one hand and Sharon's arm tightly with the other.

"It's really quite safe," Sharon assured her.

"Now, these crevasses are extremely dangerous," warned the guide, turning around again. "So everyone keep hold of the rope, and just approach the edge very slowly. You can look right down from about here." They looked down into an especially lovely crevasse, a gorgeous blue fairy-tunnel in the ice. It gave Sharon a violently mystical sensation, an urge to hurl her soul into some ultimate reality. She held Celia's arm, hoping her mother loved it too.

"They're deep and slippery," said the guide, in answer to a question from someone in the group. "And they go on much further than it appears from up here."

"What happens if you fall into one?" asked the man from Pittsburgh.

"You die," said the guide. "It's pretty hard to get someone out of one of these." He had them step back carefully from the edge of the crevasse and continue up the glacier. There were now crevasses opening up on both sides of them, more and more as they ascended. Sharon breathed the colder air and it tasted sapphire blue; she felt happier than she had for a long time. But then Celia's hand on her arm trembled and she looked down to see her mother crying for the second time in twenty-four hours.

"I know it's silly," Celia said. "But these days the possibility of something unexpected happening seems so real."

"Honestly, the guide knows what he's doing," said Sharon. "You should just try to enjoy the walk." But she felt helpless to comfort her mother, whose Bernard had just slipped out of sight into the great crevasse.

While they were stopped for a brief lecture on the moraine, to learn how the gigantic ice formations had pulled along boulders and earth, shaping these mountains, a tall young man in a dark blue sweater approached them, hugging his chest as if he were cold. He bent down to speak to Celia. "Excuse me. You are afraid?" His English was accented.

"I'll be all right." Celia let go of Sharon's arm for a moment and blew her nose into a handkerchief decorated with cross-stitched flowers.

"This is your mother?" he asked Sharon, and she said yes. "If you don't mind, you can hold to my arm on the other side," he told Celia. "I can promise you that my feet are not leaving this ground. Then you will not to be afraid." He offered her his strong-looking arm.

Celia looked up at him. "I'm being silly, I suppose, but that might be a good idea." Her voice had steadied; she sounded as surprised and happy as a captured maiden saved by the sudden appearance of a prince on a white horse—a maiden who had believed all along that this was possible.

"If you don't mind, it will make her to feel better. She can walk here between the two of us," the young man said to Sharon.

"Sure. It's very gallant of you. I thought chivalry was pretty well dead." Sharon noted that he looked puzzled by her words.

The three of them walked slowly up the ice, arm in arm, twined with the rope, Sharon feeling like the tail of some odd animal. Celia's eyes had dried and she had almost completely regained her usual rather crisp demeanor, as if male attention were a type of healing ray. "Where are you from?" she asked the young man.

"Israel."

"Oh, I thought you might be!" She looked at him again. "So you've just finished the army?"

He smiled. "I see you know about it. Yes, I just finished."

Celia spoke some Hebrew to him, and he answered; Sharon, who had never paid attention to her Hebrew lessons, couldn't understand.

They were moving further up the glacier, past larger and larger crevasses, but Celia walked confidently now in her shoes with the cleats. "I'm a little emotional these days because my best friend just died," she confided to the young man.

"I'm sorry. I know how it is. My best friend died too."

She looked stricken, holding his arm. "I'm so sorry," she said.

"But you can't live always afraid that you will die, too," he said. "When I was in the army I invented a way to stop that fear. It's a little bit strange, but it works."

"What is it?" she asked.

"Well, you pretend that you already had died, your life is finished and your soul is with God. Then you feel that you only came back to life for a visit; you have nothing to be afraid of any more. So you can just enjoy to be here, whatever it's like, because it isn't serious. Maybe I don't explain it so well."

"No, you do explain it well," said Celia.

# VII

Late that night Celia phoned her friend Emma in Jerusalem. "*Hag sameach*," Emma answered the phone cheerfully. It was seven in the morning on Independence Day. Behind Emma's voice was the rumbling of what might have been a garbage truck on the Jerusalem street. Just hearing that gave Celia a thrill.

"*Hag sameach*, dear," said Celia. Happy holiday, indeed.

"Celia! It's wonderful to hear your voice; you sound like you're right down the street."

"I meant to call you yesterday or the day before," Celia apologized, "but I'm in Canada visiting Sharon. We're in Banff, and I'm afraid the glaciers have been commanding all my attention."

"Banff! I hope you brought along some good hiking shoes and tough blue jeans. You're not going out into the wilderness, are you?"

"Yes, I am," said Celia.

"Well, be careful. I'm honored to receive a call during your vacation."

Emma's voice sounded clear and strong, even happy. She's conquered grief, loneliness, not like me, Celia thought. "You sound wonderful," said Celia.

"Well, it's a terribly sad and beautiful time of year. I'm my children's eyes in Jerusalem now, and I still see many, many things that are worthwhile."

"I'm glad you feel that way." Emma asked her how she was, so she told her that Bernard had died, and Emma said how sorry she was and how fond of him she had always been.

"I remember how we used to get together on Thanksgiving Day to eat bagels and lox and watch the parade from your windows," continued Emma. "Bernard was always there, and he was so gracious. He'd always tell you the history of the parade, of New York. He knew everything. I get homesick for America just thinking of watching the Thanksgiving Day parade from your windows with Bernard."

"Yes, he knew everything about everything," Celia agreed.

"I remember how shocked he was when he heard how we consulted each other about when to get pregnant." Emma laughed. She and Celia were dedicated young teachers then, in an experimental arts program in a poor neighborhood. Since they were afraid the program wouldn't survive if they both took a leave of absence in the same year, they alternated their pregnancies. They decided that Celia should go first, as she'd been married a year longer. But when it took her nearly a year to conceive, Emma accused her of holding out!

"I guess he thought it was like gambling with our children's lives." The memory made Celia smile, sitting alone in her motel room beneath a kitschy painting of a giant waterfall.

"He had beautiful old-world manners," said Emma.

"Yes, I really miss him. I'm supposed to be on vacation, but I just keep thinking about what our professor of Shakespeare used to say when I was in college. He was a very learned, cosmopolitan old man, but he'd never been to Stratford; he'd practically never left Brooklyn. He said travel consists merely of dragging your miserable self someplace else."

"No," said Emma, "I don't think so. You know, 'Life must go on, and the dead be forgotten'—Is that Millay?"

Celia sighed. "Yes. It ends, 'Life must go on; I forget just why.'"

"Bernard was ninety, you're seventy. You still have years left, wonderful years of joy—and pain. Use them well, dear."

"I shall try."

As they drove down out of the Rockies, the landscape seemed to shrink and soften, and Celia felt less afraid. In the distance she could see a lovely town on a lake where several houseboats floated. Behind them, the round hills covered with fluffy trees were shaped like a sleeping animal with green fur.

"Three former Nazis live here," Sharon informed her, swinging the truck easily onto the road leading toward the town, where, she said, there was a very good Greek restaurant. "A reporter found them in the phone book last year and interviewed them—they never even bothered to change their names."

Celia shook her head wordlessly.

Over lunch in the restaurant, where they ate delicious spanikopita, Celia remarked, "You remind me more and more of your father." Then, since that might have sounded strange to a daughter, she added, "A female version of course—I mean that you've become so—" she struggled to find the word, "dauntless."

Sharon sighed. "I'm not *that* courageous."

"Thank goodness you haven't had to be, dear. Though I'm certain you would have risen to the occasion. I remember having that same thought about Raymond when we visited the Soviet Union. We'd brought along gifts, Jewish books, for some of the refuseniks, and they invited us to a party—have I told you this before?" When Sharon smiled, meaning either no or tell it again, indulging her old mother, Celia continued. "The party was held at the home of a man who had just applied for an exit visa to Israel. They all knew, of course, that this would be the beginning of his harassment by his neighbors and the KGB, and that he might lose his job and be imprisoned. So they threw a party to celebrate." Celia wiped some tears from her eyes. "They were celebrating being free, they said. It was the happiest party, and Raymond really enjoyed it. I remember thinking that he would have done the same."

"I think so too."

After lunch they continued their journey, Sharon deftly guiding her big truck around the sharp turns. Celia used to drive the family out to Connecticut in the summers because Raymond would never get behind the wheel of a car. She always drove the Cadillac very slowly around the turns, beeping the horn, knowing the children were laughing at her in the back seat.

She had the strange thought that her daughter lived in an almost appalling state of freedom out here. "Is there anyone, ah, significant in your life now?"

"No." Sharon kept her eyes on the road. "Just a very sexy little buck deer who comes around to the clearing near the cabin. He's very young, about my height, with beautiful velvet antlers and big brown eyes. He likes to sneak up on me. I'll suddenly turn and see him between the branches, staring at me from about two feet away with those liquid eyes. He's lovely."

"*Sharon!*"

\* \* \*

FOR CELIA'S FIRST VISIT to the woods the next day, Sharon had planned a beautiful, gentle walk that she hoped would remind her mother of summers in New England. She got up early while Celia was still sleeping at the motel and filled her mountaineering rucksack with a Thermos of tea; a waterproof tarp; a new sketchpad and a drawing pencil she'd had gift-wrapped in town; a paperback titled *Great Nature Poems*; two cream-cheese-and-olive sandwiches for Celia and one for herself. To the outside of the rucksack she strapped a very small folding chair she'd found at a recreational vehicle store. She tried to think of everything, as if preparing for a wilderness expedition.

Then she drove out to pick up Celia, who had already eaten breakfast and had a long conversation with two loggers and the motel proprietors. As Celia climbed on her step into the truck, Sharon noticed that something had changed. The New York style was gone, replaced by a country-looking knit dress and a fringed tartan shawl.

"Nice outfit," Sharon commented, as she turned the truck onto the highway for the five-mile drive back to her place. It was a cool spring morning; the bare patches on the hills were turning bright green, and the river was full and blue in the sun. The entire valley was at its opulent best, cooperating.

"Thank you. Estelle insisted I'd need some sturdy clothing, and the shawl was a present from Anna. This is just beautiful; it reminds me of going to the country with Mother and Yale. Since we'd seen the countryside, we always knew what the poets were talking about when we read them later in school."

Celia looked as relaxed and happy as if she were sitting at the head of her First Friday table, retelling the story of this trip over the plates of petit fours. She exclaimed over the Hammond farm as they turned in through the first gate, which Sharon got out to open and then again to lock. "It's wonderful. Very modern-looking. Mother always insisted we go to a real farm, with a swimming hole and horses we could ride, and an outhouse."

"These people tore down their outhouse a long time ago," said Sharon. As they drove by, Charlotte waved from the doorway of one of the barns; she'd already invited Sharon to bring her mother over for tea some afternoon.

Celia was gracious about the cabin, too. She touched the big logs hewn in 1928 and walked around the three small rooms Sharon had worked so hard to renovate, her sensible crepe-soled shoes—bought at her maid Sophia's insistence—

quiet on the varnished boards. "Sophia kept telling me I was going to your dacha. It *is* a lovely little dacha, though I don't suppose too many actual dachas have this much computer equipment." Sharon laughed—she was surprised at how loudly.

Celia then looked at Sharon's bookshelves, built around a large bronze statue of Kwan Yin, the Chinese goddess of mercy, which Celia and Raymond had given her, and an oil painting Celia had done years ago of children fishing at a lake in Connecticut—the childish figures were Marc, Anna, and Sharon. "You know," Celia said, "I wouldn't have thought it possible to create such a little island of culture here. It's very interesting. I'd like to sketch you sitting right there in front of the window, with the mountains outside."

Sharon sat where Celia indicated, so her mother could visualize the sketch. She placed her hand on the arm of the chair and noticed that she was trembling.

Afterwards they drove up the dirt road into the hills on Sharon's land, then parked the truck and walked slowly into the woods on a flat, well-traveled deer trail, Sharon carrying the rucksack. The meadows between the trees were filled with purple lupines. Each flower held a drop of dew in the center where the petals met, and the fields of flowers seemed to shimmer from a distance. Sharon and Celia came into a clearing where they stood looking down at the swollen spring river.

"Everyone said you were just going to leave me on the edge of a glacier and run off," Celia confessed.

Sharon looked at her quickly. "Is *that* what they said?" She was accustomed to the idea that her Eastern relatives thought her not respectable, perhaps not right in the head, but she was shocked at the sudden springing up of these little poisonous mushrooms.

"Yes. That's what they told me. They said you might not even come to meet me at the airport." Celia was standing up to her knees in lupines, looking at the distant mountains where thick veins of snow were still visible. "Of course I see it isn't so."

"No. While they were filling your head with gossip I was building your step and loading up on chocolate graham crackers. Would you like to try out this little folding chair?"

As Sharon untied it from the rucksack they both began to laugh. "Of course, as soon as I saw the step I knew they were wrong." Celia laughed again, trying to balance herself on the tiny camp chair that tilted on the pine needles.

"Everyone said things like that?" Sharon asked.

"Nearly everyone."

"I'm amazed you came at all!" But Sharon couldn't help laughing, it was so awful.

"Yes, and they said I'd need lots of tough blue jeans. I was quite worried because I've never worn blue jeans. I have one pair in the suitcase."

Sharon let out a howl of laughter. "Don't worry, I won't make you put them on. I can't believe this!"

"Well, never mind. I'm the one who has the pleasure of being entertained in your lovely living room." Celia gestured toward the forest. "They'll be envious when I tell them about it."

They drank the tea and ate the cream-cheese-and-olive sandwiches, listening to the wind softly whistling through the trees. Sharon thought of a few choice things to say to her brother, sister, and other relatives, but after a while she stopped thinking of them. She felt liberated from Eastern conventionality by the victory of Celia's visit. From down on the farm rang a steady thwack, thwack, thwack of a hammer, echoing in the hills. When they finished eating she gave Celia the sketchpad and pencil, and then, at her mother's urging, went off to sit on a rock outcrop some distance away. "I want to sketch you surrounded by the trees," said Celia, and Sharon knew she also wanted to show her that she felt secure here.

For a long time Celia drew, her arm moving deftly under the plaid shawl. It was strange to see her not surrounded by things, by people. After a while she seemed to have finished the picture, and she sat looking out at the water flowing through the valley. Sharon was surprised at how easy Celia looked in the landscape, as if she felt she were seven years old again instead of seventy, sitting by a country river with her mother and Yale, alone in her thoughts as children are.

Sharon examined a patch of earth cupped in a hollow in one of the big rocks, where a white strawberry flower had bloomed. The strawberry leaves had a wavy circular mottling. She poked at the earth with a pine needle, not thinking at all, feeling the sun strengthen and heat her skin, the rock, the flower. There was a tick crawling up the leg of her blue jeans, and she crushed it with her fingernail. When she looked up again she saw that a small owl had landed right on Celia's shoulder! It was only about six inches high—a pygmy owl. Celia sat very still, as did the owl, and Sharon, none of them moving at all.

# VIII

## BOUNDARY VALLEY, BRITISH COLUMBIA

At first the woods seemed strange, with an alien, almost pressurized quiet. Celia spent hours studying the hillside beyond the motel window, where Queen Anne's lace bloomed and old pine trees grew, awkwardly twisted together. It always amazed her to see how many decrepit trees grew in any forest. One morning she looked up from her typing about Sonia Delaunay's theories and saw a porcupine sweeping its quills along the ground, a giant paintbrush making a design on the forest floor. Within a week she had established a routine of Sonia in the early mornings, then breakfast at the café next door, then more Sonia; there was simply nothing else to do. On the afternoons when Sharon wasn't working she picked up Celia after lunch and they went exploring in the truck, finding hidden lakes, abandoned Dukhaboor settlements, and once, a museum in a small town to which Japanese Canadians were banished during the war. Celia was moved by the inlaid wooden bowls and lacquered tea sets the deportees had carried with them out to this wilderness.

Today was Saturday, and instead of Sonia she was sketching for a new children's book she planned to call *Rachel's Deer Friend*. The book was about a girl who befriended a fawn and learned the language of the deer, such as turning her head away in greeting to show she wasn't a predator, as well as good deer manners, like walking softly. Celia didn't think her vegetarian granddaughter Rachel would mind lending her name for such a pro-wildlife purpose. In between sketching, Celia ate handfuls of cheese-flavored goldfish crackers and read *Northwest Farm and Country*, which had the latest news about the British Columbia Ostrich Breeders Association and the Farm Women's Conference. The picture of Delaunay and her cat was propped against the mirror, and Celia's clothing and books were everywhere. Sharon said that after one week the motel room already looked like Celia's bedroom on Central Park West.

After a while she felt satisfied with Rachel's face appearing between two trees, watching her deer friends. Celia looked up and saw a doe staring straight at her through the motel window. The doe was chewing grass, her mouth moving around and around; her deep brown eyes, Celia fancied, expressed surprise and amusement.

"Hello, Mrs. Doe," said Celia.

The doe ducked her head quickly, then brought it up again, still chewing, eyes alert. On her flank was the sharp dark curve of a wound that had healed.

"I was just thinking it was time for breakfast," Celia told her. The doe lowered her head and quickly brought up another mouthful of grass, chewing and looking attentively at Celia. "Maybe you tried to jump a fence that was too high for you. Is that what happened?" The doe seemed to nod a bit, looking very distinguished with the large curved scar in her reddish coat. She reminded Celia of a Holocaust survivor she knew in New York, who was crippled in both legs because the Nazis had experimented on them when she was a child. This survivor had the kindest but most penetrating gaze Celia had ever seen in a human being, and she carried herself, on her walker, with the innate dignity of this magnificent scarred doe.

When Mrs. Doe had wandered off, Celia put on her shawl and went over to the Gold Pan Café for breakfast.

She sat at a table with a view up the valley, the river winding through blue-gray hills. After a long while a waitress she hadn't seen before appeared, a teenage girl whose nametag said *Keturah*. Celia smiled, delighted with the name—"incense" in Hebrew—as the girl brought out her order pad and pen. Her parents must be Christian fundamentalists, Celia thought; Sharon had told her this was the edge of the Canadian Bible Belt.

"Hello. Would you care to order at this time?" Keturah spoke in the deep tones of a Hollywood beauty.

Celia ordered tea and french toast, then said, "Your name is very lovely—Abraham's second wife, as I'm sure you know. Your parents must know the Bible well." The girl herself was lovely, with golden hair and a rosebud mouth, deep blue angelic eyes; and she knew it too, carrying herself like a higher being.

Keturah smiled. "Hardly anyone ever knows who Keturah was, except for my dad. He knows the Bible better than anyone around here, except for some friends of ours who went to Bible college in Alberta and know *everything*—I mean, they can tell you right off the bat exactly how many wives and how many concubines King Solomon had."

Celia laughed. "I don't know those things myself."

Keturah shrugged. "Solomon's concubines aren't really so important. My parents—my mother's dead, but my father knows all about the life of Abraham because we're Jewish, so Abraham is very important to us."

"How nice," Celia said. "I'm Jewish too. I know I shouldn't be surprised there are Jews anywhere, but I am surprised—and very pleased—to meet you. Are there other Jewish families in the valley?"

"No, we're the only one," said Keturah. "I'm *very* pleased to make your acquaintance. Do you live in this area?"

Celia said she was from New York and was visiting her daughter. Keturah said she'd never met Sharon but thought she might have seen the red truck parked at the general store. She also remembered meeting a woman with the last name of Rosenbloom, though that was up in Greenville, not around here.

"I would be terribly afraid to set my foot in New York," Keturah confessed. "My dearest wish is to go to Israel and start an orphanage there. Do you think it would be possible to do such a thing?"

"Probably," said Celia. "Or you could work in an orphanage. I love Israel myself—I wanted to live there when I was your age. I was there for a year with my mother and my brother when I was fifteen, which was in 1935, and again with a friend of mine in 1938."

"Oh my! I imagine you had to travel there on a boat?"

"Yes. Of course the harbor at Jaffa wasn't completely dug out yet, so when we arrived the ship had to anchor fairly far from the shore. Then each person had to climb into a sort of basket, and they lowered you like cargo into a smaller boat. It was terribly exciting."

"Why did you go? I mean—" Someone called to Keturah from the kitchen, and she excused herself to deliver an order to another table. Celia watched her balancing plates of pancakes and fried eggs carelessly, putting them down in front of the wrong people and then switching the plates, all the while smiling graciously at the customers as if conferring favor upon them.

When she returned Celia resumed her story: "My father was a Zionist and wanted us to learn Hebrew. He sent my brother Yale to Palestine first, when Yale was sixteen. Yale was supposed to be studying in a gymnasium, which is a high school, near Tel Aviv. But this gymnasium was very strict, very Germanic. All the students had to stand when the teacher came into the classroom, things like that, which Yale wasn't used to because we went to a very liberal high school in New York. So he ran away from the gymnasium without telling my parents. He just disappeared, and no one knew where he was. My father decided that Mother and I should sail immediately for Palestine to find Yale. We got ready within ten days!"

"I can't imagine anyone I know standing for a teacher, either. Did you find your brother?"

"Oh yes. When they lowered us in the basket he was waiting for us in the little boat. It turned out that he was living with a family in a nearby village. He'd learned to ride a horse and was serving in the Guard. Of course Yale had learned Hebrew because he'd really become part of the life of this village. So my father was satisfied, and Mother and I stayed on with him and had the most wonderful time that year. It was a *very* romantic place."

"How absolutely incredible," Keturah sighed. "Ketty!" called someone from the kitchen. She excused herself and returned shortly with pancakes instead of french toast, and coffee instead of tea, but Celia did not complain.

While she was eating, three men came into the café, one of whom had no hands. The half-empty sleeves of his denim field coat dangled against his sides. The other two men carried a stack of paper flyers, a roll of tape, and scissors. After some discussion they began taping up their announcement while the man with no hands watched.

Keturah came to refill Celia's coffee cup. "That's Billy McBride over there by the door," she half-whispered. "He lost both his hands in a car accident out on the highway last winter. The insurance company just gave him a huge settlement, and he's going to throw a gigantic party. That's what those flyers are about. The party starts on Saturday night, and the whole world is invited."

One of the men hanging up flyers moved toward Celia's table. He wore a baseball cap and a mechanic's suit. "Hi, Ketty."

"Hello, Jim," she replied. "I'd like you to meet a friend of mine from New York, Celia Rosenbloom."

"Hello, nice to meet you!" Jim said heartily to Celia. Then he turned to Keturah. "I didn't know you knew people in New York."

"Jewish people tend to know other Jewish people from all over the place," said Keturah.

"Yeah, I guess they would. Wandering and all that. Well, if you're going to be here next Saturday night," he continued, looking at Celia, "Billy over there is throwing the biggest barbecue and—if you'll excuse me—drinking party this valley has ever seen, or probably ever will see. He just came into a large piece of cash, so he wants to celebrate, and he wants everyone to celebrate with him."

"Thank you." Celia pulled the tartan shawl more tightly around her shoulders. The tall trees waved in the wind outside and even they looked slightly sinister.

Billy flapped his sleeve at them from across the café. "Coming to my party, Ketty?" he called.

"Yes, I think so," she called back. "My boyfriend's coming down, so we'll probably drop in for a while."

After the three men had left, Keturah filled everyone's coffee cup and then returned to Celia's table. "Of course, a party like that will be too wild for us by the time it really gets going. My boyfriend Yishai is a rabbi's son and he doesn't do a lot of beer drinking. But Billy is a good person; he has a good heart, so we'll go over there for a while."

"Where is your boyfriend's father a rabbi?"

"In Greenville."

"That's where my daughter works. She commutes three times a week."

"Yishai's father says I'm not Jewish, and he's correct about that, according to Jewish law," she confessed simply. "We don't have any Jewish relatives. But my grandfather decided he believed in the Jewish way, and I've always known that I'm Jewish."

"That's extraordinary." Celia looked with wonder at the young angel in the waitress's uniform, who had almost certainly swooped down from the mist atop the timeless blue hills. But who was she, really? Celia feared the forest, the town, and its people, and at the same time believed warmly in Keturah, whose words were curiously both the breaking of silence and silence itself.

ON WEDNESDAY, CELIA came into the café in the late afternoon for a cup of tea and spotted Keturah in her waitress's uniform. This time the girl had coiled her hair on top of her head, leaving ringlets dangling over her forehead and neck. Celia wondered briefly who was meant to be charmed by all this style.

"Celia! I was hoping you'd arrive soon. Please do sit at one of my tables. Would you like coffee?"

"Thank you, but I always drink tea. I'll have some *tea*." Celia watched Keturah write it down.

"Will you have a slice of homemade fudge cake, too? It's extremely delicious."

"Homemade fudge cake! I really shouldn't, but I will." Celia felt indefinably happier just saying the word fudge.

When Keturah brought the tea and cake, she hesitated for a moment next to the table. "Celia, do you eat Sabbath lunch at any particular time?"

Celia, who had already begun to read the *Vancouver Sun*, looked up, startled. She had never heard any Jew of her acquaintance say Sabbath before: Orthodox people said Shabbos, Israelis said Shabbat, and Jews of her own ilk said Saturday. "No, I don't think so. I simply eat whenever the mood strikes me, and as you see, that's far too often."

"Then would you like to come to our home for Sabbath lunch around noon? My father would love to meet you. Your daughter's invited, too, of course. This coming Sabbath."

Celia said she would love to come, and while she was writing down her phone number at the motel, the café door opened and a tall woman wearing slacks and long black rubber boots entered. Keturah gestured for her to come over to Celia's table.

"Hello, Keturah. You look like the debutante of the month," said the woman.

"Mrs. Hammond, I would like you to meet a friend of mine, Celia Rosenbloom," said Keturah. "She's from New York, and she's staying at the motel for a while." Turning to Celia, she said, "Mrs. Hammond is my science teacher."

"Hello. Nice to meet you," said Mrs. Hammond, who, Celia realized, was probably Sharon's neighbor Charlotte. "Did you say Rosenbloom? You must be the mother of our hermitess. I'm only joking. Are you enjoying your visit?"

"Yes, I love the country," Celia replied. "This reminds me of summers I used to spend on farms when I was a child." She was eager to make a good impression on Sharon's neighbor; in this remote place where one had hardly any neighbors, they were important.

"Very nice," said Charlotte. "Well, I'm sure it's a change from New York, and as my father used to say, a change is as good as a rest. I hope you'll come down to the farm some afternoon for tea."

Celia said of course she would and that she would love to see the new lambs. Looking at Charlotte Hammond in her slacks and long boots Celia felt too citified, almost effete.

"Some very dark men wearing turbans drove up to our house the other day and asked if we're the farm that sells kosher meat," Charlotte informed Keturah.

"They must have been looking for us," Keturah replied easily. "I think they did find their way—was it on Sunday?"

"It was," said Charlotte. "How do you make meat kosher?"

"My dad knows how. He worked on a farm once where they were selling lots of kosher meat to Jewish people in Calgary, and the rabbi came out to the farm and showed them how to do it. A lot of Sikh and Muslim people have been buying meat from us—they figure it's closer to their own laws than meat from the supermarket."

"Amazing," said Charlotte. "But are you sure you're doing it properly? It's probably not really kosher if there isn't a rabbi." She looked at Celia as if expecting her to voice an opinion.

Celia shrugged. "There's a saying: 'Two Jews, three opinions.'"

Charlotte and Keturah laughed, and the tension distorting the conversation seemed to recede; words shrank back to their normal significance. "Well, I didn't know you were so well versed in Jewish laws," Charlotte said to Keturah.

"She's my teacher," said Keturah to Celia, "so she doesn't think I know anything." The blond spirals on her forehead bounced as she began wiping off a nearby table.

"On the contrary," said Charlotte. "I think she knows far too much."

After lunch, Celia walked along the path next to the creek behind the motel. The water rushed under big old pine and fir trees. Smaller trees with tender new leaves overhung the water, which ran over rocks into a hundred little waterfalls, making a sweet roar. There was something elegiac about the scene, beautiful as it was. She passed an elderly couple sitting at a picnic table near the path. Probably retired, they had parked their large motor home and were eating a lunch spread out on a red checked tablecloth. She glimpsed a paper plate of pickles, two cups of coffee, the man sitting on one bench and the woman across from him.

"Hello," said the woman, nodding her head briefly at Celia.

"Hello." Celia nodded and walked on. The woman was eating a sandwich, and so was her husband across the table. Celia herself was walking upstream on the dry path, feeling nonexistent yet perceived, like Billy's missing hands.

CELIA LIKED THE WAY Rabbi Bernstein was grilling a wire carrier full of vegetarian hot dogs in the community Lag Baomer fire. First he crouched low near the coals, his long legs folded up and the flames leaping into the darkness above his head. Then he suddenly sprang up, thrusting the hot dogs impatiently into the bright yellow flames. His wife Tanya said he was a suffering vegetarian. "You've dedicated your life to children," the rabbi said to Celia. "That's the highest state of blessing."

"I think so too," she said. She was sitting on a lawn chair Sharon had unfolded for her. It struck her as strange and delightful to find a Jewish community out here in these hills. The picnic area by the lake was filled with Jews cooking and eating; except for the Bernsteins, they all ate kosher hot dogs imported from Vancouver. Interspersed with the rise and fall of conversation, Celia could hear the lake waves rattling pebbles on the shore. She was eating a hot dog smeared with yellow mustard, and it was deliciously burnt.

"Well, I have to tell you about our brush with royalty, then," said Rabbi Bernstein, whose name was Zach. "Speaking of children."

"Yes! Tell her!" said Tanya, who sat on a log near the fire eating a hot dog speared on the end of a fork.

"We were traveling through England and Wales one summer, and one of the English princes and his entourage were coming through a town near by. So we went to see the prince, and it just so happened that it was not only his birthday, but it was also Gabriel's birthday." Celia had already been introduced to their three sons, Gabriel, Itamar, and the famous Yishai, Keturah's boyfriend. Keturah and Jacob couldn't come to the community Lag Baomer fire because this was lambing season, and there was a lot of work to do.

"It was very exciting when the prince passed by," continued Zach.

"It really was," Tanya agreed, and they both laughed.

"And I held up Gabriel to him—he was four then— and I said, 'Prince, it's this child's birthday today, too. He's four. Will you make a special wish for his birthday?' And the prince looked at us and said, 'What do I care?' And he walked on."

"Oh, no," said Celia. She was eating potato chips and feeling very well entertained, even though Sharon was talking to some other people on the opposite side of the fire.

"Yes. But the press heard," Zach said. "They took Gabriel's picture, and it made all the papers. They even phoned us up for an interview after we got back to Canada. They spoke to Tanya."

Tanya laughed, her eyes shining in the firelight.

"This reporter asked Tanya if she would make a special wish for the prince's next birthday. And she said—tell Celia what you said, Tanya."

"I said, 'My wish is that on his next birthday, the prince will receive the finest, most amazing, most valuable gift a human being can possibly ask for,'" said Tanya. "'What is that?' the reporter asked me, and I said, 'He will learn to see the world through the eyes of children.'"

Sharon threw split wood onto the fire and it flamed up, sending sparks into the cool damp night. Tanya organized the children on the fallen logs that served as seats and taught them a Hebrew song, which they ended up just clapping to and singing "la la la." Seated on her lawn chair, Celia told Zach, who seemed a most spiritual man and had studied at the Jewish Theological Seminary, how she and her friends had studied there in the forties. She described what a wonderful relationship they'd had with their teachers.

"There was one marvelous Talmud teacher who took up so much of our time that all our husbands resented him very much," she said. "So we decided to teach him a lesson. We invited him to dinner in one classmate's apartment and prepared a very fancy meal. But we covered the walls, the floor, the tablecloth, everything, with the papers he'd assigned to us over the year. Our husbands came to the dinner, too. The entire apartment was just plastered with this teacher's assignments—I think we even got some onto the ceiling. He took it very well."

Zach laughed, and then two ladies came over with plastic cups of coffee and tea, and he introduced Celia. The ladies were in charge of the hot water and the roasting of marshmallows, which Celia said sincerely that she was anticipating with great pleasure. They put lumps of sugar into her tea and told her about their sons who were doctors and lawyers in Greenville, Winnipeg, and Toronto, and about a very good recipe for cherry pie, as cherry season was just beginning. When faced with certain types of ladies, Celia understood her own mother, who had almost never spent time in female company. Instead of coffee klatches, her mother had spent her free evenings attending lectures on history, literature, and philosophy at the Henry Street Settlement House. She did walk to the lectures with another woman, but Celia remembered that their friendship was entirely formal and they always called each other Mrs. Newman and Mrs. Sanders.

After hearing the recipe for cherry pie, she had a talk with a nice country gentleman who told her and Zach about growing up on a farm on the prairies. He said they used to drive to town during mud season and that sometimes the mud would freeze and there would be two frozen ruts just large enough for the truck tires.

"You'd have to just get into those ruts and go; you couldn't move out of them at all until you got to town. You could only drive about twenty-five miles an hour, too."

"So you had to be in the rut if you wanted to go anywhere at all," Celia commented. "How interesting." Sharon had handed her a toasted marshmallow on the end of a green stick, and she ate it, relishing the odd combination of sugar and stick—peeled by her daughter's pocketknife.

"Well, I've been going along slowly in a type of frozen rut," she told Zach after the country gentleman had gone off to toast a marshmallow. "I'm glad to hear it's the only way to get anywhere." He said, "Yes?" and looked at her with wide calm eyes as she told him about losing Bernard and coming to the wilderness. While she spoke he ate in quick succession four toasted marshmallows that Yishai handed him.

"You will get somewhere," he said, licking marshmallow off a finger. "This time, the time of the Counting of the Omer, is also the ascent out of the narrow place, Egypt. Each day you come a little closer to Shavuot, to the Temple, carrying your accumulated harvest. Do you see?"

JACOB WAKEMAN, KETURAH'S FATHER, was carrying a full pail of grain in each hand when Celia and Sharon approached the farmhouse; *he* seemed the quintessential bearer of the Omer. He wore a dark blue velvet kippah with a Star of David embroidered on it, and around his neck was a small stained-glass star made of blue and red triangles. When Celia complimented the glass star, he said he'd made it himself and that Keturah had sewn the kippah. "I only wear them on Sabbath," he said. His smile seemed to emanate from his eyes and his whole body, right down to his feet in leather boots. "I'm glad you could come. We don't meet too many like-minded people around here." He did not say Jews but looked as if he found his omission very amusing.

Celia grinned, feeling a strange sense of intimate hilarity. "The last thing I expected of the wilderness was an invitation to Saturday lunch," she said. "I'm delighted to be here." She looked around the farm, at the barns built of weathered wood, smaller and older than the Hammond barns. There were sheep in pens and on the grassy hillside behind the house, and little lambs were everywhere. It really was delightful. She had celebrated holidays on farms—sometimes her family had gotten on so well with the farm families they stayed with in summer that they were invited back for Christmas or Easter—but she'd never experienced anything Jewish on a farm.

Sharon had shaken hands lightly with Jacob; this habit of hers Celia found oddly sweet and feminine—not that it was intended to be.

"You *are* the bear, aren't you?" Jacob said, and they laughed at something Celia didn't understand. "Your mother blew your cover."

"You were the bear at Purim!" Keturah exclaimed.

"Yeah, well." Sharon looked flushed in the spring air. "My mother creates these events; it's impossible not to be swept along on the wave."

"Well, I'm just bringing some grain up to some of the sheep—one of our prize-winning sheep, Hulda, gave birth last night." Jacob picked up the pails he'd set down. "I was out here at two in the morning helping her push the head out. Do you want to come and see the lambs?"

Celia, Sharon, and Keturah followed him up the path toward the barn closest to the house. It was made of beautiful old boards that had weathered to a dark brown with black streaks. This is a Frost farm, a Longfellow farm, Celia thought, feeling glad of her sensible shoes as she stepped around the muddy areas. Sharon had at first declined to come to the Sabbath lunch, saying she didn't want to risk ruining her reputation in the valley as a hermitess, but then she'd suddenly changed her mind. She came to pick up Celia at the motel dressed rather strikingly in tooled cowboy boots, black jeans, and a white silk shirt. Keturah was wearing green and blue eye makeup blended into an elaborate swirl around each eye, the design looking as if she'd copied it from a women's magazine. Aside from the eye shadow, she wasn't dressed up at all; she wore faded jeans, a sweatshirt of indeterminate color, and old basketball sneakers. Of course, Celia knew from experience that with the young you never knew what was intended as fancy dress.

"These are some of our prize sheep," Keturah said, gesturing toward some large, thickly wooled ones that stood nursing their lambs in an outdoor pen. "That's Zipporah, that's Bathsheba, and that's Dinah." Celia and Sharon were given to understand that these plump young matrons and their offspring were worth thousands of dollars each and that the Wakemans were experts at breeding them. In the next pen was Absalom, a handsome ram with thick curling horns that he butted against the railing.

"I can't let Absalom eat too much fresh grass on the hill in early spring, or he'll eat so much he'll make himself sick," explained Jacob. He was distributing the grain, pouring it into the troughs.

Hulda lay in the straw at the edge of the barn with her lamb; both of them looked up at Keturah, and Hulda ate grain from the girl's palm. Hulda then let Jacob place the lamb in Celia's arms. He did so with delicacy, only withdrawing his hands after the lamb was settled against Celia's bosom. He moved about slowly, with deliberation. His simplicity and concentration on nature seemed very like Sharon, who stood next to him and seemed to watch him closely. The lamb was soft and light. It bleated faintly, its heart racing next to Celia's own.

\* \* \*

IT HAD RAINED most of that morning, and now, out in the freshened air, Sharon felt a lifting, a reprieve. It was a bit like stepping outside for the first time after a long illness. Celia and Keturah had walked down the path ahead of Sharon and Jacob, as Keturah wanted to show Celia the chickens, but now the girl turned, shouting something and pointing to the sky. Sharon and Jacob followed her gesture and watched as a faint rainbow gradually deepened its bands. They stopped walking and looked at the seven colors, the end of the bow plunging into a cloud over the barn. Sharon saw the blocks of hay stacked up both inside and outside the barn and remembered her fantasy of some kind of fertility ritual against the hay he'd grown and molded.

"This is quite a change for a New Yorker," Jacob remarked.

"Well, by way of Vancouver," she explained.

"I was there for a while myself. But the city seemed pretty grim, all those cars and stores and people, everyone frantic about something. When I think of Vancouver, I just see neon signs behind the rain, like colored tears."

"The last time I lived in the city things were moving so fast I hardly knew who I was anymore," Sharon said. "I was never less reflective in my whole life."

"Well, in the country you can reflect as much as you want. I like being outside with no one watching or trying to talk to me," Jacob admitted.

"Me too. And if my eyes rest on something it's just a tree or a rock. It's not in opposition to me." Above them, the rainbow gradually dissipated. For a moment, Sharon felt that the day was so ordinary and yet so alluring; it could repeat itself endlessly into a time she would live in and gladly forget about all the other, more dramatic times.

\* \* \*

"THE LAST TWO THOUSAND years have sort of passed us by. But Yishai won't teach us anything," said Jacob as he served lunch, which was barley soup, lamb cooked with onions, salad, and something he baked himself and called Sabbath bread. This looked less like challah and more like some thick dark Russian loaves Celia recalled vaguely from childhood. They had pressed her for information from the moment she approached their doorpost: What did she think of their mezuzah? It was hand written in English on a small roll of paper inside a varnished wooden case Jacob's father had made. Celia admitted it was not what most Jews would do but said it was interesting. On the windowsill sat a seven-branched brass candelabrum Jacob had bought at a Dukhaboor antique shop, liking its similarity to the one in the Great Temple. Keturah said they lit all seven candles every Friday night, and Celia, amazed, said that was very interesting too.

"Well, Yishai wants us to stay exactly the way we are," Keturah explained. "He says we're in a pure biblical state. Aren't there some special prayers before we eat?"

There was no wine, and neither Celia nor Sharon remembered more than the one key line of the Shabbat kiddush. Keturah poured out lemonade, and after a moment's hesitation Celia sang the first Hebrew song that came to her mind, an old Palestinian tune she'd learned in the thirties. The words meant, "Work is made for the Pioneer, the Pioneer is made for Work."

"Of course it's not traditional for the day of rest," Celia said, laughing afterwards, "but it does seem appropriate to sing that on a farm." Celia then recited the blessings for wine and bread, while they watched her raptly.

"Is that all?" Keturah asked when she'd finished.

Jacob handed Celia a plate with steaming lamb. "It must have been fascinating to be in Palestine."

"Yes. This lunch is absolutely delicious. It was a very idealistic place when I was there. Mother and I once met a concert pianist who was very proud to be working as a garbage man. He was secretly longing for a piano, so we arranged for him to practice in the apartment of someone we knew who owned one. You should have seen him run for that piano!"

"Do they have many sheep there now?" Jacob asked.

"I don't know. I imagine there are kibbutzim that still raise sheep."

He shook his head. "I couldn't live on a kibbutz. I'm more of a wandering, solitary type of shepherd."

"Some of the kibbutz shepherds I met weren't so pleased with their lot," Sharon remarked. "I thought it was romantic, but they would rather have worked in the truck transmission repair shop. The comrades wouldn't let them, though."

"I'm very curious," said Celia to Jacob, "about how your ancestors happened to come to British Columbia. Were they always farmers?"

"Yes. But of course they weren't Jews." He reached for the knife and cut several thick slices of Sabbath bread, offering more to her and Keturah.

"None of them were Jewish?" Celia paused with her knife and fork suspended over her plate, and she and Sharon glanced at each other. Somehow she'd imagined at least one Jewish grandparent, some actual connection. The fact that there wasn't one frightened her a little.

"No, most of them were Mormon. We're not really Jewish, according to Jewish law. Although we do have a strange story in our family about a great-uncle of mine who came from somewhere on the east coast of the United States. He made his living as a peddler, and he was also known to be very particular about his food. He wouldn't eat certain foods cooked together, things the rest of the family thought it was normal to eat. They always remarked about these strange personal customs he had."

"Hm, maybe he was Jewish." Celia was charmed by the cadence of Jacob's speech: clear, precise, with the unsophisticated impact of a folk tale well told.

"But how did your parents get the idea of living as Jews?" Sharon asked.

Jacob shrugged. "My father read the Bible. He knew it pretty well, and he found the Christian parts not to his liking. He related to Abraham, wandering through the country with his sheep and goats, a family living alone in a big landscape. Religiously speaking, he was very simple. He believed there was one God for the whole world, and it wasn't a human being, either. He said if people understood that, the war wouldn't have happened. He was in the Canadian army during World War II, and he saw a lot of terrible things."

Celia stopped eating her meal and looked at Jacob.

"He was in a unit that was hunting down SS officers. And he went through some of the concentration camps after they were liberated. He said he remembered mainly the smell. Everything else, to tell the truth, he said it was all a little confused with things he heard about later on or saw on television, but that smell he could always be sure he remembered exactly."

Celia's eyes filled with tears.

"Maybe that had something to do with his wanting to be Jewish," Sharon suggested.

"Maybe." Jacob shrugged indulgently, as if it really wouldn't have occurred to him.

Although the farmhouse had obviously been neatened for their arrival, Celia saw signs of a usual disorder that rivaled her own, had she been a farmer and had no Sophia to pick up and polish. There was an enormous and varied heap of boots, sneakers, and shoes near the front door, and another of coats and sweaters deeply piled on a rack. On their way to the living room, where Jacob said he'd bring their tea, they glimpsed Keturah's room, in which books and papers were mingled with heaps of clothing. At the foot of her bed a pile of stained mattresses and torn blankets was made into a sort of nest.

"My room is terrible." Keturah led Celia and Sharon quickly into the living room, which had no rug, just a bare wooden floor swept clean. "I have two motherless kids—twins—that have been sleeping with me at night. Dad did a caesarean on the mother, but she died anyway. They're busy chewing up my homework all night, but I feel so sorry for them."

Sharon laughed.

"They're just spoiled." Jacob was carrying in mugs of tea which he set down on a heavy, hand-built low table. "They're old enough to sleep in the barn. Does anyone take sugar?"

"Dad thinks I'm a little too—what's that word—indigent with the animals." Keturah sat in a worn armchair across from Celia and Sharon, who sat on a couch covered with a crocheted afghan. "In winter I let the little chicks come in around the wood stove, and I always have lambs or something in my bed." She rested her mug of tea on the scarred wooden arm of the chair.

"You mean indulgent, dear," Celia said.

"I'm afraid we live like two bachelors here." Jacob was stirring spoonfuls of sugar into his tea. He sat across from them in a small rocking chair. The room was so simple that the bright green meadow one saw through the window seemed like the main decoration. There were no pictures on the walls except a framed photograph of Keturah as a little girl, feeding a lamb with a baby bottle. "Do you know many other folks in the valley yet?" Jacob asked Sharon.

"No, I'm a kind of hermitess, actually." They both laughed.

Celia noticed how natural they seemed together, as if Sharon had sat in this room many times before. "Her cabin is much further from the highway than your house, and no one I've met even knows it's there. As her mother, I'm a little worried."

Jacob looked at them with blue eyes that were alert but uncalculating. "Some people are just born wanderers, and they're happiest in a place where no one knows them. I understand it a little bit myself—I've lived on four different farms in British Columbia and Alberta." He looked thoughtful for a moment, then added, "In a movie I saw once there was a guy right in the middle of New York City who couldn't stop wandering for hours at a time. But he had a very interesting system. He'd arrive at an intersection, and go immediately in whatever direction had the green light." Sharon looked startled. "How strange. That's exactly what I used to do when I lived in New York."

"She'd disappear for hours, but she knows the city better than I do," said Celia. "I wonder what made you think of that?"

Jacob smiled and shrugged.

"Dad has ESP sometimes." Keturah had brought in a plate of colorful cookies. "I made ginger snaps. I couldn't resist decorating them—I just love blue and green sugar."

"So do I." Celia bit into a cookie topped with a spray of green crystals. "My mother had ESP," she told them. "Back then we called it 'second sight.' Once, when my brother Yale was staying on in Palestine, after Mother and I had already returned to New York, Mother suddenly became frantic. She was certain he was in terrible danger, but there was nothing she could do. They had no telephones then, so she just had to wait for a cable. Weeks later she found out he'd been ill with tetanus in Tiberias and had nearly died. The young men had been using long nails—it was very stupid—to prod their horses into going faster. Mother told them not to, but they did it anyway. One of the nails was rusty, and he'd cut himself on it."

Their hosts exclaimed over that, interested in any story that included animals.

"Mother died unexpectedly from a stroke, when she wasn't very old," Celia continued impulsively. "But she seemed to know it was coming. The week before she died, she finished a whole list of things she'd been meaning to accomplish, and she went to visit a number of people she hadn't seen in a long time. I remember her saying she simply had to see them that week. And yet she was perfectly healthy."

"Hm." Jacob looked unhappy and far away. There was an awkward silence, and Celia realized it was inconsiderate to talk about losing one's mother to him and Keturah, poor things.

"I don't know how I got onto that subject." Celia took a red, yellow and blue cookie from the plate. "I meant to talk about more cheerful things."

"What are those dogs barking about?" asked Sharon quickly.

There was a yipping and howling from their dogs outside, so Keturah went to the window and looked out. Several small dogs and at least a dozen cats wandered around the house and yard. "I don't see why they're barking." She sat down again. "There's something I'd like to ask both of you."

"Yes, dear," said Celia.

"Is honey kosher?"

"Yes, of course it is."

"Well, are bees kosher?"

Celia considered that for a moment. "No."

"You can eat the honey, but not the bee?"

"I think that's correct," said Celia, "but I can't tell you why."

Sharon sighed. "People *want* all that stuff to be inexplicable."

Celia thought back to her Talmud class at the Theological Seminary. "It may be that the honey is considered separately from the bee, as something the bee produces, rather than as a part of the bee."

"Oh!" said Keturah.

"Very interesting," said Jacob.

Keturah smiled her sweetest smile. "I've *always* wanted to know the answer to that question." Her eyes seemed to glow, quite apart from the bright makeup surrounding them.

\* \* \*

As SHARON AND CELIA were leaving, Jacob took Sharon's hand for a moment and pressed it gently between his own. "Thanks for lunch," she said, feeling warm and unguarded. As at Purim, she felt that these people were both magnetic and alien. Keturah followed them outside to the truck because she had to feed her chickens. It was around four in the afternoon, and smoke was blowing in the wind that drifted up over the meadows.

"I smell burning lighter fluid," said Sharon.

"Delicious," Celia said.

"They're already starting some fires down at Billy's." Keturah said. "They've probably been drinking since about noon, if I know them."

"Are you going to the party?" asked Celia.

Sharon noticed that Keturah seemed to have a wild streak in her, along with her Talmudic mind.

"Just for a very short time." They were standing out on the dirt road that led to the farmhouse; the air was cool and smelled of flowers and manure along with the smoke. "I'm thinking of dropping out of school and doing home schooling. The kids in school are mainly doing things that aren't good for them, and you can't learn anything there. I wish I could learn about Jewish things, Hebrew, the holidays."

"I can teach you," Celia offered.

Just then they heard a strange cry. They stopped near the truck and waited, and then they heard it again, a bleating moan. "Something's wrong with one of the animals," said Keturah. "But it sounds like it's coming from down near those trees. I don't know how it got out." She began to run down the hill toward a clump of evergreen trees at the foot of the drive, and Sharon, after a moment's hesitation, walked quickly after her. The sun had dropped behind the large hill to the west, so the farm was in shadow. The world seemed motionless, timeless.

She heard Keturah scream.

"Keturah! What is it?" Sharon called.

"Oh, no!" Keturah cried.

"What happened?" called Celia, from further up the drive.

Sharon ran to the clump of trees and saw Keturah struggling to untie a ram that was lying on its side, its legs tied up with ropes. With a shudder she realized it was lying, bound, on a big pile of stones heaped up crudely in the shape of a primitive altar. The animal made a low moan but wasn't struggling. There was a bloody gash on his neck. Keturah sobbed and tugged at the ropes. "You poor thing! You're half gone." She gathered the ram in her arms and tried to move him off the fake altar. Sharon put her arms around the rump of the ram and helped her lift him.

The front door slammed and Jacob came running down the drive.

"Dad! Ezekiel's practically dead!" Keturah and Sharon staggered with the weight of the ram, dropping him to the ground. Celia came up the road behind them.

Jacob came and knelt near the animal. "He's gone."

Keturah wiped blue and green streaks across her cheekbones and sobbed out the story of the altar. Jacob's face went slack with shock for a moment. "Somebody built this evil thing right at the entrance to our road, Dad. Somebody hates us here. That ram is worth about two thousand dollars," she added to Sharon and Celia.

A car turned the corner down near the altar and drove up their road. "It's Yishai! He's in his father's car." Keturah stood up and combed her hair back from her face with her fingers as he pulled over quickly. The car was shiny and low to the ground; it looked out of place on the dirt road.

"What the—?" said Yishai, getting out of the car and looking at the dead ram.

"They tied Ezekiel up and put him on an altar," said Keturah.

"*What?* Who did?"

She shrugged. "Don't know. We do *not* practice animal sacrifices, if that's what they were trying to say."

"Those dickheads!" Yishai swore.

"Yishai, do your parents—uh?"

He rubbed his chin, which was shadowed by a hint of stubble. "They went out; they were walking across town to the Finklemans'. I wouldn't go, so they left me at home. They'll be home late—they won't know when I left."

"Yishai's not supposed to drive on the Sabbath," Keturah informed them.

"I thought so," Celia replied. "We won't say anything." Neither of them responded; there was tension in the air.

"Well, I just had to get here," said Yishai.

"I'm sure the Almighty understands." Keturah seemed absolutely certain of this point.

"There was a fight," he said to Keturah.

"About what?"

"I don't know. They all of a sudden started saying, 'Who are you becoming now? Do you still want to go to college next fall?' All this stuff."

"It's about me," said Keturah. "People just don't like us around here."

"My father says you're either going to break my heart or his."

"That's a fallacy," murmured Sharon.

"My father says Jacob and Keturah aren't Jewish," Yishai explained. "OK. So the community said maybe they could become honorary members. So now my father's pissed off at the community. He doesn't even want them to vote on it."

"I just asked about becoming a member," said Jacob. "I didn't know it would cause such a lot of concern."

"Now Jacob and Keturah can have some honorary anti-Semitism. Very nice." Yishai looked like his father, though he was the country version, a self-contained mountain-bred Bernstein: something his ancestors never dreamed of. "You know, most of these people in the community are about as Jewish as Brian Mulroney," he told them. "They don't really care about it."

"The kids don't," Keturah said. There was silence for a moment, and then she put her head in her hands and moaned. "I just can't stand it. That evil thing is still sitting there."

"Let's go down there." Yishai stood up. "Show it to me." He held out his hand to her, and the two of them walked off into the darkness.

"He's a nice boy," said Jacob quietly after the young people had disappeared. "But his parents are pretty upset about Keturah."

In the distance they heard shouts and the sound of large rocks crashing to the ground.

# IX

"I've learned never to underestimate a current," Sharon told Celia, as she steered the canoe through the shallow water at the edge of the lake, brown weeds tangling around her paddle. "Once Thunder and I bought a small motor, and we decided to try it out on a river up north. We motored up a stretch that looked calm, but the motor was straining and the canoe went really slowly. So we brought the motor back to the store. The man was surprised when we said it wasn't strong enough. Later, I went over the topographic map and I realized we'd been canoeing up the river just above some huge rapids and waterfalls. The water looked calm, but the river was just about to go crazy."

"Don't tell me any more! I'm your mother."

Sharon smiled. They were clear of the weeds now, so she pulled the engine cord several times, feeling triumphant when the motor caught and she steered the canoe toward the middle of the lake. She was taking Celia across the water to see some eight thousand-year-old petroglyphs on the other side. The canoe was loaded with waterproof Voyageur bags containing a tarp, a large picnic lunch, a stove to make tea, and chalk and paper for rubbings. Celia sat in the bow, wearing a 1920's-style straw hat and an orange life preserver over her dress.

When they reached the middle of the lake, Sharon cut the motor and they floated alone in the sudden quiet. The lake looked like a magical blue stone over which they glided with heavy grace, toward the cleft between two large terraced hills with rock faces rippling down to the water. The whole lake seemed to flow to this magnificent hanging rock.

"That's why they put the petroglyphs there!" Celia pointed to the rock. "It's their Mount Moriah. The urge toward the high place is universal." At that moment she looked almost outdoorsy, in her simple flowered dress with the sleeves rolled up and her face turned into the wind.

The water was deep and clear, and dark plants waved below them. A loon swimming about ten feet away dove under and disappeared, leaving ripples on the surface of the lake. A few moments later the bird popped up a good thirty feet away, its little black and white feathered head looking sarcastic. It let out a long liquid scream of laughter that echoed against the hills. Sharon hooted back, delighted.

Celia had half-turned on the canoe seat to look at Sharon from under the brim of her flapper hat. "Do you think you'll ever get married, dear?"

"Uh, I don't know." Sharon was surprised. "There's no one in my life right now."

Her mother didn't seem to see that as any particular obstacle. "I guess it's old-fashioned of me, but I still believe marriage is one of the most marvelous aspects of life. You have to find someone you really like, of course."

"At my age, it's hard to find a man who's not ruined," said Sharon. "Most people always seem to be clearing the path. Their lives are like a road they're always grading, preparing for the entrance of some great thing. But the great thing never does come down the road, and in the meantime they've swept it clear of everything interesting."

"Well, I'm an optimist," said Celia. "I really believe there's someone for everyone."

"Romance has a hard time in such an artificial world," Sharon observed.

"Not here!" Celia gestured into the cool wind. They were floating, surrounded on all sides by hills piled with evergreens pointing at a sky so lovely it seemed more than blue, as if all the most spectacular colors in the world were pulsing just behind it.

Sharon didn't mention that she herself felt a bit ruined. The loon, which had been paddling out in front of them as they drifted, dove under again and swam in a wide arc, popping up behind them and seeming to laugh uproariously at having eluded Sharon's big aluminum canoe.

\* \* \*

CELIA'S KNEES WERE MUCH less bothersome now. She knew how to approach the path, placing each foot carefully to avoid stone and root, slowly lifting her body higher into the hills. Each subsequent rock terrace was home to different flora: tiny strawberries on the first, each tasting like a drop of strawberry liqueur; then bluebells; and then the most lovely paintbrushes and shooting stars up around the rippling ancient rocks where the petroglyphs were carved.

The first pictures were spirals and circles, interspersed with human stick figures that looked like astronauts floating among the planets and stars. The petroglyphs almost jumped with clarity; Celia half expected a Mesolithic man to spring out from behind a Saskatoon tree.

Sharon unrolled the Voyageur bag containing paper and colored chalk, and Celia made a blue rubbing of a spiral. She felt exhilarated, perhaps from the hike, perhaps from traveling into the ancient equivalent of the forms in Sonia Delaunay's "Market." Climbing to the next ledge, she found an exquisite bird petroglyph, a beautifully proportioned form with folded wings and fanciful pluming head feathers. It seemed to be outlined by a band of white light that refused to leave her eyes.

"It's the symbol of the soul, the flight of the soul after death," she explained to Sharon.

"It doesn't look like any type of bird I've ever seen around here," Sharon remarked. "Maybe eight thousand years ago there were different species in this area."

Celia felt as if her own soul had gained altitude slightly, in response to the bird with its band of persistent white light. Oh yes, there were moments in her life when her soul had flown, separate from her body. She saw herself and her boyfriend Yunis kissing under a tree on the Mount of Olives, the moon making a faint glow on the Old City of Jerusalem below. Yunis had just been bragging that he wasn't afraid of anything, not Arabs and not spirits from the rows of graves along the hillside. Then they heard rustling and creaking among the trees. With no hesitation they dashed downhill almost as one body, both of them feeling it was not a human presence but some challenging angel come to wrestle with them, wound them. She remembered the feeling of inner lightness just before the soul-essences of both Celia and Yunis rose together above their running forms. They ran all the way back to her mother, who sat waiting up for them at the hotel in the yellow glow of a kerosene lamp, sewing a button that had come off one of Celia's traveling dresses.

"It looks a little like a peacock." Sharon held a large sheet of paper up over the bird so Celia could do a rubbing.

Celia smoothed over the design with a piece of bright green chalk. As the bird's image appeared she said, "It is a peacock! This reminds me of my trip to Jordan with Bernard, when he was the guest of the Jordanian government, as you probably remember. He was advising them on water resources. Everywhere we went they were selling peacock feathers, so Bernard bought me one which I carried around for the rest of our trip, tucked into the strap of my bag. A young man asked me to give him the feather, as a sign of favor I suppose, but I said I couldn't give it to him because it was a gift from my companion."

"Hm."

Listening to Sharon's tone, Celia felt once again how her life with men other than Raymond always seemed slightly unserious to her children, a bit of playacting. In the deepest sense, there may have been a bit of truth to that.

Then Bernard's face appeared with startling clarity in her mind's eye, just as he was that day he bought her the peacock feather in Jordan. They were staying at the hotel in Petra; the weather was hot, the air weighty. She had felt suddenly afraid, alone in her room, and had gone into Bernard's adjoining room. She told him how much she feared losing him: to death. He had smiled rather impishly and said that of course he liked thinking the world could not go on without him, but it probably could, and she too would find a way, as she had when Raymond died. He held her very close and absently smoothed her dress, which was wrinkled from the sloppy way she'd packed it.

The peacock emerged onto the paper, bright green and full of enduring detail.

Bernard left her as suddenly as he'd appeared; her mind chased his image, but it lost the movement of vision and became static as memory. To cover her emotion she rubbed and rubbed, making circles and spirals and little figures appear.

"This would make a wonderful children's book," she said to Sharon. "A girl could come to visit her aunt in British Columbia, and they would go on a canoe trip to see some petroglyphs. The girl would wonder about the children who lived here eight thousand years ago, whether they drew pictures on the rocks too." Just talking about children purified the strangeness of life, brought the imagination safely home.

"Childhood seems about eight thousand years ago," Sharon remarked.

"Children have such an enormous capacity for happiness." Celia selected a bright yellow piece of chalk from the bag Sharon held out to her.

"I wasn't so happy." Sharon looked up at the clouds as if discussing the weather. "I don't like living with servants around, and there were so many parties and people. When every minute of time is filled with people, and every inch of space is filled with things, it makes me feel like nothing new will ever happen. Nothing ever seems to get done. I can remember thinking that when I was nine."

Celia hesitated in choosing the next color, her hand hovering over the Voyageur bag. "I guess I knew that." Of course Sharon had always been the odd one, so private, the one who would ask for something like a locking file cabinet for her birthday. Yet she was always Celia's favorite: the one who'd caused her the most pain at birth and forever after.

Later they walked back downhill to picnic beside the lake, where they found the most dramatic petroglyph: a face with huge round eyes like the sockets of a skull; a nose, and a mouth opened wide. Celia stopped on the path and stared. Perhaps, she thought, it was the image of a god, hungry for sacrifice. Or maybe it represented the human spirit, placed within the sacred sphere of rock and water as an aid in the soul's travels toward the World to Come. She felt Bernard's eyes on her, the eyes of everyone departed.

"It's so naked. So unconcealed," she said to Sharon, who agreed.

Celia added, "I've spent my life favoring concealment, but I'm not sure it's best." Her voice broke a little with emotion.

"Maybe not." Sharon looked down at an ancient circle she'd found on the back of the same rock. Her fingers traced the circle over and over.

Celia walked around carefully, feeling certain it was a religious ritual to travel to this remote place and carve an image on the rocks, an offering to the power implied by the mountain, the water, the sky. If I forget thee O mountain: a route to the navel of the world, iris of the eye, always arrived at through art, the curve of a line or phrase. She thought of Sonia's pulsating circles and half circles, art as a depiction of the energy behind all existence. "This place reminds me of a story," she said, feeling strangely calm and almost rejuvenated.

"One day a few years ago, Yedidja happened to be visiting Jerusalem, and he was having a drink with some friends on the terrace of the Intercontinental Hotel. Now, the Jordanians built the Intercontinental right over a Jewish cemetery, and members of Yedidja's family had been buried there for generations. Yedidja was having a quiet talk with his friends, but suddenly he leapt up and cried out that he couldn't sit on the graves of his ancestors. He said he felt physical pain."

Sharon smiled. "Good for Yedidja. He wasn't afraid to howl that out, right in some posh cocktail lounge."

"No, he wasn't. The place was so powerful for him."

Sharon looked at her with interest. "You're beginning to like it here."

Celia nodded. "I want to spend some time by myself in your cabin, if I may. I want to see what it's like to be alone in the woods."

Sharon, who was busy spreading out the tarp and unpacking the picnic lunch from the Voyageur bags, stopped with a plastic box of sandwiches in one hand and stared at Celia. "But it's dangerous. I mean it might be, for you. Actually, I don't know why I'm saying that. Of course you can if you want to."

"Thank you, dear." Celia wanted to listen to the wind in the trees, to see if a challenging angel would visit her, like the angel she ran from with Yunis.

"I guess I always count on you to be my New York," said Sharon. "You know, the antithesis of the woods."

Celia laughed. They sat on the tarp eating hard boiled eggs and cucumber sandwiches, Sharon at one end, Celia at the other, and the gaping carved face between them.

"I probably will have a kid someday," Sharon confessed.

"I'm glad you want to."

"It's not so much wanting to; it's more like just knowing that I will." She looked momentarily ecstatic, the trees of the sacred grove reflected in her sunglasses.

In the heat of the day Celia's daughter seemed to her very complicated, amber-like, with visible wonders contained in her translucence. Celia glanced at the carved face, which seemed almost alive, a witness. My child, she thought, looking back anxiously at Sharon, who was wearing a sleeveless shirt that showed her strong arm muscles. Sharon was sprinkling black pepper on an egg. My little Sharona Begonia, don't ever get away from me completely.

Late in the day they canoed back across the lake, the water almost opaque now, the sun sliding behind the mountains. The surrounding forest seemed vibrant with the watchful eyes of hidden animals. Celia looked down into the water and saw her own mother swimming swiftly through the waving plants, her body pointed with a directness she had lacked in life. She had been pliant, tactful. Celia's grandmother, her father's mother, lived with them and was a constant torment to Celia's mother. Each Friday this grandmother gave twenty pounds of gefilte fish to a Jewish home for the elderly. Though it was Celia's mother who actually made all the gefilte fish every week, the baked golden balls of fish were delivered in the name of her mother-in-law, and it was her mother-in-law who took credit for the act of charity.

Celia remembered her mother chopping the fish in her big wooden bowl, saying philosophically that after all, her husband couldn't help having a difficult mother. In real life Celia's mother had been a good swimmer, with a slow steady crawl, so conceivably she could have shot through the water as she did now, direct as desire. As her mother vanished among the plants, Celia felt she must be happy, there in the World to Come. Celia dipped her paddle into the dark water, half holding her breath, expecting someone to grasp the flat end from underneath.

*  *  *

A SHORT WHILE LATER Sharon had loaded all their gear into the back of the truck and lashed the canoe on top. When she started the truck, though, it wouldn't budge, even in four-wheel-drive. She tried rocking the big vehicle back and forth in the mud near the shore, but she'd driven too close to the water.

"Are we stuck, dear?" Celia seemed relaxed in the front seat, reading a paperback history of the gold rush.

"Just temporarily a bit mired." But when Sharon got out of the truck and walked around, she saw there wasn't a single tree close enough to attach the winch to. She walked back and forth in front of the truck, agitated by the lack of a tree and by what she had confessed to her mother about wanting to have a child.

"Look." She came around to Celia's window. "I'm going to have to walk down to the highway to get help. I'll make you some tea before I start, and you have your book. I have a second battery so I can leave all the lights on in the camper."

"Wait a minute. I have the Wakemans' phone number in my bag." Celia rummaged around beneath the clattering container of multicolored pills. She was better in a bush emergency than Sharon would've anticipated.

Sharon looked at the piece of paper, torn from a sheet that had algebra on one side. "I can call Charlotte," she said, but in truth she didn't have Charlotte's number anywhere. She left Celia sitting on the lawn chair in the camper, reading, and walked down the road, stuffing Jacob and Keturah's number into her pocket.

"Oh dear," said the woman in the passing car Sharon hailed at the foot of the mountain. "Such a desolate location." It was a couple from Greenville passing through on their way to Spokane, Washington. Sharon didn't even tell them about her stranded mother and still they were horrified; they usually never stopped in such remote locations and always carried a mobile phone, which Sharon used to call Jacob Wakeman. He said Keturah was out with friends but fortunately he had the truck and would be there in fifteen minutes. She urged the Greenville couple off and waited for Jacob by the side of the road, in front of the provincial park sign.

The white truck approached and stopped on the gravel. For a moment Jacob looked at her over the dashboard, hovering above; then he got out of the truck. His sleeves were rolled up carelessly as if he'd been working, not expecting to see anyone. He looked amused.

"I'm glad you called," he said. "I've been thinking of calling you. But I get the feeling you like it in your hermitage, and I know that feeling so well."

"Sometimes I do," she agreed. "But life is relentless. The same force that pushed you into the hermitage starts pushing you out to see the spring, float across the water one more time. Know what I mean?"

He looked startled. Reaching out his hand, he held her elbow lightly for a moment, then quickly withdrew the hand to his side. "Sure."

"My mother insisted that I call you," she apologized. "She likes the idea of damsels in distress. It's just that there isn't a single tree on that beach close enough to attach the winch to."

"I don't mind rescuing you. And your mother is a great woman."

Sharon sighed. "She has a way of holding so many lives in her own, but she never seems lessened by all their demands on her."

"She only seems even greater."

"Yes." Sharon stood still for a moment. Crickets chirped in the cool spring evening. On the hillside across the highway she could see black shapes, the charred stumps from a forest fire several years ago. Now tall pink fireweed had sprung up in the burned areas. She liked it that Jacob was not a man of many words, but of significant words, like the sudden bubble of living sap emerging on the rough bark of the pine trees. "We canoed up to the petroglyphs today."

"That skull face, that'll chill anyone into thinking about their own mortality." He laughed.

"I know." She thought how the cyclical force, represented by all those spirals, was strongly present. If you stood alone outside the spiral you remained there until you died; but if you entered it you were carried to death anyway, maybe beyond. Remembering Celia, they both turned and got into his truck.

"Well," Jacob said, "we really shouldn't go on pretending there isn't another Jew in the valley. We can admit we know each other." There was a brief silence while no cars passed on the highway. The forest rustled and waited.

She smiled. "Sure, there's practically a whole ghetto on the east fork of the river."

This was a Purim joke, set down in the annals centuries before: her life a perfectly timed reversal of itself. He turned the key in the ignition and they started the drive uphill, turning and returning on the switchbacks.

\* \* \*

ALONE ON SHARON'S LAND, Celia walked along the deer paths; occasionally she'd hear a wheeze and crash and see deer jumping over fallen trees in their flight, white tails flashing. She collected souvenirs: pine and larch cones, bluebells and strawberry flowers, stones glittering with mica. Examining the intricate plant life on the forest floor, she saw a patch of red-edged white petals evolve into a form and thought of a miscarriage she'd had, a tiny purple-white fetus fringed with red tissue. She saw it as if it were colored ink floated onto wet paper, an abstracted, softened horror. It was between Anna and Sharon—strange to think Sharon might never have existed. Why of course, and then she, Celia, would not be here now—obviously to nature it made no difference. Next to the miscarriage flowers she found a sparkling stone that looked like fool's gold. Back at the cabin she placed it on Sharon's desk, next to the computer. The phone rang into the silence, and she answered.

"Mom," said her son Marc, "I called you three times at the motel and you weren't there. Are you OK?"

"Yes, of course. I'm just spending some time at the cabin while Sharon's at work. I go for walks and collect beautiful flowers and pine cones and things."

"What are you doing right now?"

"I'm about to mix up a bit of tuna fish salad for lunch."

"That sounds all right." He sounded unrelieved. "But do you know how to make tuna fish salad?"

"Well, Sharon left me directions." She couldn't promise anything in the cooking department, but then again, he wasn't coming for lunch.

Out walking again later that afternoon, she discovered a set of abandoned deer antlers on the path, with two branches sprouting from a circular crown, bleached white over time by sun and frost. She carried this trophy back to the cabin, planning to sketch it, and placed it next to the golden stone. But it looked so inviting as a hat that she couldn't resist trying it on. Celia had always loved hats; she was often the only woman at a luncheon wearing one. She sat in Sharon's swivel chair, wearing the crown of antlers like Rabbi Akiva's wife Rachel wearing her Jerusalem of Gold. The band of antler felt cool and dry across her forehead; she sat up straighter in the chair, feeling important.

Closing her eyes, she imagined herself as the Antler Queen. She saw her husband Raymond presiding over a great banquet. He sat at the head of a long table covered with a white lace cloth, directing people who were serving gold-edged plates of steaming food, making sure everyone got his portion. Celia knew it was the Great Feast of the Leviathan, the beast killed thanks to Raymond, everlasting hero of her life and all lives to come. The skin of the monster was stretched over poles to make a giant sukkah, in which the seventy nations sat feasting, up in Jerusalem. Somewhere, there was a world at peace that recognized Raymond as a prince of civilization. Was there in fact a place for her at his side? She couldn't quite make out whether—yes, perhaps, a small white chair. Quickly she opened her eyes again, her heart—still of this world—beating rapidly. The antlers felt heavy; she remembered they were a dead thing, and she took them off her head. A bird deep in the forest shrieked, "Raymond!"

LATER THAT WEEK, Keturah, who had already learned the Hebrew alphabet with remarkable speed, came to Sharon's cabin for her lesson with Celia. They sat in the kitchen corner, drinking tea from glasses in silver glass holders that Celia's mother had brought over from Russia, and which Sharon had allowed to tarnish rather badly. Keturah pointed out that the logs of the cabin were still only half peeled; bark clung to them sixty years after building. Yet Sharon had put down a beautifully varnished plank floor and installed modern kitchen appliances.

"Jerusalem," Celia said, glancing through a book on Jewish legends, "is also a symbol of marriage and of unity, as in the unification of the old and new cities in 1967. The city represents a person's chief joy, the gateway to the divine, like the relationship with a husband or wife."

Keturah covered her mouth with her hand, laughing in a rather unladylike way. "I'm sorry, Celia," she gasped.

"That's all right," Celia said. "Really, I'm not such a prude."

That made Keturah giggle even harder. Today she was wearing blue frosted lipstick, imitation diamond earrings, and a blouse with a ruffled neck that looked like something one might wear to a square dance.

"Have you ever thought about going to college?" Celia asked.

Keturah's face became serious; her blue eyes opened wide and momentarily had the expression of childhood, when one is taking in the world, rather than the outward expression of personality which gradually appears in the eyes of adolescents. "My whole life I've wanted to really learn."

"I wish I could take you to New York," said Celia. "You could live with me and go to school."

"Celia, I would be so fortunate. But I can't imagine it; I'd be terrified to go out on the street. And I can't leave Dad alone on the farm."

"Well, there are colleges here, too." Celia felt that it probably would be a crime against nature to remove this creature from her environment; she fit here so perfectly.

"Yes. Mrs. Hammond said I should try for a scholarship—oh, I meant to ask you something, Celia. It's not true, is it, that the Jews used to send a little goat out into the wilderness all by itself?"

"Do you mean the scapegoat? Well, it's described in the Torah."

"It is? But I'm sure it can't be what she said."

"What who said?"

"Mrs. Hammond. She said in class that the Jews used to put all their sins onto the head of a little goat and then send it out to the wilderness. I asked her where did you get such an idea, the Jews would never do a thing like that to a little animal, and she said 'read your Bible.' But I've never seen anything like that in the Bible; she must have misunderstood something. It isn't true, is it?" She looked agitated, her cheeks flushing above the neck-ruffle of her blouse.

"Yes, it is true, if you believe the biblical account. Of course, you have to remember, at that time it was common practice to sacrifice a human being, often a child, to atone for the sins of a community. So by comparison the Jews were progressive. I believe later on they used to push the goat off a cliff outside Jerusalem so it would die instantly."

Keturah was crying. "The poor little thing, to die slowly of hunger and thirst, all alone in the desert," she sobbed.

\* \* \*

SHARON DROVE UP to her cabin that evening with two pear trees and a Siberian olive tree in the back of her truck, and she saw Jacob's white pickup parked in her yard. Inside, Jacob, Keturah and Celia were sitting at her table drinking tea and eating chocolate-covered graham crackers; they were laughing about something and it looked very much like a scene in Celia's breakfast nook in New York. Sharon wasn't used to so much sound and movement in her own home.

"Hello, dear," said Celia. "We're just finishing our lesson, and Jacob came to pick up Keturah. I was about to tell the story of when I taught Sunday school to children in a poor neighborhood—you probably remember this. Well, to ensure that the children took these classes seriously, the school had them pay a nickel each week. There was one student, a girl, who talked all the time, the type who wants to answer every question. I was a young teacher, and it took me a while to figure out how to keep her from taking over the class. Finally, one day, I just ignored her hand whenever it went up. But at the end of that class she came up to me and said, very seriously, 'I didn't get my nickel's worth today!'"

Celia's foreign audience laughed heartily; Sharon smiled politely. "Sorry to take over your cabin like this," Keturah said to Sharon. "We really should be going," added Jacob.

"No, no, go right on. I have two pears and a Siberian olive to plant." Sharon started toward the bedroom to change out of her town clothes.

"I'll help you plant them," Jacob offered. "I'm not bad at digging a hole, though I can't say I know much about Siberian olives."

After Sharon had changed into jeans and work boots she and Jacob went outside, and, contrary to principles she'd held dear at one time, she watched him dig two holes for the pear trees, one on either side of her front door. He dug quickly, plunging the shovel into the earth, stamping on it, then scooping out great curving pieces of dark soil. When he hit a large stone he'd throw down the shovel, and, grabbing the crowbar, work it back and forth under the stone until he'd freed it. Then he'd heave the stone out of the hole and go on digging, his body and the shovel looking like one instrument.

After digging two holes he stopped to rest, breathing rather hard. The wild roses that clung to the front of the cabin were in bloom, their crinkly petals pink against the dark logs, fragrance from their yellow centers in the air. Sharon brought fish fertilizer from the shed and connected the hose. "When I was a kid in New York, we had a mulberry tree in the front yard," she told him. "It had thick branches, and I used to climb up there and sit, hidden in the tree. People would walk right by me on the sidewalk and I'd watch them, but they couldn't see me."

"It sounds like you." Jacob smiled. "So where do you want your olive?"

"In back, where I can see it from the bedroom window."

Again he dug, bending and tossing out the rich earth. He pulled out a boulder, then bent again quickly and pulled something else out of the hole.

It was a cracked and molding leather pouch. "Looks like someone buried something here." Jacob opened the top of the pouch, which cracked further in his hand. "It's a bit of gold dust! What do you know. Some poor old prospector hid it there; it's just a few handfuls. Won't make you rich, but it's interesting." He handed the pouch to Sharon.

The gold was dark and looked very pure. This valley had hosted its own small gold rush, she knew; the Gold Pan Café still offered tourists pans to take out to the stream, to try their luck. Sharon felt the ghosts of former inhabitants of her cabin starting to stir around her. Their shapes were bulky with mountain clothing, their voices ringing in the still air. "I think we'll just leave it where they buried it." She handed the pouch back to Jacob, and he returned it to the bottom of the hole.

Then Sharon went to her truck and got the Siberian olive, which she carried, its roots bound in a little burlap sack. Jacob watched as she leaned over and placed the tree in the hole.

"I never plant trees at my place," he told her.

"Why not?" She sprinkled in earthworm castings and potting soil.

"I'm superstitious about them. Every time I've planted fruit trees I've ended up having to leave a place within two years—I'm never around to see the fruit. I guess the Almighty doesn't want me to get too settled."

"Were you married, then?" Quickly she tamped down the soil with her hands. She usually avoided asking personal questions.

"Both times it happened I was married. After Keturah's mother died, I remarried, but it didn't last long. I have a son in Ontario. My marriages just seemed to be lasting a shorter and shorter time, so I decided I'd better take a break from marrying for a while."

"Human relationships take a lot out of a person. I find trees more rewarding, in general." She told him about Thunder, about his best-selling book poetically recounting his grandfather's and father's lives and his own childhood, the book where he also exposed what the priests had done to his people. "He used to hold court in his mobile home on the reserve, and everyone would come to him for advice, for money. They treated him as a great man. He gave away all the money he made on speaking tours, and he built a new house for his parents. But in the end he thought everyone was out to undermine him." She told Jacob about Thunder going blind and imagining her exchanging looks with his friends.

"That's too bad. I think I did see him on a talk show once."

"His blindness became metaphoric. He wouldn't have his eyes operated on."

She patted the soil down around the new tree with its matte green leaves, and she noticed that her hands had left a faint streak of gold dust on its slender trunk. Then she stood up.

Jacob took her in his arms, sweaty as they both were and covered with dirt, and they kissed. "There's always another life just a short distance away. It's like stepping through a gate," he said.

# X

One moment, Celia, out walking on Sharon's land, noted the sweet green tips of the trees pointing straight to the blue sky; the next moment the weather, that Canadian obsession, had drastically changed its attitude. Dark clouds moved in fast and the trees swayed hard, their pointed tips describing Delaunay circles against the graying sky. The birds all seemed to be flying somewhere. Celia heard voices and activity in the wind, rather like the hammering sounds that often drifted up from the Hammond farm, only now she wasn't sure how far the sounds had traveled. Deer sprang through the bush; squirrels raced up the trees to their nests. It was a warm evening, almost summer, and Celia was just descending the hill in her sensible shoes. This was her first evening here alone; she planned to stay at the cabin for a full three days while Sharon attended a Legal Aid conference up north in Prince George. Sharon had admonished Celia to wear her shawl while walking and to listen to the weather reports—her child, whom she had thought incautious!

In the dimming light the wild flowers were incandescent, orange paint brushes and purple shooting stars floating in her field of vision. Then, as she descended into a small hollow she saw a tiny wild orchid, a perfect half-inch copy of the full-blown purple orchids the 72$^{nd}$ Street florist sold!

She'd known neither that orchids grew in the wild, nor that the complexity of such a flower could exist without human care and in so miniature a form. It made one dizzy, the trees and hills so big, the orchid so small; she felt like Alice falling down the rabbit hole.

It seemed sacrilegious to think of picking the orchid—there was only one—so she stood there fixing its image in her mind. She was fascinated by such intensity of beauty in something so hidden and fragile: the adolescent girl of the forest. Yes, Yunis had said she was ugly and that he was her boyfriend just because he felt sorry for her. On her second trip to Palestine at the age of eighteen, Celia had been a wonderful dancer, not fat in those days—and how they danced on the sand in Tel Aviv! Yunis didn't dance. If she danced, he got mad; if she didn't dance, Estelle got mad and said Yunis prevented Celia from enjoying herself. She remembered the band playing swing music—the clarinetist had admired her, and he played a song especially for her. Later that night she had left the apartment she shared with Estelle in Tel Aviv and walked down over the sand and right into the water, intending to drown herself because Yunis had made her so jealous and unhappy. The clouds were backlit by the moon, heavy with light, beckoning. But the water felt cold, much colder than she'd anticipated. So she'd turned around and waded back out to life.

Feeling a drop of rain on her cheek now, she turned away from the orchid and hurried toward the cabin. The forest was still, expectant; all the animals seemed to have found shelter. Celia felt terribly lonely, fearing that no one on the face of the earth loved her. But how could a remark made by an insensitive meshugeh boy half a century ago still upset her so? Rain was beginning to fall. She heard the trumpet and the clarinet playing, their blasts so clear amid her flashes of memory. *I'm just like an apple on a bough and you're gonna shake me down somehow . . . I have no will you've made your kill* you are actually ugly Celia, *Cause you took advantage of me.* The shiny horns sounded through the darkening forest:

*I suffer something awful each time you go and much worse when you're near . . .*

Yes, Raymond was always with her, though she could seldom bear to think of him for long. Very quietly now his spirit took her by the hand and led her home to their daughter's cabin. His soul had wings that she rode upon, resting; but no, he was not calling her to come sit beside him in the small white chair that awaited her at his Feast. He did not berate her in death, just as he never had in life. Thus she rested entirely, continuously, on his wings, but could not pay attention to it most of the time.

Celia rocked back and forth in Sharon's rocking chair and watched the lightning open up the pulsing black sky outside the cabin window. The sky was cracked apart, then put back together, then cracked apart again, flaming from the highest point above the mountains right down to a spot in the tender meadow grass not far from the window where she watched. Something ought to be revealed in all this. *Bernard!* She straightened up in the chair, sensing that his soul was disturbed, angry. There he was, walking along the path in his shiny shoes, through the woods where she and Sharon had made the petroglyph rubbings. As always, Bernard was immaculately groomed and wearing his three-piece suit. He appeared to be looking for her; he touched the peacock petroglyph, and some blue chalk left from Celia's rubbing came off onto his fingers. Seeming puzzled and annoyed, he resumed his angry walk, his bright brown eyes searching the forest. She recalled all the objections he'd made to this trip and realized, with a shock that was mirrored by another jagged flash in the sky, that she probably wouldn't be here at all tonight if Bernard were still alive. Thunder boomed in the distance: *you shouldn't have!*

Then the clouds closed in over the mountains and rain was released in thick gusts, beating against the window. The thunder cracked louder, a god smashing his drum to bits each time, his huge eye getting closer. The wind blew hard with rasping, clinking sounds, and someone outside called her name: *Cee-lee-ah!* She had indeed distanced her own soul from Bernard's by running her life so sloppily, living dangerously in a cabin of which he would not approve. When Bernard was alive, he assembled all the guidebooks and maps for their destination before each of their trips, planning everything in astounding detail. He liked to quote Stefansson, the Arctic explorer who'd said that an adventure is merely the result of poor planning.

She realized that the ancient people who'd inhabited these woods eight thousand years ago had now joined Bernard in searching for her. They wanted to tell her something, reveal the secret meaning of the peacock, soul in flight to—where? She became afraid of dying; she would have a heart attack or a stroke here in the woods and no one would find her. How could Sharon have just flown away to that conference? But it was too late; Celia was already having an adventure.

The wind blew a high, almost musical note, and once again from out among the trees came the call: "*Cee-lee-ah!*"

"What?" she asked aloud in a trembling voice.

The ancients would give her a magical protective, so that death might not swallow her in this storm. She had never really known how to live; she had done instinctively, haphazardly, what she felt she ought to do: not like Bernard with his maps, not like the ancients, deliberately carving their way through the rocks. She trembled, listening to the indistinguishable voices in the wind.

\* \* \*

BETWEEN THE OPENING SESSION of the conference and dinner with some colleagues from Winnipeg, Sharon decided to explore the highway north of Prince George in her rental car. The moment she was out of town, heading north on the highway where wild roses grew in profusion, she had the comforting sense of an endless journey resumed.

She'd spent the previous night at the farmhouse. Keturah was asleep or pretending to be, and Sharon had left before daylight. Lying in Jacob's bed that night, she felt momentarily that she had slipped into the deep center of things where she could rest. He wasn't interested in analysis; he would not betray her because he was accustomed to not betraying himself. Journeying up the highway now, she felt his presence approaching her, encircling. But his whole way of being was strange to her; it would be like marrying an unseen force, saying yes with no idea of what lay ahead.

Sharon parked the rental car in a dirt lot next to a café-store, and got out to breathe the evening air. She planned to buy a cup of tea and then head back to town for dinner with the lawyers, as it was already growing dark, the bush closing in around her. The highway was a faintly glowing strip, a wish. The wind blew hard, and off to the south some wolves began a sinister opera, singing a sweet, deceptive overture. Then, altos and basses joining in, they sang a story of danger, someone in trouble. The wolves' tongues were stilettos, piercing Sharon's heart. Of course a Jew fears wolves: Russian folk tales in the blood, the bride thrown out of the sleigh into hungry jaws. Still, the animals' voices grew louder, closer, running up and down the scales in complex melodies of warning. There's probably a storm coming, she thought; she worried about Jacob and especially about Celia, alone in the cabin. Listen, *liiisten*, sang the wolves, opening their throats to cry to the full.

\* \* \*

CELIA THREW OPEN the heavy cabin door and the wind almost knocked her over; Sonia Delaunay was blown to the floor in a heap of papers. Raindrops spattered Celia's dress, but she stood there, listening to the voices calling to her from the World to Come: *Cee-lee-ah!* Every few minutes, her name blew in on the wind. The huge trees bent back, looking as if they would break in half. Many of them, Sharon said, were weakened by a pine beetle infestation and could suddenly collapse.

"What? *What?*" Celia cried out into the storm.

She thought of stepping outside; perhaps there really was a lost person behind the shed or up on the hill. But the light from the cabin shone out, revealing a river running down the dirt road and solid lines of rain streaming from the sky. She told herself she was imagining things, that even if Bernard and the ancient spirits were calling, they did not really want her to join them before her time. Yet when *was* her time? She was old, and it could be soon. Perhaps they were calling out a warning that would sear together all the disparate fragments of her life, providing the final organizing principle.

"What?" she called again. The rain blew against her, soaking her dress.

They did not answer; they faded away, or perhaps she was too cold and wet and frightened to listen. After another lightning strike she shut the door quickly. It slammed with a soft, solid sound. Where were the deer in all this? She had often seen them bedded beneath the trees outside this window. Probably they were cozy in a cave up in the hills. It seemed that every creature in the world had a safe, secure place except Celia.

"I am an old, wet woman in the middle of nowhere," she said.

She sank down into the rocking chair and cried. It frightened her to think of her own bedroom at Central Park West, her own soft bed covered with the Guatemalan blanket, her desk overlooking Central Park. Several deep cracks of thunder seemed to shake Sharon's hills. Celia waited for an earthquake, for the world to burst into flames. The Goddess of Finished Projects rose up off the screen and screamed at her against the background of thunder. The dragon was curled about the goddess's feet; she was surrounded by smoke and held a sword dripping blood the color of a child's tempera paint. But Celia's babies were gone, flown!

She thought of Rabbi Bernstein at the Shavuot service this morning, saying Yiskor for the six million Jews, three million of them children, in his Middle-Eastern style of praying where the notes wavered, descended humbly, then sprang up again toward heaven in naked anguish. Many people wouldn't have the nerve to shout at God like that. Jews hid in the countryside, in places like this: If necessary, she could hide up on that ledge Sharon had shown her, where the rocks were sheltering and wild lilies grew. It was nauseating to think of the beautiful sun flashing off the rocks and death stalking. Would they pursue you that far up the hill? She heard the Jews hiding in the forest shouting anxiously at her; she was the first person to remember them tonight. The collective unconscious: All Jewish souls heard the revelation from inside the smoking cloud, and all are collectively terrified from generation to generation. Celia felt herself approaching some kind of knowledge, getting closer, only there was a boundary set up around the knowledge which, if she crossed it, would mean something like annihilation. Still, she approached, the boundary of fear squeezing her old heart and shaking it.

She decided she'd better call her son Marc. She moved to Sharon's swivel chair at the desk and, after several deep breaths, dialed Connecticut.

"Hi Mom, I'm glad you called," he said—it was, rather startlingly, Marc's own voice. "We heard on the news there are big storms in the northwest. I can hear the thunder in the background! Are you all right? You're in the motel?"

"Yes, I'm fine," she said. "I went to Shavuot services this morning at the little synagogue in Greenville. It was very nice."

"Good. Listen, I can come to the airport on Tuesday to pick you up. That's when you're coming in, isn't it?"

"Actually, I've decided to stay a little longer. Sonia is coming along very well; she seems to like the Canadian bush. So I changed my flight."

"OK," Marc said doubtfully. "I guess there's nothing else to do around there but work. No distractions. You must feel like you've left the real world behind."

This remark, coming as it did along with a clap of thunder, gave impetus to her fear. She felt she was floating in furthest space and Marc had just cut the towline. From the dim edge of the universe she said weakly, "Well, we do go to town. And I've made some interesting friends here. Anyhow, what's new *there*?"

"We all went into the city last night. Claire's at home, by the way. We saw a marvelous off-Broadway performance of *Long Day's Journey into Night*."

Celia was chilled, as she hadn't changed her wet dress before phoning. She felt alone in the universe except for a long filament connecting her to Marc, whose voice usually reassured her but was now simply terrifying. There he was, on the safe, rational East Coast where she ought to be, only she'd changed her flight and her pride would not allow her to admit her present state.

"It was an excellent performance, but the play of course was very depressing. It made me think of how easy it is for people to descend into insanity," said Marc.

Celia opened her mouth to deny that insanity came with such ease, but she was stopped by a huge crack of thunder.

"Wow, I can really hear that storm," said Marc. "I'm glad you're safe in the motel. Is Sharon there with you?"

Somehow Celia managed to get off the phone without revealing that Sharon had gone to a conference and left her alone in the cabin. She said good-bye, sending love to Maxine and the children in her best Little Sunshine voice, and then she hung up.

Immediately a long flash of lightning lit up the whole meadow outside the window. She could see every detail: stones and grass and prickly knapweed all illuminated by a surreal light. *If I'm not insane right now, what am I?* she thought. She tried listening for the voices in the wind, but they had vanished, leaving behind only fear of themselves. *No one's going to tell me anything,* she thought, and just then she heard a loud splitting and breaking, and a crash.

Every light in the cabin went out.

Celia sat for a moment in total darkness, suspecting she might have died and gone to the World to Come, but then she remembered about fallen trees and power lines. The darkness was terribly thick. It took her a long time to grope around for the flashlight. Finally she saw it by the light of the storm, lying on Sharon's night table. Then she had one little beam in the thick blackness. Sharon had shown her how to light the gas lantern, but in the actual emergency she couldn't remember a thing. She found the matches on a shelf and tried lighting the mysterious bag of ash, but the match touched the mantle and it crumbled. Old bag of ash, she thought, tears rolling down her face. She was afraid to touch the thing again. But how long would the flashlight batteries last? She walked in a circle with her little beam of light, panicking, as if she were lost in the woods. Then she hugged the flashlight to her breast and thought: Be calm, calm. After a moment her heart stopped racing so fast and she remembered the candles in the cabinet over the kitchen sink. Slowly she made her way to the kitchen, thinking, I am conquering fear. She said it aloud, experimentally: "I am conquering fear," and then repeated it more loudly: "I am conquering fear! I am not insane, *I am conquering fear!*"

In the quiet of the log cabin, the only noise rain beating against the metal roof, she heard every nuance of her own voice, its exact pitch and tone. This voice sounded so very familiar and sensible that she began to feel a deep comfort. The very air around her seemed to change consistency; she felt borne up on a wave of wonderful, resonant sound.

Just as she was taking down the box of candles, tunelessly singing, "'They won't get lost in the wilderness, Let my people go, With a lighted candle in each breast . . .'" she heard the sound of a vehicle bumping along the flooded road outside. Then two bright headlights intruded through the uncovered window. Her heart pounding again, she walked, shaking, to the door to check that the heavy deadbolt was fastened.

*   *   *

"Heard about the weather?" asked the owner of the café, while Sharon was waiting for her take-out tea. "There's big storms all over the southern half of the province, and it's heading our way." The television behind him was flashing pictures of little people jumping out of a giant bag of chips.

"No, I didn't know," she said. "I live down there; I'm just up here for a conference in Prince George."

"Oh yes, we heard they've already sent out the emergency crews. Electricity and phone lines are down. It's a lot of fierce winds and rain, apparently, and lightning strikes." He said this with relish, as most country people would—even on the most ordinary day they truly loved to discuss the weather.

While he was waiting for the water to boil, Sharon went to the pay phone and tried to call Celia, then Jacob, but there were only strange electronic sounds on the line.

"You're trying to call down there?" he asked when she came back to pay her bill. When she said yes, he said, "Well, try again in a little while. They often restore the lines very quickly," with a suppressed excitement in his voice that this probably wouldn't be so. He shook his head, almost clucking, and she sensed that nothing cheered him more than the idea of submission to the fate nature had in store.

Carrying her tea back to the rental car, she heard the wolves still singing. She sank into the cushioned driver's seat and sat with the door open, listening to the wolves cry their warning: uuuuh-ooooooh! Yet she felt that Celia would manage in the cabin; she knew where the candles were, and surely Charlotte would drive up to check on her. Sharon feared more for Jacob, out in the storm tending to his animals.

When she'd returned to the farmhouse after driving Celia to the motel on Shavuot eve, there was only one small light on in the living room, where Jacob was reading the paper. Keturah had gone to bed with two kittens, the mother Siamese, and an orphaned kid. The full pilgrimage moon shone in on the bowl of fruit, illuminating Sharon's gift to them, her purchases of a few days ago at the Greenville market. There were two golden mangoes and a bunch of dark red grapes, as well as some kiwis and figs. She and

Jacob had cut open a mango and eaten it with their fingers, swallowing the orange flesh.

"What was it like, growing up in New York?" he asked. She knew her primary fascination for him was that she was a New York Jew; his fascination for her was that he was not. He wasn't afraid of being alone on the farm during a raging blizzard with a power outage, but he thought anyone who'd live in New York was braver than he was.

"It was like, you could never be alone. You're never in a place where no one's watching."

He offered her another chunk of the mango. "I would've thought no one paid attention to anyone else."

She considered that; in one sense it was true. "You're never free of all those people who aren't paying attention but could be."

Jacob laughed. "Maybe people get a little paranoid, eh?"

She was charmed by the contrast between the depth of his perceptions and the simplicity with which he stated them. It was enjoyable not thinking, just slipping into this very casual affair—though that caused her guilt, his assumption that the distance between them was so great that it must be casual—with a guy who actually had bits of hay clinging to the hems of his jeans. The fact that he was brilliant but totally uneducated made for interest but also a sense of unreality. What on earth was the agreement between the two of them? In one sense it was very direct, prosaic: Neither of them had been with anyone for a long time. But it also felt like some force was pushing them together, some agreement written in an old hand, letters twined with grape vines and fig leaves. It had its romance.

This they pursued after the mango was eaten, in his bedroom that, like Keturah's, was the human equivalent of what the pack rats did in Sharon's shed, where she'd find an almost expressionistic mingling of her possessions, or parts of them. Once, she thought she'd lost a small silver spoon that Celia had given her, but then she found it in the pack rat's nest. On the bedside table in Jacob's room, she found a picture of Keturah in a sequined gown—at the community holiday dance, he said—along with a pair of gardening clippers, a few smooth stones from the river, some small wrenches, and a frilly homemade valentine that said "I love you, Dad." There was a thick layer of dust on everything. It bothered her that he read the Bible, something that Jews she knew didn't usually do, or not for pleasure; it especially bothered her that he had a Gideon edition with the Christian part that had to be ignored. She made a mental note to at least buy them a Jewish translation.

Once she was naked with him between the sheets, her sexual excitement peaked and then subsided, while he wanted to go on. She took more pleasure, actually, in his talk than in his lovemaking. Sometimes Sharon thought she was like Celia, who apparently could live easily without sex. That wasn't lost on Jacob, either.

"You make a good hermitess, as Charlotte calls you," he observed.

"I know," she said apologetically. She sensed that he knew already she wasn't going to be wife material—how could it not cross their minds?

"It's good to be independent," he added.

"I don't always do such a good job of it," she explained. "But I need space around me. I can't stand so much involvement and complication anymore."

"You're happy like this," he said, in wonder.

"Yeah, especially when I can just be at home in the woods. Nature doesn't make any complicated demands. I remember one day when I first came out here, I went for a long walk up on the west ridge—you know where I mean?"

"Yes," he said. "You've been way up there? I never have time to do things like that. What's it like?"

"It was beautiful. There's a pond, and alpine meadows. You have to find your way up around the rock ledges, but there are lots of deer trails you can follow. I had a wonderful day up there, but then the sky clouded over and it started to rain. I had to find my way back, sliding down these muddy descents, over rocks and roots. *Sheets* of rain came down, and I was totally soaked and cold. But about halfway back, I started to feel really, really good."

"Probably the beginning of hypothermia," suggested Jacob.

"No, I was realizing that my whole life, I'd been reacting to other people. If I was walking down the street in the city and someone shoved past me, I'd feel annoyed. I was always in reaction to my parents, to law school. But at that moment, I realized that the rain was just itself, totally indifferent to what I did or didn't do. It would get me wet no matter who I was, and the only demand on me was to get inside and get dry. I learned I could just *live*, in a simple, non-reactive way."

He had rolled away from her then and started getting up to put on the t-shirt and shorts he slept in. He didn't like to stay up too late since he had to be up early. Outside the window, the moon was further away but still bright. She seemed to move her craters a bit, as if opening her mouth to speak. "Nature makes plenty of demands," Jacob said. "For example, if you want to grow some alfalfa around here in a dry year."

"Tell me what that's like."

"It's a bitch," he said, but he allowed her to pull him back into bed for some more talk about the land. She realized she liked him so much because he too didn't seem to demand a reaction.

Now, alone on the northern highway, Sharon sipped her hot tea.

*Listen, listen*, cried the wolves, warning of tragedies and exiles to come.

\* \* \*

SOMEONE WAS POUNDING on the heavy door. Celia stood behind it holding Sharon's heavy-duty flashlight, which alarmed her by flickering. "Who's there?" she called out in a trembling voice.

"Celia! It's Keturah!"

Celia opened the door, laughing with relief, and two wet girls blew in—Keturah and a girl she introduced as her cousin Sandra. They wore neither raincoats nor boots, just drenched sneakers, and some very skimpy tops over their jeans. Their wet hair fell across their faces, Keturah's blond and Sandra's dark, and they had brought along a plate of brownies wrapped in plastic—their one concession to the rain. They too were laughing with excitement.

"As soon as we realized your phone line was down, Dad said we should go check on you, but he has a lot of frightened animals to deal with, so we came," Keturah explained. "Fortunately we have a gas stove, so we could finish baking the brownies."

"Wonderful! It's so kind of you, I'm very appreciative." Celia went to make them tea, and the previous hour seemed to vanish. These country girls didn't know how to light the gas lantern, either. Keturah tried, tying on a new mantle and pumping, which Celia had forgotten to do, but the cabin filled with the smell of gas. Keturah said never mind that lantern, they'd end up killing themselves, and they all laughed. Instead, they lit four candles, which gave the log walls a golden glow.

"Do you know what brought down your electric line?" Keturah asked. "You must have heard the crash—there's a huge tree across the old outhouse by the fence. I mean a *really* big tree. The funny thing is, the outhouse is still standing!"

"Built to last," said Sandra, and they all giggled.

"This is just like camp," said Celia, when they were all settled around the table with their tea and brownies. "I didn't know you had cousins near by," she said to Keturah.

"Oh yes," said Keturah. "Sandra even lived with me and Dad for a while this year."

"Ah," said Celia. Sandra's pretty face looked rather pinched, she thought, unhappy around the mouth.

"My parents are divorced." Sandra shrugged. "My mom's sort of going wild, and she can't stand to ever stay home anymore. And my dad is remarried; they have kids. I was living with them, but they just wanted me to babysit all the time. I couldn't take it."

"She *had* to run away," Keturah said. "No one paid any attention to her at all. She's much better off with me and Dad."

Celia was surprised by their openness about all this, and she was confused by the details. "Do your parents mind your living with—is Jacob your uncle?"

The girls exchanged a look.

"Actually, we met last fall at school," Keturah confessed. "I asked her if she wanted to come live with us, and she did. She stayed at our house for six months—we're her family now. And then the state took her away from us a couple of months ago and put her in a foster home. It was horribly unfair. The social worker said Sandra can't live at our house because it's dirty and Jewish!"

Celia raised her eyebrows. True, the farmhouse was a bit dirty, no denying that, and the Wakemans considered themselves Jewish. Was "dirty and Jewish" the same as "dirty Jewish?"

"Living with Jacob and Keturah was the only real family life I ever had." Sandra bit into a brownie. "And I *am* Jewish. But my foster parents don't want me to be Jewish, so I ran away."

"You mean you just—became Jewish while you were living at Keturah's house?" Celia inquired.

"Yes. I've been Jewish for six months, and my foster mother knows it. That's why she tried to make me eat a ham sandwich. She gave it to me and said I had to eat it. I couldn't have anything else for lunch. I said but these are my laws; these laws were given by God to the Jewish people at Mount Sinai. I have to obey these laws, and I want to."

Celia was impressed; she hadn't even heard any real Jews make such a declaration in years.

"And then she said you're not really Jewish and you can so eat this sandwich, so I ran away."

"When did this happen?" asked Celia.

"Today." The girl tossed her dark hair off her shoulders.

Keturah took down a Jewish encyclopedia which Celia and Raymond had given Sharon for her Bat Mitzvah, and which Sharon kept on the shelf above her table along with some cookbooks and the *I Ching*. "It says here that it's traditional to stay up all night on Shavuot as a symbolic remembrance of how the community of Israel stayed up all night to receive the Torah at the foot of Mount Sinai. We're supposed to study aspects of Jewish law and history." Keturah's face was close to the thick book as she read by candlelight. Suddenly she sat up straight. "Wait a minute! It says that Shavuot has its roots in pagan festivities, celebrations of spring fertility, the awakening of the sleeping god Tammuz—"

"That can't be true!" Sandra said hotly.

"I know, the Jews don't have anything pagan in our religion, do we, Celia?" Keturah's face was flushed.

"Oh, possibly." Celia helped herself to another brownie. "But that was a long time ago, anyway. You needn't worry about it." She dipped the corner of the brownie into her tea and ate it; she was having an absolutely wonderful time.

"I suppose Yishai's father thinks *I'm* a pagan," Keturah confided. "He asked Yishai the other day if Dad and I would ever consider converting."

Sandra looked sharply at Keturah.

"What a good idea. Then you'd be accepted in the Jewish community." In Celia's mind, some strange floating patterns to which she'd been only half attentive drifted together, their curves interlocking. Ah yes, there seemed to be something between Sharon and Jacob—and what if she wanted to marry him? Celia's thoughts on this subject tipped back and forth on the patterned curves, unsettled.

"Does this by any chance have something to do with you and Yishai?" asked Sandra.

Keturah gave her an arch look, tilting her head to one side, teacup aloft—she looked like one of the café beauties from Sonia Delaunay's time. Both girls burst into adolescent giggles, their faces reddening, shoulders shaking, laughing until they cried.

Celia smiled and pressed together a bit of brownie left on her plate, bringing it to her lips. All those giggles must mean that Keturah and Yishai were serious. She tried not to think of the sexual aspect hinted at by their hilarity; she preferred not to know.

Finally Keturah quieted, wiping her eyes and turning toward Celia. "But to convert you have to learn about so many things and then *do* them all. Yishai's parents invited me and Dad to come up and spend a whole Sabbath with them sometime. We'd have to get someone to feed the animals and do the milking."

"Yes, well, you ought to talk to him about it." Celia wondered whether she sounded like a missionary. Should one just leave these people in their natural state, as Yishai thought? But of course they didn't live in a vacuum; whenever they saw some Jewish practice on television, they instantly adopted it. Their way of being Jewish was half biblical, half CBC special report.

Keturah was paging through the encyclopedia again. "Do Jews think water is holy?"

"I don't know. Why?" asked Celia.

She closed the book and looked at Celia; she wore no makeup this evening, so her tears had left no stain. "There's this dream I've kept on having, at least once or twice a year, for as long as I can remember. I don't know what it's about, but I always think it's a Jewish dream."

"What happens in the dream?" asked Celia.

"Well, I'm the only person there. And I'm walking down these narrow steps made of stone, down into this ancient little stone pool full of water. The pool has been there for a long time, built out of the rocks, maybe as long as those petroglyphs up at the lake. The water is dark and clean, fresh. Just as I'm stepping into the water I wake up."

"Like a mikveh," said Celia. "How strange," she murmured.

"What's that—a mik—what did you say?"

Celia was just about to explain when they heard another vehicle driving up the road, and headlights shone through the trees.

"I bet it's Katherine," whispered Sandra to Keturah. Her eyes were like wide, dark pools.

"Hide in the closet!" said Keturah.

Before Celia knew what was happening, the two girls had opened Sharon's closet and were pushing aside jackets and boots; but the closet was so small and crowded that Sandra, who was tall, could get only halfway in.

"Damn!" she said, "this is so small! I'm sorry, Celia."

"What's going on?" asked Celia. Whoever it was had turned off the engine outside, and there was silence except for the rain.

"Our visitor is probably her foster mother," Keturah explained.

"Well, I'll just tell her!" Sandra said. "I don't care. If they bring me back I'll just run away again." There was a knock on the door and Sandra, as if on cue, shouted, "I'm not coming back!"

A woman's voice outside was shouting something muffled by the rain. Celia went to the door to listen. "Sandra!" the woman shouted. "Can't we discuss this like normal people?"

Celia thought, if she's out there in this weather she must have some sense of responsibility. She turned to the girls, who had scuttled back into the kitchen. "She's getting drenched out there."

"Open the door then. I don't care!" Sandra said.

"Are you sure?" asked Keturah.

Celia opened the door slowly and let in a very wet woman wearing a long green slicker.

"I'm not coming back!" Sandra shouted from the kitchen. "You can do anything you want but it *won't work!*" The girl stepped forward and glared. Her mouth was so tight it had almost disappeared; her face was pale and her eyes were huge, bulging—Celia had never seen anything like it.

"You should listen to people that know what's good for you!" Katherine shouted back. "You just want to go around with your delinquent friends and wearing those skinny clothes and getting in trouble. I know what you and Nathaniel are doing; you can't fool me! Pretty soon you're going to get in some real trouble that no one can help you out of!"

The girls snorted but said nothing. "Would you like a cup of tea?" Celia offered.

The woman looked at her in surprise. For a moment no one said anything. "That's very hospitable of you, thank you. I'm completely soaked, chasing after her in this tornado. My name's Katherine Peterson, by the way. Sorry to barge in on you like this. I've completely forgotten my manners."

"I'm Celia Rosenbloom." Celia felt that her name sounded strange in this context. She urged Katherine to take off her dripping slicker and sit down in the rocking chair.

"God bless you," said Katherine. She had a long gray braid, and she wore a longish skirt and high green rubber boots.

The girls did not sit down, but stood up, leaning against the kitchen counter while Celia made the tea.

"I'm afraid you're interrupting our holiday," Keturah told Katherine. She spoke with great dignity: an actress playing the part of herself.

"What holiday?" asked Katherine.

"Shavuot. The Feast of Weeks."

"Of course," said Katherine. "The Temple was very grand, and they'd all go up there. It was filled with precious objects of gold and silver for sacrificing the animals."

Keturah winced. "Well, the Torah says we should give thanks for the harvest and bring fruits too. And they *ate* those animals. How did you find us, Katherine?"

"Your father told me where you were." She turned to Celia. "He's at least an honest man; he said he wouldn't lie to me."

"Dad says we have nothing to hide," Keturah replied. "If Sandra comes to us we'll take care of her. It should be *her* decision where she lives." In the light of the four candles her blue eyes were dark, mysterious; it was like an argument between shades.

"Well, the Lord knows we've tried to show her kindness." Katherine was becoming emotional. "But she's so stubborn about standing on her strange ways—she's not even grateful for the food that's offered to her." The girls began to object but she went on, "Let's be realistic here. Maybe Keturah and her father had some Jewish ancestors, but *you* don't." She turned to Sandra. "Being Jewish doesn't just rub off on you after a few months living in the house of someone who's a Jew." She then appealed to Celia, "She's *not* Jewish, is she? It's just a thing she's trying on like a new dress."

Everyone was looking at Celia, awaiting her pronouncement as eagerly as if she were King Solomon, sitting on Sharon's swivel chair. "It's not for me to decide," she said finally. "I'm not a rabbi."

"And speaking of dresses," Katherine, undeterred, said to Sandra, "you might think of putting one on once in a while and covering up your belly button. You might think of staying at a home where people care about you instead of running all over the place with Nathaniel. If you get—" She turned to Celia and said, "excuse me," then turned back to Sandra. "If you get pregnant it's your own responsibility!"

Even in the candlelight Celia could see Sandra's face growing paler and her lips tighter; Celia was afraid she'd faint or explode—but Sandra didn't reply. The girl's eyes bulged in fear, perhaps outrage.

"You'll give birth to that baby all by yourself and no one will help you!" Katherine threatened Sandra. Her words had a canned sound, cruel yet limp, all the bite gone out of them. No doubt this was something she'd heard as a girl herself, out on a farm somewhere, from the tongues of female relatives in cotton print dresses. They, like Katherine, would have been roughened by the harsh elements, and they would have viewed sex with the resentful sagacity country people reserved for the less convenient aspects of nature.

"There *is* such a thing as an abortion, you know." Keturah took a big bite out of a brownie, then offered the plate around to the others. No one else took one. Celia hastily went to the kitchen to get Katherine her tea, while Katherine exploded.

"Abortion is *murder*! Do you understand what murder is?"

"Jews aren't completely against abortion, are they Celia?" Keturah licked brownie crumbs off her fingers.

Before Celia could answer, Katherine shouted, "It don't matter what the Jews think—you can't kill it!"

Eager to hasten this guest's departure, Celia returned to the main part of the cabin with a mug of tea and a jar of sugar, both handmade pottery in unconventional shapes. The mug, with its slender base and flared top, looked unstable. Celia felt a bit frightened; Katherine brought an alien roughness into Sharon's cabin, which, for all its strangeness, was still within the realm of possibility. On Sharon's walls hung good paintings that Celia had shipped out from Central Park West. There were also bookshelves from floor to ceiling in the main part of the cabin: a shield of history, philosophy, and literature against the surrounding cultural wilderness. In a nook among the books stood the three-foot-high bronze Kwan Yin, goddess of mercy, which she and Raymond had collected in New York.

"Thank you so much. I hope I haven't put you to too much trouble." Katherine stirred sugar into her tea and drank it. The bottom of her skirt was still wet from standing outside the cabin door in the storm.

"Do you know how to light a gas lantern?" Celia asked her.

"Of course. Here, give it to me." She briskly pumped up Sharon's Coleman, lit the mantle and adjusted the flame so the lantern burned steadily with a pleasant hiss. The thunder and rain seemed to be pushed back as the bright light filled the cabin. "Is there anything else I can do for you right now?" she asked Celia. "I can come and check up on you tomorrow. Your daughter left you here all alone?"

"She had to go to a conference. But I'm fine. I can always call the neighbors."

"I'll come tomorrow and bring you a casserole."

"No, really," said Celia. "But thank you for lighting the lantern. This reminds me of the farms my mother and brother and I used to visit when I was a girl. Most of them had no electricity, of course."

"Well, you seem like a nice, reasonable woman," said Katherine. "I've heard about you and your daughter before. I live near Bentwood—do you know the place with a big barn near the highway? We've got a litter of pigs out in the yard now, excuse me for mentioning."

Sandra and Keturah sniggled from a corner of the kitchen. They were pointing to something in the Jewish encyclopedia and then looking at Katherine, who glared at them—but it was a tired, distracted glare.

"Perhaps you could come over sometime," Katherine invited Celia. "We'd love to have you. I have five children of my own."

Celia murmured something, not quite accepting or refusing the invitation. She was always known among her friends as Little Sunshine or Sunny Celia, who got along with everyone. Somehow, people never knew what she was really thinking.

Katherine stood up and said she'd better be going; her husband needed help with the animals and who knew what else in this storm. She put on her slicker and turned to Sandra, "Well, at least I found you and you're safe, and no one can say anything is *my* fault. I'll call Bernie in the morning and tell her. That's the social worker," she explained to Celia. "I can't fight this child anymore."

"Go ahead," Sandra said finally—the first words she'd addressed to Katherine in some time. "Tell her I'd rather live in a house that's dirty and Jewish."

Once Katherine had left, the girls came out of the shadows and sat with Celia around the wooden table. They progressed from brownies to little cucumber sandwiches which Keturah prepared with finesse.

"Dad's been having trouble at the auction," Keturah confided, holding a triangular sandwich between her thumb and forefinger. "Someone started a rumor that he uses black magic to increase his herd." She put out the tip of her tongue like a cat and licked cream cheese from between the slices of bread.

Celia looked at her and dropped her own sandwich into her lap.

"Well, our animals breed better than anyone else's. Of course it's not black magic; Dad doesn't know anything about that. He just knows a lot about breeding and veterinary stuff, and he ends up saving a lot of animals that other people would lose. Everyone knows it, too—every time there's a difficult birth anywhere in the valley, Dad goes out at night to help them deliver. But some of the people who used to buy from us at auction aren't buying anymore." She ate the sandwich with an expression of childlike remoteness from the trouble she was describing.

"Terrible." Celia shook her head, genuinely concerned.

"I also found out," Keturah said, "they tied Ezekiel to that altar thing because *someone* said we do animal sacrifices in our basement. Supposedly it was a joke, but some drunk guys heard about it at Billy's party and decided to hassle us. There are some German guys around here who are anti-Semitic."

"But who would even joke about a thing like that?" Celia exclaimed.

Keturah didn't answer at first. Then she nodded her head in the direction of Charlotte's farm. "Mrs. Hammond."

\* \* \*

SEVERAL TIMES DURING the meal of moose meat burgers and salmon steaks, Sharon left the restaurant table and tried to phone home, but she found the lines were still down. The television news playing in the hotel bar said the storm was moving north. In the back of her mind the wolves sang, imploring her to heed, but she couldn't fly out because the airports in the south of the province were all closed. She was increasingly worried about Celia. Why hadn't she written down the instructions for lighting the gas lantern?

Back at the long table filled with lawyers, bottles of wine and beer in front of them, she sat across from Don, a colleague from Edmonton and the person she liked best to hang out with at conferences. Don was Chinese-Canadian; he'd grown up on the prairies in the only Chinese family in town, helping his parents in their restaurant.

"I'm worried about my mother," she told him.

He looked sympathetic but spoke philosophically. "It's not so much isolation you have to worry about. That's when someone will rise to the occasion. You have to worry more what people will do when their designs overlap lots of other people's. Surviving a blackout in a storm is simple by comparison."

Sharon smiled. "I suppose," she said, and they both laughed.

"I'm sure the neighbors will check up on her," he added, removing a long translucent bone from his salmon steak.

\* \* \*

ANOTHER PAIR OF HEADLIGHTS approached through the darkness, and shortly there was more pounding at the door.

"Sharon! It's Charlotte Hammond!"

Once again Celia opened the heavy door, and the neighbor, clad in a long dripping slicker, came in with a gust of cold rain.

Charlotte looked surprised and displeased. "Hello," she said to Celia. "Hello, girls."

"Hello Mrs. Hammond," Keturah replied. "Would you like a cucumber sandwich?"

Charlotte waved away the idea of cucumber sandwiches, and the girls whispered something to each other and giggled. "Are you all alone here?" she asked Celia.

"Well, I have my friends with me."

"It's the holiday of Shavuot," Keturah told her teacher, "and we're studying the giving of the Torah, which is the Old Testament."

Charlotte nodded. "The foundation of all the world's injustice." She sounded almost regretful.

Celia sensed that Charlotte thought her insufficiently grateful to her for having come out in the storm. Yet it was difficult to thank the neighbor for anything. She made one feel it ought to be understood that no one was ever really grateful, that words were hollow stylizations and nothing more.

"I think there were a few injustices around before Moses," Celia argued. "That's what he was trying to correct."

"Yes of course. Replace injustice with a new injustice and call it progress—that's what we humans do," Charlotte said.

Giving up, Celia asked her if she'd like a cup of tea. Charlotte didn't answer, but Celia went to get her one anyway. When Celia returned to the main room, Charlotte was asking Keturah, "How is your father?"

"Fine." Keturah closed her mouth after the one word.

"He's a generous man. I heard that he went out to save twin lambs the other night at MacLaughlin's."

"Yes." Keturah looked daggers at Charlotte, but they didn't seem to pierce her.

Charlotte thanked Celia for the tea and drank some. "I heard a rumor that your daughter is somewhat less of a hermitess these days. My son ran into her and Keturah's father down at the lake the other night."

"They went out for an *ice cream*," said Keturah.

Celia objected, "My daughter isn't a hermitess. She's up at a conference right now with three hundred other lawyers."

"All right, all right. Well, I won't keep you from your studies." Charlotte stood up and put on her slicker, which was still wet. "Do you need anything else? Do you want me to check up on you in the morning?"

It interested Celia, the way nothing was allowed to interfere with these country manners. She said she'd be fine, and she thanked Charlotte for driving up to the cabin in the storm.

Soon they heard Charlotte's truck starting up and bumping down the road. Keturah sprang to the door and opened it again. Hail was falling. Little white ice balls hit her sneakers and bounced over the wooden threshold into the cabin. The wind blew in, strong and cold.

"Ketty, what are you doing? It's cold!" Sandra exclaimed.

The wind seemed to shriek, and another volley of hail hit the cabin's threshold. "Don't *covet!*" Keturah shouted after Charlotte, as the tail lights of her truck disappeared among the trees.

# XI

## GREENVILLE, BRITISH COLUMBIA

Zach blessed the One Who brings forth bread from the earth, and then he swung his long right arm over the *challot*, slicing rapidly. Celia thought he looked like God's representative, the knife an extension of otherworldly strength. A pile of sliced bread accumulated, and Zach passed it out quickly, as if his guests were starving in the desert and he was the triumphant witness to a miracle. His outstretched arm holding up the plate spanned the table to Jacob and Sharon, to Keturah, Celia, and his own three sons with remarkable ease. "Delicious," they all agreed. Tanya had made sweet spiraling loaves as if it were a holiday, which in a way it was. They were spending this hot summer Shabbat at the rabbi's home. It was several weeks after Shavuot and the storm which had knocked down trees on Sharon's land, including the ancient fir that fell on the outhouse. Already Celia had been sojourning out in the bush for long enough that she felt both excited and strange to be in town, enjoying what Sharon called a "talk-fest."

"Your tablecloth is lovely," said Celia. "Very unusual." She'd been admiring the rows of embroidered black and red triangles.

"It was such an intense experience." Tanya had risen from her chair to go to the kitchen. "We bought this tablecloth in Hungary, in the same town my grandparents lived in. A woman sold it to us on the street, and then she brought us to the building that had been the synagogue. This cloth became a holy object." Tanya then brought out bowl after bowl of steaming matzah ball soup, over which the guests exclaimed. A steady heat from a large warming tray filled the house, compounded by the summer sun shining through the dining room windows. Greenville had its own, northern-desert microclimate which made it much warmer than Sharon's woods. It took some determination, Celia thought, to sit inside and eat hot matzah ball soup while the rest of the town was down at the beaches. Driving to town last night with Keturah and Yishai, she had enjoyed the fullness of the orchards and vineyards that sloped down toward the big blue lake. Celia herself wouldn't have minded a long cool swim that Shabbat, the length of the whole shore and back again.

"What *are* these things?" Keturah poked at a matzah ball, first with her spoon, then her finger, which was tipped with blue nail polish. She made an unpleasant face as Celia explained what they were made of. Keturah was like a five-year-old about food.

"Matzah balls are a very important part of being Jewish," Celia concluded. "If a bit heavy." Yet as she ate her soup she forgot about the swimmers in the cool blue lake. She grew very warm and, sweating, inwardly rose to a place she'd visited many times, a place always more or less the same: Jews sitting in chairs slightly elevated above their daily existence, sending up poetry to a God who, like everyone, wanted to be praised.

"This reminds me of my friend Hilda Reinlieb's family," said Celia. "You may remember this," she said to Sharon, who recalled rather less of her childhood than Celia would have liked. "Hilda came from a family of thirteen children. They lived on Long Island. And every Friday night they all went home to their parents' house for Friday night dinner, even after they were married and had children of their own.

This mother made each week—by herself—enough food for all thirteen of her children, their spouses, and all the grandchildren. We used to go there sometimes too. And each week she would have baked enough challah that everyone could even take some home!"

"Nice." Zach ate a big forkful of soufflé.

"Incredible," said Tanya.

"Of course, your lunch is equally impressive." Celia accepted more of a wonderful concoction of local tomatoes and peppers that Jacob passed to her.

"This is just her usual," Zach boasted quietly.

Keturah was slouched in her chair and, it seemed to Celia, just picking at the food on her plate. "You do this *every week?*" she asked Tanya. "You must like to spend a lot of time in the kitchen."

"It's a Shabbat like people used to make," Celia explained. "It reminds me of wonderful times."

"Well, I don't know if I always *like* it," Tanya said to Keturah. "But I always do it. Last spring around Pesach I found I could take out these audio books from the library to listen to while I'm in the kitchen, and that really helps. I'm so busy, you know; at certain times of the year I just turn into a human baking machine."

*  *  *

AFTER THE CHALLAH, matzah ball soup and the appetizers, Sharon definitely felt she'd eaten enough, but there was more: stuffed mushroom caps; sweet potato tzimmes, and salads arranged on little round blue plates. All this gourmet vegetarian food covered the table and it seemed almost a holy obligation to eat—Zach urged it on them. This rabbi was clearly as determined as he was portrayed in the stories his son told about him. One night recently at Jacob's house when they were all sitting around drinking tea, Yishai told them that Zach had circumcised Yishai himself when Yishai was eight days old. Celia blushed, and Keturah said you'd think Zach would have felt too nervous to do it. She and

Yishai had laughed like two loons over that. Jacob's opinion was that it was a test of trust, like Abraham's test of faith. Yishai said yes, my father trusts God, but he doesn't trust too many human beings. He says there's too much democracy.

She overheard Yishai's two brothers, Itamar and Gabriel, softly discussing skateboards on her right. There was a new kind out with a curved tail, and you could do some cool spins on it.

"Matthew has one. He and a bunch of kids are meeting in front of the pizza place in the mall, and then they're going out to where they're building condos and there's this fantastic asphalt sweep," Gabriel, the youngest brother, said quietly. "Matthew can really spin on two wheels. Did you know he's Bahai?"

"No," said Itamar. "That's cool." His lips hardly moved when he talked. "You should go meet them." Yishai had told them once that Itamar was always going out to the mall on Shabbat, against the rules of his home, and that this was a gossipy town, so Itamar was doomed.

"I don't think I can get out of the house with my skateboard," whispered Gabriel. Celia was telling everyone else how she'd walked up the glacier full of crevasses.

"I know how." Itamar's brown eyes shone; he flashed Sharon an enigmatic look and then laughed out loud. She laughed too, surprised a fifteen-year-old had such charm. Yishai had told them that Itamar played jazz clarinet in a band and that about five girls from his class always came to his rehearsals. Gabriel, too, had a big shiny drum set in his room upstairs which he wasn't allowed to play on Shabbat.

"Sometimes I think this town is just a fool's paradise," Tanya was saying on Sharon's left, "but then I—"

"—hide it under the porch—" Itamar whispered to Gabriel.

Sharon glanced at Jacob, who was quietly eating tzimmes. Wearing his homemade kippah, he looked almost hippyish, out of place here. Clearly he didn't know what to say to Zach and Tanya, nor they to him. Zach and Tanya would have been more at ease with people from any other culture than with this self-proclaimed Jew who felt free to invent his own way. What charmed Sharon and Celia out in the bush was beyond the pale to this rabbinic couple, she sensed. Following this thought further, though, she realized in her heart that she too couldn't take the Wakemans completely seriously, she who had Kwan Yin in her cabin and was sleeping with Jacob.

She heard a soft drumming, an accompaniment to her idly uncomfortable thoughts. It was Gabriel, his fingers curled underneath the seat of his chair, drumming a complicated rhythm that made his shoulders tremble. Yishai said Gabriel shook the house when he practiced his drums, and their father sitting downstairs studying Torah always said it was a message but that he didn't know for whom.

"What is that? Gabriel? What are you *doing*?" Tanya looked around behind Keturah to where Gabriel sat. She seemed uncharacteristically agitated.

The pounding slowed but didn't stop. "Practicing my new song. 'Pack of Lies' by Vulture Row."

"That's not very *Shabbosdik*," Zach said. "Save it for the rest of the week." The drumming became less furious but still continued. "Gabe, I *mean* it."

"Did you know, in the days of the Beit Hamikdash all the young girls would come out dressed in white and dance a sexy dance on Yom Kippur." Itamar spread a large chunk of butter on a slice of challah and bit into it. "And they played instruments, too."

"That was in the time of the Temple—everything was different," Tanya objected. It looked like the religious rebellion simmering in her teenagers was getting to her.

Gabriel was still drumming. "It's a great song about a guy who can't stop telling lies. This is what *I* find restful," he said, giving the chair several whacks followed by silence; this seemed to be the finale.

"*Ga-bri-el!*" exclaimed Zach and Tanya at the same time.

"—the boys would watch the girls dance and decide which ones they wanted—" Itamar was explaining to Keturah.

Sharon noticed that none of the young people had eaten much; maybe they'd already been out eating burgers somewhere.

"Shabbat," said Zach, "is like the special, ancient sacrifice of the Red Heifer. It has to be done precisely. We have to be very careful not to let in weekday things." His voice was softer now but intent. "We should always be listening for what we have to do." For a moment everyone else stopped talking and turned toward him. He had a true gift, Sharon thought, for conveying the essence of spiritual attentiveness. For a moment she too wanted the mystical ashes of a red cow. They would be soft; she would spread them over her skin and obliterate the errors of her past.

Yishai and Keturah started talking with their heads close together. Keturah wore a plain white sundress that was tied in little bows over her shoulders, and her hair was swept back from her forehead casually, as if she'd just woken up. Jail bait, Thunder would have called her. "I have no feeling in the second toe of my right foot," Yishai was saying. "Didn't I ever tell you? My parents used to let me go on winter camping trips in the Kootenays, and a couple of years ago I froze my foot."

"Well, we didn't know exactly how few matches you were bringing." Tanya, calm now, passed a salad to Celia.

"Whatever did you do?" asked Keturah.

"Well, I would allow myself only one match for each day. If it was a three-day trip I'd allow myself three matches. I figured that if I couldn't get a fire going with one match, I didn't deserve that fire."

"A fanatic," said Itamar.

"I wasn't a fanatic," Yishai replied. "I was just trying to do something—precisely."

"It's like what happened at Meribah, which is also in this week's *parasha*," Zach said. "Moshe didn't listen to Hashem's exact words. He struck the rock instead of speaking to it, and in doing that he destroyed the proof that the flowing water was a miracle. Every word and every action continues into spheres we can't imagine."

Sharon noticed that Tanya was sitting very straight and watching Zach as if he were a fascinating figure she'd just spotted in a crowd.

Gabriel's long arms hung at his sides, but he was soundlessly drumming a complicated pattern on the edge of his chair. Itamar sat with his head resting on one fist, his eyes moving around the table, up the stairs leading to the bedrooms, then out the front door. "It's to show that Moshe was human," he drawled.

"That's right, he was very human," Zach agreed. "He could make a large error in judgment only because he was a great human being. Of course we don't really know. His mistake may have been in saying *we* will bring forth water, as if he were a magician. He forgot there's always a reason why something happens."

"Maybe the text is trying to have it both ways," suggested Sharon. "It shows that Moses had some kind of special power, but it undercuts that by punishing him for it." Tanya said that was interesting, but Zach just looked at Sharon with his eyebrows raised, as if she'd said something heretical. "Power always comes from Hashem," he said.

"Maybe his mistake was that he didn't show respect for the rock the Almighty made," Keturah said. "Of course, you have to feel sorry for Moses. He had it so hard out there— the wilderness just got to him. I'm sure the Almighty understands how tired people get fighting nature. Maybe it was really a reward, getting to die up there on a nice mountain where he could feel free."

"Yes, nature can be very difficult," Celia murmured.

"It couldn't be a reward not to be allowed to enter the Land of Israel." Tanya sounded a little nervous. She and Zach looked pleased and disturbed that Keturah had spoken.

"But you know, there were large cities there," Keturah said easily. Sharon saw that the girl felt certain of her own charm and of their eventual blessing. "It wasn't the same as being out in the quiet where he could always hear the Almighty's voice," Keturah concluded. Yishai looked at her and smiled. The inheritance was actually his, Sharon saw, and in another world he would have been simply Keturah's man: unassailable rabbi, father of new nations.

\* \* \*

CELIA TRIED TO UNSTICK her legs one by one from the chair without anyone noticing. "My mother's father was taken away by the Russian army when he was about seven years old," she told them. "He was with a number of other Jewish boys. By the time they were teenagers they knew nothing about Jewish tradition, but they remembered that there was a holiday in the spring. So each spring they would pick a day and fast. They'd mixed up Passover and Yom Kippur."

"Incredible," said Tanya.

"But your mother's mother probably knew something about Yiddishkeit," said Zack, "because *you*—"

"Oh, no," said Celia. "My mother's mother was the daughter of someone who'd also been taken away to the czar's army. He distinguished himself militarily, and because of that they were permitted to live in St. Petersburg. So my grandmother grew up without Jewish traditions too, and so did my mother. Later on, my father taught her about it."

"I had some idea that you'd grown up in a fairly observant home," said Tanya.

"No, not really," said Celia. "We did whatever we wanted on Saturday." Hoping she wasn't offending her hosts, she added, "But it was very important to my father to have a kosher kitchen and a real Friday night dinner. He wanted any immigrant to feel at home in his house."

"I can sense his presence in you, even now," said Tanya. She was very slender and seemed hardly to eat a thing herself; Celia's mother had been fat, of course, loving the food she gave to others with love. Last evening, Tanya's slim fingers had circled the candle flames three times, for holiness and, she said, the three-stranded cord that cannot be broken. Celia, standing with her in the window at twilight, felt the holy circling of Tanya's hands concentrated around her own shoulders, holding her safely like a mother, only this immediacy was something even her own mother had not possessed. It was the past pulled out of the ground like the knives Bernard's mother had kashered in the earth: a purified object, tradition passed on by the young to the old.

"You're all right out there?" Zach leaned toward Celia; he wore a white shirt and his eyes were very dark. She felt he understood her perfectly, buttressed her. "Isn't it lonely?"

"No." She paused and bit into a delicious pickle. "I'm becoming more of what I really am: an old lady who says what she thinks."

"My life is so involved," Zach lamented. "I need trees, water."

"Your roots are thirsty," said Tanya, and they both laughed.

\* \* \*

"WELL, IT'S WAR," Yishai said softly to Sharon and Keturah, while his parents were telling Celia something about the community. "My father said the other night, 'You have to go to college. You're not just going to stick around here like some local, marry a girl right out of high school and go to work in the minimarket.'" Like Itamar, Yishai could speak while hardly moving his lips.

Sharon sighed. What could she say? Where to begin?

"I said, 'I might just do that. What's wrong with it?' I asked him. He couldn't tell me. He makes it sound gross on purpose. It doesn't have to be the minimarket—I know lots of kids who've gotten decent jobs."

"Besides," Keturah added, "I don't think there's any law against married people going to college, I mean *if*—" Her cheeks reddened.

Sharon did not know why, when she was faced with Keturah and Yishai, they seemed so eminently sensible. Their view of life seemed as pure and compelling as the Boundary River moving south to the sea. They themselves were like the deer Sharon watched from the cabin, pausing to nuzzle and graze, but inexorably making their way down to the water below.

"I was in Grand River on Tuesday, waiting for my wheat to be ground at the mill," said Jacob, "and as I walked down the street I noticed a book in the window of a shop. On the book's cover was a picture that looked like two Sabbath breads under a cloth and two lighted candles, so I went inside. It turned out this old fellow was originally from somewhere in Russia, maybe Ukraine. He left after the war and came to Canada, and he's never been back since. But the odd thing is, he wrote this book about the Jews and published it at his own expense because he believed they weren't around anymore. He was real surprised when I told him that Jews still exist."

Sharon placed her hand on the back of Jacob's chair, feeling a little jump of electricity. No, he was not naïve, just unhampered by rancor.

"*He* wrote the book?" Tanya held her teacup in mid-air.

"Who is this person?" demanded Zach. "Where was he during the war?"

"I think he must have been with the Russian army," said Jacob. "He said he saw all sorts of terrible things happening to the Jews, and he tried to help them. Anyway, it was nice finding a kindred spirit sitting out in Grand River. He paid to have this book about Jewish culture published because he thought he was one of very few people around who remembered anything about it."

"It does sound strange," said Celia to her hosts, "but on the other hand, if he wasn't really in the Russian army and was actually a Ukrainian Nazi, why would he bother to write a book about the Jews?"

"*Guilt!*" said Itamar, in the clear ringing tone of the student with the right answer.

Keturah said, "Dad, this reminds me, did you give Elijah his medicine before you left?"

Jacob looked instantly more alert at the mention of one of the animals. "No, I didn't have time. I'll do it as soon as I get home this afternoon. He'll be all right."

Zach winced. "Do you really have to drive back before dark?"

Tanya smiled sadly at the guests. "We've had lots of discussions about this."

"Well, the animals would get pretty hungry if I didn't," said Jacob.

"How could a really observant Jew be a farmer?" Sharon asked her hosts. "You couldn't ever go to a synagogue or even visit other Jews on Shabbat."

"But there were always Jewish farmers," said Celia. "My father told me about some who lived in the country, outside the town where he grew up, in Ukraine. They'd drive to town in their wagons on the holidays and stay over with Jewish families."

"I guess Jews aren't really supposed to live in isolation—not from each other, at any rate," said Zach. "The community is all-important."

"Well, Abraham lived in isolation," Jacob asserted. "I'm not sure there were so many rules back then. With all due respect. It's not easy to live as Jew in the country. I'm losing money because people are happy to believe I'm cheating them with black magic," Jacob explained to the Bernsteins.

"That's insane," remarked Tanya.

Sharon was afraid; she'd already heard him say he might have to go somewhere else if this black magic business kept up. Come with me, he'd said to her one night; we'll buy a farm on the prairies. She couldn't quite imagine this final leap into remoteness.

"I've never run into anything like this, though of course I've heard of it." Jacob spoke without bitterness.

"Yes," said both Zach and Tanya, but she knew they found Jacob puzzling. There was an otherworldliness about them: They lived in a spiritual landscape that was the metaphorical reflection of the human soul. They walked through the blue marble corridors of the King's palace, their minds always peering at you around a column, through a brightness.

\* \* \*

CELIA WAS EATING her second of Tanya's heavenly cinnamon rugelach. Her mind was wandering, floating through the heat: On this day I eat, drink, speak an old woman's truth. Yes, and I put red ash and water on my brush, and paint God's gift to the world. Zach looked at her, eyes wide, a dark ancestral burning. He was adorable. She reached for another little cake.

Yes, it was true: Sitting in the Gold Pan one morning last week, Celia had overheard a strange conversation among several people at the next table. He runs circles around you, said a man in a tan Stetson. Offers a cheap price so you'll buy more, he's making a killing off of the people around here. A woman added, some people have decided they won't buy his animals anymore; they're afraid to. They have their reasons, she said, pursing her lips in what looked like a parody of Speak No Evil. They conferred softly for a moment, and Celia couldn't make out what they said. Then the woman exclaimed, "—but the devil *does* exist!"

After the tea and pastries, Tanya passed out little song books. Ah, Celia remembered this from camp; she sang along tunelessly, with heart. *This day is honored above all other days, the Shabbat of the Rock of the World.* All the girls would dress in white and sit at outdoor tables by the lake, where the damp, still eastern forest and the souls of the Indians had seemed to listen.

\* \* \*

The Bernsteins didn't sing any better than the Rosenblooms. As the voices in the room scraped and scratched, Sharon sang along politely, feeling tired and thinking *sing for your supper*. Jacob and Keturah didn't know the songs, so they studied the English side of their books.

Between choruses they heard a low steady knocking on the door. Zach got up, still singing, and went to answer. Sharon glimpsed Jeffrey Meisler, the president of the Greenville Jewish Community, wearing the same yachting club sweater he'd worn at Purim when Elise delivered her baby in the community center library.

"Good Shabbos, Good Shabbos." Jeffrey waved to everyone around the table. "Sorry to interrupt, but we need our rabbi." Jeffrey looked at ease, happy to be in the rabbi's house on Shabbat. He was a thirty-eight-year-old multimillionaire who owned a chain of amusement parks throughout western Canada, and he was also the major donor for the Greenville synagogue and community center.

"Sorry," said Michael Ackerman, who'd worn the moose antlers on Purim. "We're so sorry to interrupt your Shabbos, but this is really—" he shook his head. With him were a man he introduced as Dave something from WGRV—Greenville's radio station—and Bertha and Gillian, the coffee-and-cake ladies. They were all simultaneously explaining something to Zach.

"Wait a minute, wait a minute." Jeffrey held up a hand. "Let's start at the beginning." He spoke in a smooth, authoritative board room tone and it worked, even on this fast-talking crew. He explained the problem: a leaflet that had arrived in that morning's mail from a local Conservative MP's constituency office.

"He's quoted *Hitler*," said Gillian, taking a brochure from her purse. "'Determination and hard work are the keys to success. Adolf Hitler.'" She stood holding out the brochure to Zach as if it were a piece of evidence he could use, to her only slight regret, to have someone executed.

"Who *is* this?" Tanya set down a tray of tea and cake on the living room table.

"*Werner Gross!*" Gillian enunciated each German syllable.

That one, thought Sharon. There had been a conflict of interest scandal in the Vancouver area, she recalled. He'd arranged for the rezoning of farmland in the Agricultural Land Reserve and then sold the properties at some enormous profit. "Not surprising."

"Shameful," Zach said.

"Well, let's slow down," said Jeffrey. "I suggest we wait and see what Werner himself has to say about this."

"Hasn't he contacted you?" asked Zach. Everyone looked at Jeffrey, who had close ties to the conservative party that had dominated the valley for years. Twice Jeffrey had won the government's Outstanding Business Award for Familyland, which had rides, water slides, fire-eating jugglers, and rock music playing in a laser room. He was always inviting conservative MLAs and MPs to speak at Jewish community events, where they received plaques and commended Jeffrey for his contribution to activities for Greenville's youth. Sharon had wondered if she were the only Jew who didn't vote conservative, but Jacob said he guessed not.

"I don't know him personally, but I know some of his close associates," Jeffrey explained. "I spoke to Greta Larson a couple of hours ago, and she said Werner never saw that leaflet before it left the constituency office. Apparently somebody working there just added this quote to the text without asking anyone. Werner had nothing to do with it. Greta said he's planning to return my call as soon as the hysteria dies down a bit."

"There's a demonstration going on right in front of Werner Gross's house now," Bertha was telling Tanya, Celia, and the others. "We wouldn't get involved, of course—we just drove over to have a look—but there must have been a hundred people!"

"It *was* gratifying to see how many friends we've got." Jeffrey was looking at Dave from WGRV. "Though of course we're giving the party a chance to explain before we—"

"Not *all* of us are giving him a chance," said Gillian. "In fact, a number of our younger members are already out carrying placards in front of Werner Gross's home."

"Really? Who's out there?" asked Tanya.

"Mary and Anthony Gleuck, Michael Schwarz—and Katie Applebaum was out there by herself."

"It's always this way," Bertha explained to Celia and Sharon. "The non-Jewish spouses are the quickest to get angry."

"Not very *Shabbosdik*," said Zach.

"Rabbi," said Dave, adjusting the strap on the tape recorder hanging over his shoulder, "Excuse me, but would you mind if I asked you a few questions about this incident? Strictly off the record and unofficial, of course. I'd just like to get your feelings about this."

"My feeling," said Zach in a hushed voice. He paused and looked around. "My feeling is that you have just interrupted me while I was alone with my bride."

Only the reporter's eyes showed surprise; his mouth kept smiling.

"Our Shabbat, our Sabbath, is like a loved one who comes to us in privacy, intimacy, and we look forward to the highest form of enjoyment with her."

Jeffrey cleared his throat. "As I told you," he said to Dave, "Rabbi Bernstein would probably rather talk to you later tonight."

"Sure, no problem." Dave looked around the Bernstein's wall-to-wall carpet as if he'd dropped something.

"We're sorry, Zach," said Michael Moose Antlers. "We just thought since it was such an important issue you might make an exception. People out there are pretty upset."

"There can't be any exception for Shabbat," said Zach in a gentle, dreamy tone. "She's like a queen wielding her scepter over us. We can't appear in her presence in a way she hasn't commanded."

"I understand completely, Rabbi." Dave looked amazed.

"Come back after ten-seventeen tonight and I'll talk to you." Zach and Jeffrey escorted the reporter to the door.

"What if Werner doesn't return Jeffrey's call?" Michael asked the others. "I think the whole community should have a meeting tonight so we can prepare a public statement and coordinate our response."

Tanya brought in more fruit and cookies, even though no one was eating. "The problem," said Bertha, "is that we just had the floor in the community center polished."

Michael and Zach had returned and everyone was sitting on the couches and chairs in the rabbi's living room except for Sharon and Jacob, who stood near the foyer leading to the front door. All the men looked at Bertha, seeming not to comprehend what appeared to Sharon to be—amazingly—real.

"It costs six hundred dollars each time we have the floor polished," explained Gillian. "It shouldn't get all scuffed up just for something like this meeting, especially when we're renting it out to the Christian Caucus on Monday night."

Keturah and Yishai were obviously not giggling. Tanya's eyes were wide; she often looked as though she were straining to understand the most appalling transgressions. Jeffrey looked confused. "Well," he said, "I guess we can have the meeting at my house."

"There *is* the building fund fee we're charging all the new members," objected Michael. "I don't know much about floor polishing, but I'd assume three thousand per family would cover a few extra polishings. We have to be able to walk on our own floor."

Sharon wondered: Why was Jacob hanging around this community waiting for a vote on honorary membership? He wouldn't be able to afford the honor even if they conferred it.

"This is definitely *not* what we should be talking about on Shabbat," Zach protested, but no one—not even Tanya—seemed to hear him.

"So who else was there?" Tanya asked.

"Janice was there, carrying a big sign. I think it said, 'Greenville is not Wannsee.' By herself, of course," said Gillian.

"I've never seen them together for more than thirty seconds, have you?" asked Bertha.

Tanya shrugged and took a tiny bite of a cookie. "I don't know."

"Never," said Gillian. "I've never known a stranger couple. She goes to Vancouver all the time without him, too, did you know that? By the way Michael, has somebody phoned Benny about all this?"

"I tried," said Michael, "but I think they're away for the weekend."

"Speaking of strange couples," said Bertha.

"When I was teaching Sunday School last year their kids would come all the time without having eaten any breakfast," said Michael. The coffee ladies clucked.

Jeffrey said, "You know, this is such an important event for the community—you wouldn't believe how many friends we have. There must have been ten phone calls when I got home from shul today, church people, other MLAs, business associates. I had to say over and over that we're not going to give an official response until we've heard from Werner."

"You're too nice," Zach objected.

"Well, I won't give him much longer."

"It wasn't that long ago we were afraid to go public at all," said Gillian. "Before your time, of course," she told the Bernsteins.

"Why was that?" asked Celia. She was sitting in the largest armchair beneath a painting of an arched doorway surrounded by stones—Jerusalem, probably. Celia looked at home, as Sharon had always seen her look in other people's houses.

"Well, you know, this is the Bible Belt," Michael explained. "We weren't sure, is all. But it's worked out amazingly well. They've welcomed us with open arms."

Celia nodded and said how wonderful, and the others immediately credited Jeffrey and Familyland. Sharon decided it was time to return home to the valley. "We have to get going," she said in her mother's direction. A look of surprise and pain crossed Celia's face and then disappeared, like the passing harsh beam of a headlight, seeming to Sharon to briefly illuminate the fact that she had a man while Celia was alone.

"Drive carefully," said Celia. "I always like to beep going around the turns, but I suppose that's too old-ladyish for you."

"I wish you didn't have to do this," said Tanya.

"The animals think I do," said Jacob. "They're expecting a regular meal, like the rest of us just had."

Tanya looked caught off guard by the mention of something like animal meals. Zach just sighed.

"*We* parked three blocks away and walked from there," said Jeffrey. The others laughed and looked hesitantly at Zach, who said, lightly, "Oy."

As Sharon and Jacob sped down the highway toward the mountains, she felt she was shedding layers of New York, of childhood. But how could she follow this man into the wilderness, enclosing all thought in the elemental? He often said how great it was to grow crops, animals, children, all together. Her feelings weren't wild enough to follow him to what she thought of as the godforsaken expanse of the prairies, to grow things. Yet she had a sensation now that something new was pushing up in her to the outside; she had an unfamiliar feeling of personal expansiveness.

\* \* \*

NO ONE ELSE HAD made any move to leave Zach and Tanya's living room. Celia, seated in one of the rabbi's comfortable armchairs, was starting to understand the attractiveness of living in a small community like this; this odd collection of Jews all *needed* each other in a way one seldom saw in New York. "As a matter of fact," said Jeffrey, "I was just talking to Oliver Jones, from the church up at Half Mile Creek. He phoned me right away to express his support for us. He said he'll do whatever he can to let people around here know they can't print things like what we've just seen."

"Good," said Tanya.

Jeffrey cleared his throat, rubbed the side of his nose, and added, "Oliver had something else he'd like us to think about. There's a Russian woman, a friend of some members of Oliver's church, who wants to leave the former Soviet Union and come to Half Mile Creek. The only problem is that the church can't afford to sponsor her themselves—she has a family, too, and they'll probably need about two thousand dollars a month. This woman, Irena Vassiliev is her name, had a Jewish grandmother. So Oliver was wondering if our community might agree to help with this good deed, financially."

There was a moment of silence. Then Bertha said, "It's a little confusing. Does she want to be a member of the Jewish community?"

"No," said Jeffrey, "she wants to be a member of the church at Half Mile Creek. She's Christian, for all practical purposes."

Tanya sighed and looked skeptical, but said nothing. Zach asked, seeming very sincerely not to believe it, "She wants us to pay for her to live as a Christian?"

"Well, it builds friendly relations between the two communities," Jeffrey explained. "I'm sure she'd come down here and meet us."

"It's rather a large amount, is all," said Gillian.

"They could go to Israel instead," suggested Bertha. "That way the government would pay their expenses, if she does have this Jewish grandmother."

"But she wants to go to Half Mile Creek, where she has friends," Jeffrey said. "She wants to come to Canada."

The word *Canada* vibrated a little in all the corners of the room. Celia thought about Jeffrey's sentimental Jewish heart; he wanted to share Canada, the joy of being an ocean away from the nightmare of European history. He was generous with Jewishness too. Sharon had told her how Jeffrey was one hundred percent in favor of giving honorary membership to Jacob and Keturah, which Zach opposed. Jeffrey had arranged for a vote to be taken on this issue around the High Holidays, when people were back from their summer vacations. His sentimentality was beautiful, yes, except for the fact that he didn't question it. Celia's own father had once agreed to help sponsor a group of Ukrainian Christians who'd asked for help, but he'd been torn between the kindness of the act and its historical absurdity. Sitting here in Greenville half a century later, Celia sensed how the word *Canada* made these Jews similarly impulsive, only now there was no inner struggle except in Zach. And herself. She couldn't help it; she didn't want an honorary Jewish son-in-law.

"Well maybe," said Michael, "we can raise a little money for them, even if it's not the whole amount."

"Yes, of course," Jeffrey agreed.

Celia noticed Keturah's eyes on Jeffrey, her lips smiling slightly. Yishai was seated in a leather sling chair and she was draped delicately on the arm, almost touching him. Behind them on the wall was a glass-fronted cabinet containing several brass hanukiot, a tall olive wood cup, and a silver filigree havdalah set. Celia felt affection for her young pupil but was also aggravated by her. The girl believed she could be accepted by this community in a way that even conversion, much less honorary membership, would have difficulty bringing. But she sat soft and straight as a young fir, sure of her claim to a spot on the Jewish earth.

"But this person has chosen to turn away from the Jews," Zach objected. "And we have lots of Jews in this province who need *tzedakah*. The Jewish Food Bank in Vancouver is begging for donations. I got a letter yesterday."

"It's true, and there are a lot of Jews who want to get out of Russia and live as Jews, not Christians," Bertha asserted. "I admit it's a bit off-putting—but I feel sorry for her."

Keturah straightened up on the arm of Yishai's chair. "I know my opinion doesn't really count. But in *my* opinion these people are asking *us* for help, not any Jews anywhere else. Only us." Everyone in the room had fallen silent and was looking at her. "So could it mean," Keturah went on, "that if these people are turning to *us* for help, that the Almighty means for *us* to help them?"

Still no one spoke. *The Almighty*, Celia thought, for a moment willing to believe there might be one.

Keturah looked triumphant. "*I* would be happy to donate my tzedakah box money, though of course it isn't much. It's just what I put into a little kitty-cat bank when I figure what I've saved by using a tea bag over again or not buying a candy bar. But it's a start."

Celia had heard before how Keturah put the money into a porcelain cat she'd had since she was little, then donated it to the poor through the Farm Women's League. All the older people in the room seemed to be looking at the floor, perhaps slightly puzzled or ashamed, picturing the coins dropping into the slot between the cat's ears.

## XII

By August, the forest was being burned alive because of Familyland's conservative buddies, who were always out to trim the fat from the public belly. Why pay some freeloader to sit up in a fire lookout all summer, reading books at public expense? So the freeloader was removed, and an unnoticed fire ignited thirty miles east of Sharon's land and became a moving, consuming inferno. Sharon couldn't actually see the fire, but she breathed its stinging smoke. It was ninety-eight degrees in the shade, with a yellow-gray haze filling the sky.

One afternoon, the fire was still a few miles away, but it was quickly licking its way west, jumping from tree to tree, hilltop to hilltop. Sharon and Jacob watched the news on his TV, the firefighting planes tunneling into the gray smoke, spraying a red chemical.

"Well, as long as I can get the animals out at the last minute," said Jacob, "I guess I can accept the Almighty sending fire down into our bones." They were both sitting on the edge of his couch, staring at the flames on the TV screen. Sharon's throat stung from the smoke. "I feel like I'm about to be burnt at the stake," she replied.

If the fire came much closer, the wild animals wouldn't be able to get down to the river. She pictured the deer with their red summer coats fading, their bodies thinning as they walked through burned meadows, led by feeble stags.

Around eleven that night she was cooking eggs back at the cabin, feeling sick just to look at them bubbling in the pan. She'd been feeling so off-balance lately that her doctor in Greenville had ordered a pregnancy test, just in case. Maybe it was just low blood sugar from not eating much all day, she thought. Then the phone rang into her nausea.

"Sweetheart, the RCMP were just here," said Jacob's voice, sounding steady but far away. "They said the fire is just on the other side of the hills, across the river. If it looks like it'll jump the river, they're planning to evacuate all of us."

"Jacob, I—"An egg popped on the black oiled surface and her stomach set out on a voyage across a roiling sea.

"Are you all right? This smoke is terrible. They said they'd been up to Charlotte's already, but it seems like they don't even know your place is there."

"That's OK." She turned off the gas under the fry pan. "Don't need any royal police up here. You sound strange," she realized as she was saying it.

"I just had quite a discussion with Ketty. But I'll tell you about it in person—it's not something for over the phone."

Not over the phone; jumping over the river, she thought, her head feeling murky. "Jacob, I'm going to pack up some stuff and bring it to the office in the morning—just my computer and legal books. Do you have any valuables you want me to keep for you up there?"

"Maybe Hulda and Bathsheba, but I'm not sure how your colleagues would like it. I'll bring over a carton in the morning." He sounded hurried. Even this partial evacuation seemed like it could be the beginning of their exile from this valley. What if both their properties burned to the ground, the fire leaving nothing but black stumps? Jacob would surely go to Alberta rather than starting over here, especially with all the black magic rumors harming his business. She cried a bit after putting down the phone. She wanted to keep Jacob, but at the same time she had a strong urge to jump out: evacuate herself while she was still sanely single, baby or no baby. Possibly at thirty-nine she was too old and crotchety to build a life with a man; on the other hand, maybe she was too young to settle for a life that didn't fit precisely. It had been an adventure, being an educated, urban Jew in her country surroundings, but she wasn't sure she could really go native. At bottom, she didn't completely understand why people *got* married.

After eating haphazard bits of her dinner like a child, she got some cartons from the shed and started packing. Of course it didn't stop with the legal books. She had stuff here like it was her parents' apartment on Central Park West: a gold-initialed Florentine leather bag that was a gift from Raymond and Celia; her Connecticut rock and mica collection from childhood; and what to do with Kwan Yin, goddess of mercy? It was very dark outside, the moon obscured by clouds of smoke, and there was a heavy smell of burning. She called Celia at the motel to say she'd pick her up in the morning, and then at some point Sharon just fell into bed, the cartons still unsealed.

She dreamed of herself and Jacob making a dugout in a hillside, like early settlers on the prairies, hollowing out the earth to form a protected space to live in. She set up her computer but then discovered there was no electricity—she couldn't plug into the wall made of packed earth. A prairie storm started whirling around them and water seeped into the dugout. Soon it became a thick greenish pond with tiny beings floating in it, made of shimmering protoplasm, their hairy tentacles waving. Yes, it was the way she and Marc used to look through their microscope at drops of water from the scummy pond near their Connecticut house, hydras and amoebas fleeing across the lens.

In the morning she awoke later than she'd planned, feeling nauseous and with a mental image of herself vomiting amoebas and hydras. Just as she was finishing making the bed, coughing from the smoke, she knocked a glass off the night table and it cracked to pieces on the board floor.

Crouching to place the shards into a paper bag, she suddenly had a vision of herself, cleaning up what a child had broken. She swept the floor carefully, looking for bits of broken glass. Then, trying not to think, she picked up the phone and punched in the number of her doctor's office in Greenville.

"Good morning!" said a cheery voice, probably the nurse who wore the gold half-heart charm dangling next to the cross.

"I had a pregnancy test yesterday morning. Sharon Rosenbloom." Her own name sounded strange—the name of someone she didn't know.

"I'll check," said the nurse, and put her on hold. The ensuing computer music ran up and down Sharon's throat.

Then the music ended abruptly. There was a silence and a little smacking sound at the other end of the phone, as of the nurse finishing something she was eating. "Sharon Rosenbloom?"

"Yes," Sharon whispered.

"Congratulations, *Mom*!"

Sharon slammed out of the cabin and climbed up the hill fast, panting in the smoke. *Oh my God, it's close*, she thought. She hadn't eaten a thing this morning, but she stopped to vomit nothing by the side of the path, then continued up to a rock ledge where she could look out.

"God!" she called. The flames were so orange, so huge; how could something such a soft green as the grove of larches on the opposite hill have exploded into those hot orange tongues? Wagging tongues, certainly. She'd never thought of the future, oh no. She'd grown casual—it had seemed unlikely, even faintly desirable. Overnight the fire had spread until it was just the width of the river away. The approaching inferno on the opposite hilltop would consume her cabin, the olive tree she and Jacob had planted, everything. Looking at the fire, Sharon shed tears of mourning.

\* \* \*

CELIA WOKE THAT MORNING smelling the smoke, and, glancing at her date book while she dressed, noted that today was Tisha B'Av. She recalled going to synagogue in Brooklyn with her father and seeing the ark draped in black cloth, hearing the wavering song of *Lamentations* that she imagined rising up to God, who floated just under the domed ceiling. Her father was a founder of that synagogue but had scrupulously refused roles like the presidency because he doubted, for example, the hand of God in the history of human beings.

When she entered the motel dining room for breakfast she was shocked by the sight of the orange flames consuming the tops of the opposite hills. It was an ugly, unreal vision framed in the plate glass windows. The waitress said good morning and brought Celia's tea as if nothing unusual were happening, but people at other tables were discussing the possible evacuation. The white saskatoons would burn; the pale pink and purple wild flowers would become dust. Sharon had told her last night that the petroglyph site was on fire. Sipping her tea and looking at the flames, imagining the blackened peacock, Celia realized she would have to return to New York, evacuation or not. This fire marked a division, a time when she must gather herself, half-healed, to return from her exile.

Keturah appeared, wearing her white waitress's uniform and nametag. "Good Mor-ning!" she sang. Then she sank into the chair opposite Celia and folded her arms on the table, as if concealing something within them.

"Good morning, dear," said Celia, coughing. If only her father's questionable God would send rain, a descending blanket of dew, something.

"How are you today?" Keturah asked with more intensity than usual. She nodded toward the window. "You could paint a picture."

"It's dramatic," Celia agreed. "But I'm afraid I've always preferred pictures of the lighter side of life."

"I agree with that. We're not meant to be dismal all the time." The dining room door opened, letting in a hot wind, and wisps of hair blew in front of Keturah's eyes. She brushed them away and sighed, looking lightheartedly tragic.

Celia started to say that she had to order breakfast soon because she was driving to Greenville with Sharon this morning, but Keturah interrupted her. "Celia, I must tell you something. I hope you won't hold it against me, but I simply can't think about anything else."

"Of course not, dear. What is it?"

"I'm pregnant," Keturah whispered, looking at her with such intense blue excitement in her eyes, a profound and beautiful color. When Celia said she understood, Keturah giggled like a child taking a dare. Once, Marc, Sharon and Anna had confessed to jumping from some high rocks into the reservoir in Connecticut—oh, had she been angry—and they'd giggled because any future moment was so unreal to them.

"I assume—" Celia began.

Keturah nodded quickly. "Yes, Yishai. But he's a very responsible person. You know, he already has a job in the hiking store, and he wants all of us to live together. I'm going up to Greenville tonight; we have to tell his parents after the fast." Playfully, she winced. "I'm trying to fast for Tisha B'Av, but the smell of all this food is making me sick."

"But are you—will you marry?" Celia asked.

Keturah laughed, showing all her white teeth, her lips the straightforwardly seductive red of the lichens bursting out on the old gray rocks of these hills. "You never know!"

Celia was more shocked by this than by the pregnancy: marriage as an afterthought, an option; how many shares will you buy in your beloved? Ah, she couldn't understand the world any more. "Well, I wish you both the best. But as your friend I'm a little concerned." Poor Zach and Tanya, she thought.

"I think everything will be OK. We can always live with my father. I think he's happy about—" she whispered again, "becoming a grandpa."

"Are you sure you want to go through with this, dear?" Celia felt she had to ask.

Keturah folded her hands on the table and sat up straighter, a maiden in a moment of meditation or prayer. "I couldn't have an abortion. I'm not against it, but I just *couldn't.*"

Celia saw that Keturah's entire life had been a preparation for these moments. They were the inner image her outer form was built to house, and it was no use imagining any other manifestation of her essential being. She would hatch with this startling crack into a lovely young mother.

"Celia. Were you frightened, I mean before you gave birth?"

"Oh yes, it can be difficult. But you just have to remember that it's *so* worthwhile." This moment was completely surreal: the peaceful hillside bursting with orange flames, and Celia talking to this pregnant child as if she were ten years older and a married young matron. The entire valley seemed in a perfectly natural state of dreamlike destruction.

\* \* \*

INSIDE ONE OF JACOB'S CARTONS, on top, was a photo album that Sharon peeked into. There were pictures of a young woman with a face as lovely as Keturah's, though less defined: a garden rose rather than the smaller, intense wild flower face of the daughter.

"You said you had quite an evening?" Sharon turned to Jacob. They were out in front of her cabin, where he was sealing another carton before loading it into her truck.

He immediately stopped, the extended roll of strapping tape in one hand, smiled faintly and sighed. "Ketty told me last night she's pregnant."

Sharon realized she looked absolutely shocked. She had been sitting on her hilltop, but now she was tumbling down into the burning valley. She was a little plant growing on the ashes of herself: an ordinary country wife.

"I'm not really worried," Jacob said, by way of soothing her. "We can handle it. Yishai's a good person; he wants to take responsibility, and I can help them out." He shrugged and added, "Keturah's mother was only seventeen and a half when Ketty was born."

A nauseous anger flared in Sharon at this mention of the garden rose. "Jacob, *I'm* pregnant."

He was so surprised that he dropped the scissors. Then he laughed, coming over to stand close. With both hands he smoothed her hair, but she could feel his fingers quivering. "I want to marry you, anyhow."

Sharon sighed. It always seemed unreal whenever anyone said this, and now even more so. Like saying, let's slaughter an animal and sacrifice its entrails and make a fragrance unto the Lord. No friend of Sharon's even barbecued steaks anymore. Except Jacob. Some of her friends *had* gotten married, but apologetically.

Jacob kissed her.

"You'd become a father and a grandfather at the same time," Sharon pointed out. "It's like that song, 'I'm my own grandpa.'"

"It's not that bad." He withdrew his hands.

"I don't even know if I'll go through with this." How people would sneer and scoff, and she would too, at herself. On the other hand, she couldn't bear thinking of the destruction of the fruit of her body. Her soul was thinning to its bone; if she destroyed the incipient child, would she even be capable of other acts of love with this man? Passion was at the distant end of an uneven voyage.

He was silent for a long time. Then he said, "I hope you will keep it. As soon as I know about it, it feels like a soul already alive in the world."

"That's because you're really a Christian fundamentalist," she replied, unreasonable anger flaring around the spot in her belly she didn't want to think about. "The Jews believe it's not yet a person at this stage—it's only four weeks. The soul enters when the baby is born."

"I'm not a fundamentalist," Jacob said, "and I'm not Christian. If you feel you can't keep it, I'll understand. But I doubt Rabbi Bernstein would tell you that."

She wept because he was so sure that God was taking care of him. "Jacob," she said, "people have already lost their homes just on the other side of those hills."

He put his arms around her and held her. "Sharon, Sharona," he said, but she could feel something unyielding in him. His whole zeitgeist said, let the fire sweep over you and new life spring from the ashes. She could not make him feel urban angst.

A moment later, Charlotte drove up to the cabin and got out of her truck, slamming the door. No greetings were exchanged. She raised her arms in a wordless question to indicate the situation. Sharon, dizzy, realized she still hadn't eaten a thing since last night.

Charlotte smiled, seeming certain of the natural world's insincerity and probably spoiling for heroism against it. "Sharon, could we move the sheep to your upper flat? We had to bring them across the river last night, and there're too many down below."

"Sure, Charlotte, go ahead—you could have even started last night."

"Well, I thought I'd ask you first. Lots of folks wouldn't want two hundred sheep tramping through."

Sharon shrugged. "The sheep were here before I came and I suppose they'll be here after I'm gone."

"Yes, indeed," said her neighbor, nodding as if Sharon were finally being sensible after a long lapse. "Actually, we wanted to buy this place when it was up for sale but we couldn't afford it. It would've been convenient for forest fires—and other times, of course."

Ah, so the Hammonds had territorial ambitions. They'd like to buy her out, bulldoze her cabin, and erase the few traces of the camping place that she felt belonged to her, not by right of having worked the land but by having *not* worked it—having experienced it in a way that left no marks on it, only on her. Even Jacob was more real to her neighbors; she herself was a nice raiser of unicorns, pleasant but a useless obstacle.

There was a short silence, and then Jacob said, "Yes, I've already moved my animals up above. Better safe—"

She interrupted him. "Well, some of us don't have as many resources."

For the first time Sharon saw Jacob visibly anger; it was a flush on his neck and face, a brightening of his blue eyes as he tried to prevent his own destruction from baseless hatred. "That isn't called for, Charlotte. I've helped you many times, and Sharon's helping you now."

That was a lot for Jacob Wakeman to say. They both felt the closing in of their enemies and the imminence of their departure, even obliteration. It seemed to Sharon that in the end, Charlotte was the one who'd endure.

"It's true, I should be more—" Charlotte ducked her head. "Yes, I'm sorry. I really do appreciate—" She simultaneously conveyed the heartfelt thanks of a neighbor with two hundred sheep to move and parodied those thanks, her quick brown eyes moving across Sharon's face. "How are you feeling? You look a little peaked."

"This smoke is awful," Sharon said.

Charlotte turned to Jacob, "Yes, I happened to be in the ladies' washroom at the Gold Pan yesterday, and Keturah was there, sick as a ghost, as my kids used to say. She said it was the smoke, but I've never seen a person—well, thank you; thank you very kindly." She swung herself into the truck, still talking, and drove away making clouds of dust down Sharon's access road.

Sharon was trembling. "I've left so many things unfinished here. I wanted to build a new woodshed, and a back porch..." She looked up into the hawthorn tree, usually a comfort, but its leaves were covered with fine dust and the birds' nest was dry, abandoned.

"I know, a person can't help but wonder what he's done to deserve this. It seems like collective punishment," said Jacob.

"Yes," she agreed. His hand felt uncomfortably hot on her shoulder. You needed your little vine and fig tree in this life, if only because so few people would grow a thing, return each day, keep the faith.

"Those rumors Charlotte started are hurting me," Jacob said. "I mean, I don't care what she *says*, but hurting in the sense of the bank balance. I can't survive here, especially if there are going to be more—responsibilities."

It was the way he said the last word that let Sharon know her child would be born. This was a wordless, sensual knowledge, like seeing the exact spot where you would dig into the front yard and plant another tree, breaking the surface of the earth, tossing up clods and roots. Yet she still didn't know how she could metamorphose into a mother. And Charlotte would complete her destruction, exiling Sharon's man before she had a chance to figure out whether she wanted to marry him. "Maybe we can take her to court for promotion of hatred."

"No, I can't prove anything," said Jacob. "And the Hammonds are a very powerful family in this valley. A lot of people have needed political favors from Charlotte's husband when he was alive, and now from her son. He's the one to talk to if the Ministry of Highways wants to put a road or a high-tension power line through your land. He knows everybody in Victoria."

"There's a fire going through my land right now. I don't see him doing much about that."

Jacob shook his head. "They wouldn't say anything against her. People are afraid of the Hammonds. Charlotte's husband was known to shoot out people's tires if they drove down his private road. They're—"

"She's jealous." Yes, Charlotte wanted to show that she was the boss: *You're going back, bear, and I'm going forward.*

\* \* \*

Sharon picked up Celia after breakfast, and they drove by the general store on their way to Greenville, the big red truck loaded with things Sharon and Jacob wanted to safeguard from the fire. Celia looked closely at the children sitting on the front steps of the store. They were assorted ages, wearing shorts and t-shirts with cartoons, and each child was eating a multicolored ice pop and watching the fire burn on the opposite hills. This was their summer vacation entertainment. Why was it, she wondered, that people wanted to watch? They sat for hours at the café, too, watching orange flames consume the soft evergreens and blacken the dusty hills, which were now a midsummer parched brown instead of the spring green they'd been upon her arrival. Her trip had been a fruitful month that turned into three. She'd return to New York soon with Sonia Delaunay captured, her wheels of light and color set down in words, as well as a persuasive proposal for the Board of Education—not to mention *Rachel's Deer Friend*. Celia felt confident that the Goddess of Finished Projects was about to have mercy on her at last.

"It hasn't spread much in the last few hours," Celia remarked.

"Well, even if it doesn't jump the river, I'll be looking at black hills for a long time," Sharon replied.

"The vegetation comes back quickly. Last time I was in Israel I visited a place on the Carmel where there had been a forest fire. Our guide pointed out that the burned things acted as fertilizer, and there were more flowers than ever that spring."

"Celia." Sharon sounded rather anxious or annoyed.

"I'm sorry. Yes?" said Celia. I'm an old mother retelling her false comfort too many times, she thought.

"It seems that I'm pregnant." Her daughter drove swiftly around a narrow bend. They were out of reach of the fire now. The leaves were glittering madly in the August sun, an improbable paradise flashing by.

"But that's—" said Celia. "*Keturah* is. You are too?"

"It's Jacob's."

"Yes, I would have guessed." At first Celia felt a sick dropping feeling, as if Sharon were seventeen and unmarried. But then she thought of Jacob, and in spite of everything she felt reassured. It came to her that he loved Sharon. Celia had seen them together and hadn't wanted to perceive it, but now she thought, well, after all, he's practically Jewish. Her heart warmed toward the embryonic grandchild: so late, so unexpected. She would send it children's books from New York. It would come to visit her and she'd take it to see the dinosaurs at the Museum of Natural History, the mummies at the Metropolitan—it would have the best of both worlds. Perhaps it would be rather remarkable, like its parents. Celia would help shape that originality, doing a better job than she'd done with Sharon. Suddenly her mind returned to the present. "Will you marry?" she asked.

"I don't know. I'm not really sure what to do." Sharon took her eyes from the road for a second and gave Celia a close look. "Even if I do have the baby, I think I might be too old and set in my ways to marry."

"Anyone under fifty seems young to me. Besides, people marry at any age." Celia meant to save her embryonic grandchild and give it a proper family life.

"I'm not really the mother type," her daughter objected.

Celia looked out the window at the forest flashing past like green cubist lace. Looked at one way, each bough was still, separate, but if she shifted her focus, each branch existed as part of a continuous unfolding of color and shape. "When you become a mother," she said, "you start to feel as if you have to be five women at once, and it seems impossible. But then one day you realize you've *become* those five women, and life is *so* much more interesting."

Sharon was silent, accelerating uphill. They passed a place that sold hubcaps of every shape and size. There was an old farmhouse covered in hubcaps, with stacks more in the yard.

"I'd be *very* sorry if you decided—" Celia realized she was being presumptuous. But she couldn't help starting to cry, flooding the green cubes.

"*Celia!* I'm *going* to keep it, I'm just not ready to say I'm keeping it—do you understand?" Sharon sped around another turn. They were going downhill now, fast.

"No," Celia sobbed. Then she realized what Sharon had said. She calmed down and the forest re-focused itself. "I think Jacob loves you."

"But does that mean I should become a prairie farm wife?" Sharon continued. "He can't stay here, you know. Charlotte did in his business; it's a damned mess."

Celia thought. "Well, you could become a prairie lawyer and farm wife. That's not such a bad combination. You could live near Edmonton or Calgary. I met a lovely woman on the plane whose husband is an expert in chickens at—"

"It's too flat out there," objected Sharon. "The roads are perfectly straight, and there's maybe just a little tree now and then. *Grain elevators*. It's not my landscape."

"You're not sure about Jacob," Celia observed.

\* \* \*

SHARON PILED HER AND JACOB'S cartons along the wall in her office, beneath the Indian paddles and masks, emblems of old passions. She sensed a thickening of skin within and without her, an increasing bulbousness of the emotions. Too tired to care whether or not she liked herself as she felt now, drifting apart from every hard idea in the world, she lined up her and Jacob's separate lives and wondered whether and in which direction they'd be setting off. Apparently pregnant women imagined not so much that they would bear a child, but that there would emanate from this thick bulb of feeling a bit of magic, flick of the unseen Hand, a being of cool fire who could heal and meld, attaching one firmly, even passionately, to the world. It was irresistible; she did not decide a thing and yet everything was decided. When this child, this essence, was born, she would have been wandering the earth for almost exactly forty years.

* * *

CELIA GUESSED THAT ZACH knew about the Other Embryo by the way he said "Yes, come over. It's so important," when she called him from the motel in Greenville the following morning. When she arrived, Zach and Tanya both greeted her with emotional hugs.

"You know everything, right?" said Zach. "Keturah drove up here last night and they told us. They said you knew before we did."

Celia nodded. *Oh dear*, she thought, wondering how determined he was to be hurt by that.

"It was Tisha B'Av yesterday." Tanya's voice was heavy with meaning and wonder.

"I know," Celia said.

"They told us right after the break-fast," said Tanya.

*Considerate*, Celia thought. You sit down after no food or water for twenty-five hours on a blistering August day. Then, within minutes of diving into your bagel spread with delicious kosher cream cheese and lox imported from Vancouver, you've tasted illegitimate grandparenthood.

"I had just gotten home from the airport," said Zach. "I had to fly to Vancouver yesterday to do a funeral. Twenty-seven years old, the son of Holocaust survivors. Committed suicide." They were sitting in the Bernsteins' living room, and Zach held a vegetarian hot dog in one hand like a cigar. He ate them straight from the package.

"Terrible." Celia shook her head.

"He'd joined a cult on the island," Zach went on, "and they discouraged him from seeing his family. His parents hadn't seen him at all in about a year. This cult has a very ascetic routine; they get up at five every morning and swim in the ocean. He left a poem that said something about the waves washing his wounds, and then when the rest of the group started swimming back, he turned and swam further and further out. They called to him, but they couldn't bring him back."

The waves at Tel Aviv were so chilly when Celia walked in to drown herself over Yunis. How badly this young man must have felt, the Holocaust heightened in him by meditations, just as her own troubled love and inadequacy—so she thought!—were inflamed by the romance of Palestine. How delicate the young were, no match for their own strongest emotions.

"They dragged the bay and found his body," said Tanya. "Then his family asked every single rabbi in Vancouver and Victoria, but not one of them would give him a Jewish funeral. Finally someone gave them our number."

"I got their call around ten at night, and I said I'd fly out the next morning to do the funeral," Zach continued. "In the next two hours I got six threatening phone calls, saying there would be consequences if I did this funeral."

"Who were the calls from?" asked Celia.

"Rabbis," said Zach. "I did the funeral, and I got home just in time to break the fast. Keturah and Yishai were here." He looked out the window at the round hills covered with evergreens, the orchards and vineyards, brilliant and orderly in the sun. "They said they wanted to talk to us after the break-fast. Itamar and Gabriel went out to skateboard."

"We had no idea what it was about," Tanya added. "We'd just taken our first bites of food and then they hit us with this news." Tanya did not seem to be crying, but she wiped her eyes.

There was no comforting them, Celia realized. It was like stepping into a house of mourning, where people were struggling to affirm the great wisdom behind destruction. "Actually, Sharon is pregnant too."

"What? Sharon? Oh, my." Tanya was still very capable of surprise, as one would be, attributing a great purpose to every event.

"Does she want to marry Jacob?" Zach asked.

"I don't really know. But I hope so."

"There seems to be something very alluring about these people." Tanya was now laughing and crying at once, wiping her eyes again.

"Tanyale." Zach put his hand on her shoulder. They were sitting far apart on the sofa but he could easily reach; his arm reminded Celia of Moses' arm plus the rod, spanning the waters.

"I know it's a difficult situation," Celia said. "But Keturah is really a very nice girl, and she's very intelligent."

Zach and Tanya sighed. They were young but they comprehended everything Celia's own mother would have known, and more. True, Yishai had a job at the hiking store and Keturah waited on tables at the café, but they were going into their senior year of high school. It was as if Celia had married her first love, Yunis—heaven knew she seriously considered it at the time, with the logic of madness.

"Where are they now?" Celia asked.

"They went out somewhere; they have a day off," Zach said vaguely, waving them away with another veggie hotdog. Celia had accepted a cold stuffed grape leaf left over from Shabbat. It tasted of the dry summer hills and rich lake vegetation, and she felt rather sorry to be returning soon to New York.

"They went to play miniature golf at Familyland," said Tanya. "I'm afraid we should have moved east when we had the chance."

"Really, I want nothing but love and peace between us," said Zach. "But if she won't convert I can't accept it. I talked to her for three hours about it. She seems to have a kind of selective hearing."

There was an ominous edge to his voice—Celia saw Tanya looking at him, her large eyes tired in anticipation. "Keturah's a very unique person," Tanya said. "And her individuality is important to her. She actually has a strong identity already."

Zach shook his head and turned to Celia. "What's the fire doing?"

"They think it may jump the river. People living further up in the hills have already lost their homes."

"Tisha B'Av is the destruction of the world as we know it," said Zach, "and we bring that upon ourselves through hatred, which is the negative momentum in human life."

"Yes, but we don't just leave the world in ruins," Tanya pointed out.

Yes, yes, said Celia's heart, she thinking of her floating cherry, seeded fruit, mysterious visitor-of-the-future. If only Sharon were like Keturah, emotionally incapable of getting rid of the embryonic combination of herself and her beloved.

"I'm so hesitant to say *anything*," Tanya told Celia. "Yishai is quite fierce about her, and she's quite fierce about keeping this baby. I think he's leaning toward getting married. He's a very serious, responsible person."

Zach made a sound of irony and objection.

"I think I'm always superstitious about interfering with a betrothal," mused Celia. "There's a strange story about my grandmother in connection with that." She paused, saw her audience was with her, and her voice wound back into czarist Russia. "She was engaged to marry a man whom she loved, but it became apparent that he had tuberculosis. So her parents forced her to break off the engagement, and eventually she married someone else. She never knew what had happened to her first fiancé. But after she'd been married for some years and had a family, her husband also contracted tuberculosis. And she thought—" here Celia always paused, emphasizing the poor woman's guilty conscience, "—that she'd been cursed because of what she'd done to her first fiancée. So she went to the rebbe—they were Lubavitcher Hasidim—and told him that she was afraid her marriage was cursed because of her having broken off the engagement to someone with tuberculosis. And the rebbe, although of course he was a very mystical person, gave her a very modern answer. He said, '*There's no such thing as a curse*,' which I think is extraordinary. He also said, 'If you feel badly about what you did to him, you should try to find him and ask his forgiveness.'"

"Wow." Tanya was leaning forward, listening as if Celia were a rebbetzin, a Bruria, lips forming wisdom. It was always charming to be listened to, even if you knew you weren't really a wise old woman, only old.

"It turned out that her first fiancé lived in a town quite far away, and she traveled there by herself. I think she had to take a train and then go the rest of the way in a horse-drawn wagon. Eventually she found him. He was married, with children, and completely well! He'd been cured of his tuberculosis. She asked his forgiveness for having broken their engagement—it was because of her parents' insistence, after all—and he forgave her. Then she returned home, and her husband died."

"I believe in fate." Tanya's eyes often had this look of seeing into another dimension.

"I do too, but I'm always interfering with it," said Zach. "I think it's my fate to interfere. I just told them at the board meeting that I still don't think we should give the Wakemans honorary membership." He looked at Celia. "Before I *knew*. But I'll say that even now, Jeffrey and almost everyone else are all behind it. They wanted to hold this board meeting on Shabbat, because Sunday is the day they spend with their families. I said I couldn't. So now they want to wait and vote on the Wakemans at the end of the summer, when more of *them* are back from their vacations."

*Them*, thought Celia, noticing the clarity of the division, like fire and water.

"They think I'm a fascist," Zach said. "The Temple was destroyed and this long exile happened, which is really the education of the Jews, all for these people."

"And they *want* to be so loving." Tanya's voice was a tonal counterpoint to her husband's. "They really do."

"They love every god but their own," said Zach.

"It's always like this," Tanya sighed. "It starts like this and within a year we'll be out of a job."

Celia was startled, even schooled as she was in the ways of Jewish communities. It sounded exaggerated: a trial of the Bernstein dybbuk, a blowing of the black shofar. "Well, I wouldn't necessarily—"

"Yes," Tanya insisted. "In every Jewish community everywhere in the world there are certain stock characters. You may not notice them at first, but they always eventually appear. And there are certain ones who spell our doom every time. They step out from behind the curtain and that's it; we know our final exit is coming soon."

Celia understood Zach and Tanya's lamentation: The cruelty of your society is your own earning, mothers eating their children, trees glowing red with fire falling onto the painfully scorched earth, not a drop of sanity left behind for the enemy to capture. But she would fly this child in for the seder, send it to Israel for the summer as she had the others. *I have passed on my tradition*, she said to herself, and the resulting emotion caused her to see, for a moment, the most amazing cascade of Delaunay blue rectangles.

\* \* \*

WHILE THE FIRE RAGED, Sharon and Celia stayed in a motel in Greenville. One evening, they amused themselves by going to the Greenville mall, the entrance to which was a giant brick-and-glass mouth reflecting the distant hills. Sharon wanted to buy some African pancakes because they were the only food she could possibly imagine eating, and Celia needed some padded removable inserts for her shoes, as she'd already worn out one pair here.

"I sometimes enjoy being where there's nothing naturally beautiful to look at," Sharon remarked, as they passed glitzy stores.

"Zach and Tanya were talking about the destruction of the Temple on Tisha B'Av, which was yesterday," Celia told her. "It was really the urge to appropriate beauty, of course."

Sharon laughed. "They're still talking about the Temple. Amazing."

"Ah, it's wonderful to think of. I mean the materials the priestly class had at that time. Imagine living in a house built of cedar and acacia, eating off gold and silver plates, and sleeping in a bed covered with fine silk."

Crossing the food court, where ethnicities were crammed into cubicles and served with mustard-ketchup-mayonnaise, they spotted Keturah and Yishai, sitting at a little table in front of South of the Border. She was smiling and tearing off bits of a tortilla to eat with her fingers.

"They look like two contented rabbits in a hutch," said Celia.

"Hey! How's it going?" Sharon said to them.

"Hi," Keturah said calmly, as if she'd known they were coming. "Good." Some tinny music was playing, creamed flutes and drums. The hexagonal food court slurped up the public, then released it in five streams of purchasing power. Next to Keturah on the table was a cheap white teacup in a saucer, both daubed with green and gold.

"I just bought this cup at the Dollar Store." The girl stroked the cup's rim with her forefinger.

"Fantastic," said Sharon.

"I think it looks homey. I'm imagining I'll have a shelf in my kitchen someday with all different cups and things lined up."

The white handle was stuck on crookedly, Sharon noticed. Yes, if you could give them goblets of olive wood and silver, they'd drink Coke out of them. Keturah would be rosy and distant with pregnancy, wearing a silk gown with little bells at the hem, cherubim grabbing at them as she swung from room to room.

Celia sat down next to Keturah, who offered her a sip of piña colada soda pop. "It's interesting," said Celia.

"It has a rather decadent flavor." Keturah turned to Sharon. "You've heard the news, I imagine?"

"Sure." Sharon smiled, couldn't help it—she really was pleased, apparently. "Mazal tov. I have similar news. I'm pregnant too." They both looked at her while Celia, seeming confused, picked up Keturah's piña colada soda and swallowed some as if it were her own.

"Oh, really?" said Yishai. "How interesting. Mazal tov to you too."

He was so cool he was dour, but Keturah had leapt up and was now reaching across the tortillas to hug Sharon. Her hand rested, heavily, for a moment on Sharon's shoulder. Then she sat down again, shook her head, and wiped some golden powder from the corner of her eye, which was circled with green and gold, like a Disney forest pond. "I'm over—overly wised."

"Overwhelmed, I think you mean, dear," corrected Celia.

"Yes, thank you. It's been that sort of day, I suppose. I cried yesterday too because I couldn't decide what to do about the fast. On the one hand, the Jews were exiled from Israel and the Temple was turned into a stone pile. On the other hand, unborn babies get hungry, Yishai says."

"I think they do," he said. "I also think on any fast day a pregnant woman might be able to eat something about the size of an egg. Or maybe it's only an olive. But I didn't exactly want to ask my dad."

Sharon and Keturah first snickered, then shook with giggles as if they were sitting next to each other in sex education class.

"I simply cannot believe this," said Keturah. "Are you going to marry my dad?"

"I don't know," Sharon murmured. With her body she would take in the whole world, mothering Keturah the mother-to-be, and mothering—

"There's an interesting story about an architect friend of mine in connection with the Great Temple," said Celia quickly. "You remember Sandor Stern," she said to Sharon, who of course didn't. "Some wealthy American retirees living in Jerusalem commissioned Sandor to design the Third Temple. He envisioned it as an enormous Plexiglas structure that would enclose and protect the Western Wall, the Dome of the Rock, the El-Aqsa Mosque, everything. He designed all sorts of transparent walkways and platforms, winding staircases where people could stop and look out, or meet and talk to each other. There would be Muslims, Christians, and Jews together in this big transparent house. As you walked from one sacred site to another, you'd always be able to stop and see the others from a fresh vantage point, and you would also see your own sacred place from new angles."

Sharon shook her head. "The Temple Mount as a mall."

"Sandor thought of it as freeing the essences of these places, erasing the whole linear concept of history." Probably only Sharon could hear the tremor of nervousness in Celia's voice. In general, she handled illegitimate pregnancies and other socially awkward events as if they were burning objects for which she had instant asbestos gloves. "Of course they discovered in the end that building the Third Temple is illegal according to Israeli law."

"*Why?*" Keturah demanded, instantly indignant.

"Well, they're supposed to maintain the religious status quo," Celia went on explaining, her voice still quavering a bit.

"Look, are *you* going to marry?" Sharon asked them.

"We don't know yet," said Keturah rather irritably. "We're like children. We want one thing one day and another thing the next."

Celia, of course, rushed to fill the awkward silence. "Sandor was so disappointed." She paused for a moment while the tinny mall music beat around them and laden shoppers rolled past the table. "He said if he could have proceeded it would have been the final slaying of the Angel of Death, the re-emergence of the Garden of Eden."

# XIII

Sharon drove more carefully now, guiding the red truck carrying herself, Celia, and her unborn child around the curves slowly, slowly. Of course, not far along the road to Greenville she had to pee, so she pulled off to the side of the highway. It was very early on a beautiful summer morning, and the river, lower than in spring, moved slowly beneath the overhanging trees. "Sorry, but I can't make it to the rest area," she told Celia.

"That's fine, dear. I think I'll go too." Celia sounded easy, and she slid down from her side of the truck, landing with both feet on the ground before Sharon could even think about getting out the little step she'd built. Celia was leaving today. She was dressed in the New Yorkish spring suit she'd worn when she first arrived in Calgary, along with the blouse with the droopy tie and a round straw hat with a white feather. They'd decided that she would return home through Seattle, since there was no way Sharon was driving over the Rockies to Calgary again in what Celia jokingly called her condition. First Celia would have to catch, in Greenville, a twelve-seater plane that flew very low over the Cascade Mountains to Seattle. In keeping with the more adventurous personality she seemed to have developed out here, Celia said cheerily that this was no obstacle. Sharon herself had taken that flight more than once and thought it the most thrilling ride in the world, as the plane route wove through narrow passes around the glaciated peaks.

"It requires a bit of courage, though," she'd warned Celia. "And I'm worried about thunderstorms this time of year."

"If I can survive a blackout in the middle of a storm in the woods all alone, I can survive a little plane ride through the mountains to Seattle," Celia had insisted staunchly.

Each squatted in privacy behind her own large tree. It was quiet, except for the faint sounds of the river and the birds, and the occasional burst of chatter from a chipmunk. The air was clearer now, as the forest fire was contained far to the east and would likely soon be put out. It was a strange relief to have been prepared to lose everything and then suddenly to return to the cabin, all just as she'd left it. "There's nothing like a nice pee in the bush," Sharon remarked. "The earth receives." She could see just the corner of Celia's skirt poking out behind some leaves.

"That's true," Celia replied. "It's one of those experiences a person doesn't want to miss in life."

Sharon laughed, and they both emerged into a small clearing, adjusting their clothing. Though she was accustomed to parting from her mother, she felt terribly sad that Celia was leaving. It was harder to be the one left behind than the one traveling. Whenever Sharon spent time with her mother, she realized how much she missed family and a certain kind of culture, which she'd exchanged for freedom. Inside Sharon was a New York Jew who craved intense conversation, conducted with the arrogance that sometimes hid ignorance but was fun nonetheless. Yet it took only a brief visit to the East to remember how tired she'd become of the assumption that everyone had the highest professional ambitions; how weary of the competitive conversational knocks that chipped off your individuality, little by little.

\* \* \*

THE DRIVE TO GREENVILLE to catch the plane seemed longer than usual, and Celia was filled with a sense that she was failing her daughter. How could she not have prevented Sharon's having a child alone and living alone in the bush—everything alone, alone! "Do you think that you and Jacob will get married?" she asked. She figured since she hadn't asked that question for a while she might as well ask again, just to see if anything had changed.

"I like him very much," Sharon said cautiously. She shifted into a higher gear as they sped along a straight patch. "I love him in a way, even though we're very different. But I was already on a certain trajectory when I met him. I'm happy with my life as it is."

"I thought maybe you just needed some time alone after Thunder," Celia remarked.

"No, I think I chose Thunder because I wanted to be alone—he was so wrapped up in his own world, very different from mine. And so is Jacob. Look, if I wanted to, I could even find a nice Jewish lawyer in Greenville and settle down; the place is crawling with them. But I've realized in the last little while that I *like* being independent. I feel guilty about Jacob and the kid, that's all. Maybe I've just stayed single too long, but I keep wondering exactly *why* people get married. You'd think after all this time human beings would've found some better way to relate to each other."

How natural that sounded, here in Sharon's environment. The truck was climbing into the higher hills now, with small stunted trees and a wider vista. Celia rolled down her window and breathed the clear air with satisfaction. She'd forgotten how wonderful it was to be a freethinker, which she believed she herself had been prior to her marriage to Raymond, who'd had very definite ideas about things. He had excellent ideas, really, but they were not her own and yet she was swept along in them for forty years. Just what *was* marriage, anyhow?

"I'm reminded of a conversation I had with your father before we were married," she said. "I believed that friendship was just as important as marriage, and I also thought that men and women could be friends without a romantic involvement. That was of very high value to me."

Sharon smiled. "You kept all your men friends, didn't you? Like Sol and Ephraim."

"Oh, yes. I insisted on what was important to me, and Raymond understood."

"That's great. But you *did* marry him."

"Well, yes, of course. I wonder if I would now, though." Celia remembered her father's opposition, not to Raymond but to their marrying before she'd finished her PhD. He turned out to be both right and wrong: She did finish her degree eventually, but it did take a decade longer, with the three children. "I think I would still have married him now," she concluded, answering her own question, "though it might be a different *kind* of marriage. You know dear, I've had a marvelous time out here. I admire the environment you've created for yourself. It's not my sort of life, but I can understand why you're here." Sharon glanced at her and smiled, obviously pleased and surprised.

\* \* \*

IN THE AIRPORT, after Celia checked her luggage, they hugged each other and both shed a few tears. But almost immediately, Celia met another passenger who was flying to Seattle, a curator who turned out to have worked with her friend David's last exhibit. It seemed to Sharon that the New York world was already reaching out to pull Celia back into itself, to hold her close as a valued member while Sharon remained on the outside, watching but unable to participate. The tiny plane was perched out on the runway, and the passengers exited the building and walked over to it. Sharon stood on the tarmac, watching Celia climb the narrow metal steps. At the top, Celia turned in the doorway and blew Sharon a kiss. Then she entered the plane and was gone.

THE FARMERS HAD ASKED Jacob to judge the hogs at the Fall Fair; since he didn't raise hogs himself he was assumed to be objective. While he was busy with that, Keturah and Sharon strolled together through the fairgrounds. The forest fire was reported to be completely out after the last rain, but the melancholy burned mountains rose above the big field.

"Next summer it'll be full of fireweed," Keturah said, "but of course we won't be here to see it." They walked through the open barn with the domestic displays. Both of them wore loose men's shirts, and Keturah said you couldn't tell either of them was pregnant unless you looked carefully around their eyes. Keturah maintained that pregnancy in both humans and animals was easily detectable around the eyes; Sharon, perhaps because she lacked farm experience, couldn't see it. Apple pies with latticed crusts and jars of golden honeycombs caught her eye: She was now both herself and a sugar-loving child.

"I like that one." Keturah pointed to a carved wooden cradle with a design of apples and pears stenciled across its hood. She rocked it with her fingertip, and Sharon noticed that the finger trembled. Keturah wore her hair swept into a high swinging ponytail tied with a blue ribbon—first prize for young matron-to-be—and she acted happy.

"Did Dad tell you all about the new farm?" she asked Sharon.

"Yes, I heard. Two hundred acres and a double-wide." Jacob and Keturah had flown to Edmonton last week and found a farm that was perfect for sheep and goats, with enough acreage for them to make their own hay, and with a good auction nearby. Last night Jacob told Sharon that he couldn't wait any longer for her to decide whether she'd share a life with him and the child; he was going through with the move to Alberta before he lost any more money. She felt a stubborn resistance to going along that was almost outside her own will to control. As Jacob's wife she'd become like him, another strange fixture in a small town. The women would ask her if she wanted to do needlework for the Farm

Women's League or the Fall Fair, and they would invite her to events at their church. She tried to comfort him by saying that Edmonton wasn't far and they could visit.

"You're not coming with us?" Keturah was looking at her, pregnant eye-to-eye.

Sharon shook her head. "I can't right now, I—"

"You don't have to explain. Dad says we all go where we have to go, and we may never know why."

"I might come, eventually." They were standing in front of the quilting display. A wheel of triangles turned before her eyes, then turned back: optical illusions stitched perfectly into place. Keturah reached over and hugged her with arms that felt soft and young.

"I suppose not everyone hates us here," Keturah conceded. "We won first prize for Abner."

"Mazal tov!" said Sharon. Abner was their ram. She'd watched Keturah getting him ready for the fair, cleaning mud out of the ripples in his long curved horns, combing bits of grass and leaves out of his wool. Abner had stood, handsome and polished in the fall sunlight, radiating testosterone. For just one moment, the male beauty of the ram made Sharon want to lay her own life on the circular altar of a close farm family.

They wandered out of the wide barn and past the riding ring, where the horse-riding competition for twelve to fourteen-year-olds was underway. Each child gripped the horse with his or her knees and made the same wide arc, hooves raising the dust; it seemed that each child might fall but none did. Would Sharon's child too, ride and raise the dust? She could not imagine it was actually human, with features that could be set into its own particular expression of concentration, galloping at a dramatic angle. They watched for a while and then walked on. Sharon found herself staring at a furry teat, fascinated, as a man's brown fingers stroked out a thin stream of milk.

"Want to try?" he asked. "This a friend of yours, Keturah?"

"Hello Bill. Yes, this is Sharon." Keturah giggled. "Do you want to try? Go ahead!"

They both looked at Sharon, laughing. Bill was giving out blue ribbons that said *I milked a goat at the fair.* Would she or wouldn't she milk? She felt she wouldn't be the same afterwards, that it was a loss of virginity.

She did it, grasping the tough skin of the teat and stroking. "You won't hurt her," said Bill. It somehow gave Sharon courage, seeing her hand producing the thin-looking milk that splashed a bit out of the pail and onto her jeans. Her hand could do it just like Bill's, Keturah's, Jacob's; the white stream seemed to make a purer thing of her existence.

"What's the matter?" Bill was saying.

"Nothing, it's fine. Just splashed a bit," said Sharon dreamily.

"No, I'm talking to—"

"Just a stomach-ache," said Keturah in a squeezed voice. She'd sat down, Sharon saw, on the low fence nearby, her face pale as Jacob's old white shirt that hid her belly. Sharon let go of the hairy teat and went over to her. "Maybe we'll take a walk, it'll feel better," Keturah said, but all her words, again, sounded squeezed, stroked from her throat in a thin stream.

"Wait, here you go." Bill pinned a blue ribbon to Sharon's collar. "Feel good," he told them.

As they walked away, Keturah was still pale. "I had the strangest pain."

They both went to the washroom, and after they came out and were standing by the sinks, Keturah said, "There was a little drop of blood." She seemed rather panicked.

"Just come outside and we'll lie down," said Sharon.

"I really want this baby. Do you think I might be going to lose it?"

"I don't think so. I read that sometimes there's a little bleeding. Probably you should see the doctor—she's out here tomorrow morning." Sharon led Keturah over to the edge of the fairgrounds, which were bordered by a farm. Between the two there seemed to be an abandoned apple orchard with old, gnarled trees. The orchard had apparently reached the point where it no longer produced much, but it was allowed to stand, and the birds came and pecked at the few small apples. Though planted by human hands, the trees appeared inseparable from their surroundings. "This reminds me of Connecticut," said Sharon.

"It reminds me of apple trees around here," Keturah asserted. She seemed in a rather strange state. Pointing to a spot on her belly, she asked, "Is this where the baby is?"

"Maybe. Do you want to lie down and rest for a few minutes?" Both Sharon and Keturah lay in the long dry grass beneath a large apple tree. The ground was hard, rising up under Sharon's back in just the spots that seemed to need the reverse pressure. It was comfortable to yield, exchanging one's upright ranging for something infinite, bringing down favor from between the branches of the old apple tree. Lie down and be bound, Sharon thought dreamily. Her limbs felt heavy and hot; she was burning and she didn't care.

Keturah said, "I don't know what will happen with Yishai, but I'm going to give the baby Yishai as its last name. Maybe David, or Adrian Yishai—I think it's a boy."

"Really?" Sharon lifted herself on her elbow to look at Keturah, who lay still with her eyes closed, the shadows of apple branches across her face and arms.

"He told me this morning on the phone that he's not ready to get married. He's been talking to his parents." She held her hands over the spot on her belly that she'd pointed to earlier. "They offered us money, but I don't want to take it."

ON ROSH HASHANAH Sharon went alone to hear the shofar at the services in Greenville, with the paradoxical child who was right there inside her yet far from the world. Neither Jacob nor Keturah would come with her.

Sharon knew that the community was rife with rumor, but just that fact was reassuring. She liked waking up and seeing the clear autumn hills, the larches turning yellow, and knowing that somewhere not far off were a bunch of Jews and their Day of Blowing—it made her feel more wonderfully isolated. It was a little like the red chemical marks on the opposite rock face, left from the firefighting: a delicious imperfection that made her feel she knew her own landscape and possessed it.

She arrived just in time. Zach was up on the bimah wearing a long white robe, his dark eyes looking like he was about to blow the black shofar of excommunication. Sharon had forgotten it might actually be scary to hear *him* blow the shofar. There in front were his family members, with the errant and now unengaged Yishai. Well, she didn't really expect to be able to dive into the Jews like Long Island Sound on a hot day, that rather acrid, briny, East-Coast sea. No, she wanted merely to hear the sound that was made by none of them, really, the cry from the Jewish gut, and then she'd get out before they could ask her any Eastern-sounding questions. But first she listened to it all, the screeching and bellowing and trumpeting, Dr. Moose Antlers holding the siddur and calling out "*Tekiah!*" Yet even after the big tekiah she was still there, swimming out further now like a big-bellied mother fish cruising the holiday waters with her eggs. It was pleasant to think of death and destruction on a brilliant fall day.

. . . how many will pass from the earth and how many will be created . . .

. . . who by water and who by fire . . . who by stoning . . . who will rest and who will wander, who will live in harmony and who will be harried . . . who will be impoverished and who will be enriched . . .

She thought of Celia, sitting in her father's shul in Flatbush where she went once a year on the High Holidays. Then she thought of Charlotte, who couldn't come to the Fall Fair to judge the jams as usual because last week she'd fallen from a ladder while painting the trim around her garage. She thought of Thunder, but he was only a far-away rumble; she was too tired not to be at peace. Just outside this Katie-Applebaum- and-Jeffrey-Familyland lurked the demons, blasted into the corners by Zach's Tekiah. Yet the lion and the deer still struggled in a recess of her heart. Eventually they'd stand together in peace under the Tree of the Knowledge of Good and Evil. Would she go to Alberta eventually, or wouldn't she? I am not the wife type, she explained to God.

"'On Rosh Hashanah will be inscribed and on Yom Kippur will be sealed...'" the congregation sang in Hebrew. Nibbling sustenance, Sharon lurked unobtrusively at the bottom of this Jewish sea, right up until the moment the service was over and they served sweet wine and *challot* spun into golden snails, the pieces dipped in honey. She stayed on, always hungry these days, filling a plate with pieces of fish and sweet noodle kugel, eating her symbolic fate: Might she be as the fish-head and not the tail. No one could tell she was pregnant in her loose India-print dress. Yishai stayed very far away from her. Tanya kissed her and wished her a *shana tova*, as did Zach, but they didn't linger, either. She guessed they had no more taste for rumor and scandal than she had, the spread not wanting to be the spreader. Having accomplished Yishai's sensible disengagement from a pregnant farm girl who refused to convert, they wished to move on to next week's portion, a fresh set of interpretations. Surely they knew that Jacob had bought a new farm in Alberta and that the Wakemans were moving away, but she doubted they'd have mentioned either their personal anguish or its upcoming relief to anyone else in the community. As to herself, perhaps Celia had given them some details, though Sharon could hardly supply her mother with information she couldn't even locate in her own heart.

She was eating a forkful of stuff that tasted very Jewish, sugary and pickled at the same time, the symbolic foods with their opposed tastes merging like Sonia Delaunay's artistic theory of "simultaneity," as Celia might say. Sharon missed her mother, who would come back to be rewarded with her new grandchild in the spring. The family back east were eating the same plateful of harmonious opposites, hoping for new inscriptions in the Book of Life.

Bertha made her way through the crowd toward Sharon. "I think we'll be able to call a meeting about the Wakemans sometime this month, maybe even the week between Rosh Hashanah and Yom Kippur. But didn't either of them come with you today?"

"Uh, no. It's hard, with the animals. I think they have some sick sheep." This was partially true.

"I see." Bertha had a habit of darting out her small pointed tongue and touching the top of her upper lip before she spoke. "You know, there's a very good chance that your friends can become members of this community. Jeffrey Meisler is one hundred percent in favor of it, and so are the Gleucks and lots of other people—I've heard Benny say he is, and Katie Applebaum."

"Well, but I think actually Rabbi Bernstein is opposed to it." Sharon was momentarily caught up in the idea as theory, an argument interesting in its logic. "So I'm not sure that in the end his view wouldn't sway the others."

"No, no, that's not exactly—"Just then, Gillian, the other coffee-and-cake lady, appeared at Sharon's elbow, and Bertha said, "I'm trying to explain to Sharon that her friends the Wakemans have a very good chance of winning their vote for honorary membership."

"That's very true," Gillian agreed. The three of them had been standing near the dessert table, and now they moved off a little distance. "You see," Gillian confided, "more than half this community might not want them. I mean, ordinarily they might not stand up to be counted on this—no offense intended. But right now, these same people won't vote with Rabbi Bernstein on *anything*. And they'd love to vote against him."

"Why is that?" Sharon asked.

Gillian had to think about it for a while before answering, as if it were either a conundrum or too obvious for words. "Well, he's just always not on *their* side. You know, there's been a lot of controversy about when to use this building, as you've probably heard. The floor polishing alone is a sizeable expense, and Rabbi Bernstein and his wife—I'm not saying they're not good, well-meaning people—but they think we ought to be open here all the time for classes and discussion groups. They never even think of the number of extra shoes going over these tiles, and for events no one's paying for! And of course there are various other problems. He was giving Hebrew homework to our children in Sunday school that the parents couldn't even *understand*—well, it's all politics, anyway. But just so you know, I think your friends don't have to worry. People would love to vote them in as honorary members."

"Also," Bertha added, "the Bernsteins are here on a five-year contract that ends next spring, and the way things are going—"

"I see," said Sharon. "But the fact is, the Wakemans are moving to Alberta. They've bought a farm north of Edmonton, and they're selling out of the Boundary Valley."

"Oh my," said Bertha.

"We didn't know," said Gillian. "Of course, there are plenty of others who want honorary membership. There are some Christians who know Hebrew, from up north somewhere. They've driven two hundred miles down here to see a Shabbat service, several times. Fundamentalists. It's a big problem for this community to figure out where to draw the line."

Gillian looked rather gleeful about that. Sharon had seen those northern people; they'd watched with shocked, attentive eyes while the candles were being lit and the prayer sung, as if they'd chanced upon an ecstatic primitive ritual in a cave.

"Don't say anything about the Bernsteins' contract," warned Bertha. "You never know who you're talking to around here. Everyone's trustworthy, of course, but some people are more trustworthy than others."

Bertha and Gillian excused themselves, sliding away on the waxed floor to open more cream and fill the honey bowls.

Then Zach was there, standing next to Sharon at the herring with wine and onions, a black-eyed angel in white robes spearing a piece of fish with a toothpick, then another and another. He swallowed herring as if he were famished from the long trek down from the heavenly sphere where he'd been chorusing in judgment. "*So shall you cause to pass, count, calculate, and consider the soul of all the living,*" she thought, watching him eat two more bits of herring. He smiled at her mercifully, his head actually crownless but far up, among leaves.

"Hi," she said, spearing herring herself.

"This time of year is so crucial," he replied softly. "It's all about the scales, you know, tipping one way or the other. The fate of humanity depends on whether one side goes up or down, or finds equilibrium."

"It's hard to be balanced," she agreed. "You balance yourself only to find you've unbalanced someone else in the process."

"Complete equilibrium is something only the *mashiach*—the messiah—can bring. But for that reason, every little movement up or down is important. We're always moving toward that still, perfect place, with every judgment."

Ah, poor Zach: Rosh Hashanah came on the seventh sign of the Zodiac, seventh month of the Hebrew calendar; today was even, as it happened, the seventh day of the month of September. How he stood there in his white robe hoping for luck! He longed for a spiritual line from the upper divine emanations, drawn taut between them and himself here in this world. He didn't know yet that these Jews were going to give him the boot.

On that same Rosh Hashanah, Sharon and Jacob stood together beside the creek that ran through her land. Rain had fallen lately in the form of summer thunderstorms, and the water hit the smooth stones in a loud rush of crisscrossing foam. There was a soothing violence in the sound that drew into a whole the river, mountains, sky, and the two of them, reaching outward to gather every place they'd ever been and everyone they knew, all part of this precise pattern submerged in sound. It was a hopeful noise that made Sharon feel release was imminent.

She was in the middle of trying to explain things to him. "I'm not used to being taken care of," she said loudly.

"It's different when you have a child to care for yourself."

"Like the food chain, eh?"

He laughed. "Sort of. But that's what life is like—your connections spread outward until you're—pretty well connected."

"Connected," she repeated, trying out the word. "Look, I can fly; there are planes from Greenville to Edmonton all the time. We'll see what happens. I don't know who I'll be five months from now."

He shook his head. "You sure don't, in my opinion."

They stared at the flowing water, splitting and rippling out around the rocks, then rushing together. In her belly the fetus fluttered and trembled in its own water, and her heart fluttered in response.

Jacob held a bag full of bread crumbs from the big spiral challah Keturah had baked for the holiday, and Sharon read the prayer from her *siddur* that would help them release their sins. "'... *You do not maintain anger forever* ...'" she read, holding the handful of crumbs Jacob had given her. "'*None shall hurt or destroy in all My holy mountain, for the love of the Lord shall fill the earth as the waters fill the sea.*'"

But the rushing water seemed also to warn of the potential for flood and destruction. Together they threw the bread crumbs into the stream and watched them bounce and tumble away, appeasing the ancient river demons. They emptied the bag, and then they each brushed their hands together until they were clean.

"*Tashlich* always seems to be over so quickly," Sharon remarked.

# XIV

## NEW YORK

On *Kol Nidre* night, Celia dreamed again of the Indian holy place with the petroglyphs, the site across the lake to which she and Sharon had canoed. This was also where Bernard seemed to be looking for her that awful night of the storm on Shavuot, when she'd seen something like a vision of him. Yet in her dream Kol Nidre night she saw not Bernard but someone more shadowy whose features she could not discern. He looked the way one might imagine an emanation of divine light in the form of an angel. His body was angular, like a human figure from one of the stone carvings come to life, his hands describing eternity in spiraling gestures. He was building a fire, first making a cone of small twigs as she'd seen Sharon do on one of their lunch trips. The cone of twigs began to flame and the mysterious stranger added larger sticks of wood, weaving them into a flaming lattice.

She reached over to warm her hands at the fire—in the dream her hands were damp and cold—but before she could feel the warmth she woke up in her bedroom at Central Park West. It was a strangely vivid dream, probably the result of skipping her usual bedtime snack of crackers with jam and cottage cheese, after standing for so long in the synagogue last night for the official breaking of all vows. There she'd felt a brief sense of freedom in her still-beating heart: gratitude for having returned to her own spot in the world, her soul hovering once again over Manhattan.

Her eyes rested briefly on an amulet hanging near her bed, a *hamsa* she'd brought back from Israel years ago. It was a brass hand with little brass fish hanging from each of the fingers, decorated with designs of soldered copper wire. At a certain age, the children and grandchildren always wanted to play with that hand, so she'd take it down from its nail, warning them to be careful with the good-luck fish. She imagined she'd return to the woods when Sharon gave birth, and she tried to sculpt this news—which Sharon had asked her not to reveal yet—into a group of prettily dangling phrases that warded off the evil eye.

Celia didn't exactly fast on Yom Kippur, but she did eat less than usual, and by *Neilah* she felt rather faint, having eaten only a small tuna sandwich while alone in her apartment during the break in services. She stood in front of her seat in the second row that had the plaque bearing her mother's name, beneath the glow of the eternal light dedicated to her father. Although he had refused to be synagogue president on the grounds of his agnosticism, he did allow them to dedicate the light to him.

Celia, like her father before her, still hadn't arrived at firm beliefs. The door to the ark was open, the Torah scrolls arrayed in white satin like a closet full of miniature brides. Sharon said she was not going to marry Jacob, at least not right away; but of course Sharon was Sharon and it would have embarrassed her to be a white-clad maiden dancing in the fields on Yom Kippur afternoon, an object of potential desire. Yet you never knew what would happen in life; the earthly realms were indeed governed by mysterious laws, and the Book of Life was an unfolding poem, an oblique Modernist work.

The seat next to Celia's with her father's name on the plaque, reserved for her brother Yale, was empty, as Yale couldn't breathe in a synagogue and couldn't talk to God with so many people shuffling, sniffing, scratching, and glancing. Celia didn't really pay attention to the words of the service; she just let the general Yom Kippur feeling wash over her like a refreshing mist—all except for "We are your flock and You are our Shepherd," her favorite song which she looked forward to each year. "We are your vineyard and You are our Watchman," she had sung hopefully. That was better than the recitation of the forbidden sexual practices from Leviticus 18, which would have embarrassed her had it been read in English. She looked now through the white Gates of Compassion and thought of Sharon and Jacob with a wish for completion, wholeness—yes, happiness. Of course the gates were always open, but one ought to get up and walk through while one's legs could still carry one lightly, gladly. "We are your clay and you are our Potter," the song went. Celia walked through the doorway herself, visiting them in a nice weathered farmhouse, the kitchen filled with pottery dishes. Celia and the little grandchild sat at a round table covered with a checked cloth. Sharon carried in the clay platter Celia would give her as a wedding present, filled with delicious goat-meat shish kabob which Jacob had barbecued outdoors on skewers, with alternating slices of tomato and green pepper, singed in the fire. The Torah itself was written in black fire on white fire, the sages said.

 The final blast of the shofar came like a universal breath of relief. She wished a *shana tova* to a good number of people she knew and then, after a wonderful few bites of challah with honey, floated out onto the street and into a taxi home for the break-fast. She was having just a few people up to her apartment. Estelle and Yedidja would come; he was nearly the only person she knew who really fasted twenty-five hours without food or water. He was a charming, serious person, his Sephardic boyhood so alive in him still. She had almond milk and herring in cream sauce for them, and all she had to do was put it out, as Sophia had arranged the table before she left yesterday.

Arriving home, she saw that the elevator man wasn't at his post, so she waited downstairs in front of the big mirror framed with bronze vines and leaves, near the podium where they kept the book listing expected guests. She felt hungry but light-hearted, and the strip of thick red carpet that crossed the black-and-white tiled lobby of her building seemed to rise and fall slightly, as if preparing to give her a ride. An older man was let in by the doorman and walked over to wait beside her for the elevator. The two of them were reflected together in the mirror: an old man and an old woman, waiting. He looked older than she but somehow distinguished, his white hair combed back from his forehead, his face angular. She'd seen him somewhere before—on the elevator, no doubt.

"I'm quite accustomed to thinking in terms of ages lasting millions of years," he remarked, "but our elevator man seems to want to expand even *my* mental concept of an age."

Celia smiled. He held himself quietly, hands folded in a gentlemanly way, and his remark was nicely cadenced. "Yes, he wants to be certain we'll appreciate our ride. I wish he'd hurry; I'm waiting to break a fast."

"Of course," said the gentleman. "I don't fast on Yom Kippur myself, but I do meditate on the mind-boggling age of our earth, even our most recent rocks, and on the fact that even the oldest human designs etched on a rock ten thousand years ago are like the scrawl my grandnephew made on the wall—an up-to-the-minute newspaper for our planet."

The red lobby carpet seemed to ripple happily up and down a few times with Celia on it. "I've the feeling we've met before. I'm Celia Rosenbloom."

"Stanley Wallerstein." He bowed his head to her slightly—all his gestures seemed just right.

"You seem very interested in the ages of things. And in carved designs." She looked at his hands, which were spotted and gnarled with age, and noted the way he held his fingers in loose spirals at his sides, reminding her of the man in her dream the previous night.

"I'm a prehistorian, actually," he told her. "My specialty is Alaskan petroglyphs. I'm retired from Columbia, but I'm still working on a book about identification methods. We can even analyze prehistoric DNA now, and that changes everything."

The elevator man had finally arrived. Stanley stood aside and waited for Celia to go in first. "I saw the most wonderful peacock petroglyph while I was visiting my daughter in British Columbia," she said. "I'd love to tell you about it."

He looked excited. "Was it a lakeside site, by any chance?" When she said yes, he said it was quite rare and that he was certain he'd read about it in a journal once—a rather remote and inaccessible site.

Celia felt that the bird had landed between the two of them and fanned out its stone feathers into luxuriant blue-green. "I'm having a break-fast for a few friends," she said as the elevator man swung back the metal gate and pushed open the wooden door to let her out. "I'd be very happy if you could join us."

Stanley hesitated, his fingers a polite spiral in the air. "Well, as I said, I'm not—I don't exactly fast on Yom Kippur. I wouldn't want to join you under false pretenses."

He and Celia both laughed. "You're very welcome to come," she assured him. "I don't think any of us really fasts completely except my friend Yedidja—and to my way of thinking the break-fast is just as important a part of the holiday as Kol Nidre." By now he had stepped out of the elevator with her and she was unlocking the three locks on her apartment door. They laughed again as the door swung open, and she walked across the threshold with a new and admirable admirer.

He helped her to arrange Sophia's lovely platters of fish, challah, and fruit salad on the dining-room table, carrying plates and glasses from the pantry as if they were the rare finds he handled with delicacy and knowledge. The prehistoric meal, she thought, sensing the beginning of a new epoch for the first time since Bernard died. This fish we will have eaten together ten thousand years hence, my dear.

It was still a bit early for her guests to arrive, so they sat side by side on the mahogany chairs with red velvet cushions, spearing herring in cream sauce on silver fish forks, hungry for the future. The whole neighborhood seemed quieter than usual, and up here in the apartment she noticed the spaces between their words. She told him how she'd gone to British Columbia to visit her daughter, with a picture of Sonia Delaunay and piles of papers, and how the woods first destroyed all her thoughts and then made order of them. He seemed to understand; he had spent six months on a remote island in Alaska once, studying petroglyphs on a foundation grant.

"But I didn't like it," said Stanley. "I had all this time to investigate the sites. My first wife, who was my assistant, and I were alone in this beautifully-appointed cabin with all of our equipment. It was so *quiet*. I felt that I should be grateful—we discovered some new sites and it was all very exciting. But the solitude frightened me, all that freedom to come to my own conclusions. I think perhaps it was too early in life to have been given such a gift."

"My daughter's life frightened me, too. Maybe it still does. But I also find it inspiring. After all, Sonia was a complete mess before I went out and confronted her there all alone."

She and Stanley laughed. "Oh yes," he said, "I can believe that."

"I've discovered, also, that you have to complete the process of giving birth. I've given Sharon to the world, and she's found her place under the big trees. And I'm still at the other end of a delicate line." As she tried to describe this she sensed a turning, a big Delaunay Spanish-market tunnel of marvelous violet and pink, undulating over a distant background of red fire: fate brightening, perhaps.

"Yes." Stanley looked at her more urgently. "My daughter is single and lives in Brooklyn, and my son has been living with the same woman for ten years in Kyoto." He'd already told her that his second wife had died several years ago.

"Oh, my. Meanwhile we try to send ourselves out into life one more time, and then another."

"Yes. We're single, and our children are so singular," said Stanley. "They never mind about anything besides their own uniqueness. I don't even have any grandchildren yet."

"Well *I* am about to have my first illegitimate grandchild. It's a secret."

"Ah. I envy you. Really, I do."

They each laughed a little uncertainly, and then they were both roaring. Celia felt the warm cacophony of colors circling in her breast, heating her. How different she was from Sharon in her desire to relate, to complicate. "Such mirth. And on Yom Kippur."

"'Present mirth,'" quoted Stanley slowly, "'Hath present laughter. What's to come is still unsure—'"

He was looking at her seriously, expectantly; he had deep hazel eyes, investigative and changeable. The quotation reminded her of sitting together with Raymond on a blanket, eating cold chicken at Shakespeare in the Park. Was it really possible to love again, and then again? It seemed at this moment impossible that it shouldn't be so. One last time, she would dance in her white dress as an unmarried maiden of Israel. She knew what came next in Shakespeare: *In delay there lies no plenty; Then come kiss me . . . Youth's a stuff will not endure—*

## XV

## BOUNDARY VALLEY, B.C. & NEW YORK

On a cold autumn night Sharon lay on her bed in the cabin, her mind wandering down labyrinthine hallways, inward to a white-marble palace. That's how Zach would have it. "Pregnancy is another world, isn't it?" he'd asked. "Come to our sukkah party," he added. "We invited three hundred guests, and it's the only one in Greenville." But she was too tired to stay in town after work. Lying here, she appreciated the company of predictive angels, surrounding intelligences made half of fire and half of water, hard at work on her life. Paint a stone with the circle of completion, they instructed, and put it in your pocket, a stone with mica sparkling. You will go deep into the water—of course you are afraid—and this magic well will save you and your child; you'll become beloved outcasts.

Turning slightly, she picked up Keturah's last letter from the slice of cedar that served as a night-table. That was a gift from Thunder, who, if he could see her swelling inevitable belly, would say, "Wow."

*Dad and I built a sukkah like we always do. Of course it isn't the real thing, just old boards nailed together but we like it and feel proud. We hung up some strings of frozen cranberries as decoration and they stayed frozen! It's so cold that we're mostly in the house and we have the wood stove going all the time. The little lambs and chicks find their way in to get warm. I don't have the heart to put them out, and neither does Dad. So we have a real menagerie in our kitchen. We make hot soup and bring it out to eat in the sukkah. Sometimes Dad builds a fire right outside the door to keep us warm—or to keep warm the part of us that's facing the fire! Of course as soon as it's out we're headed back to our nice warm kitchen with the wood stove, and all the chicks and lambs. We thought of our ancestors wandering in the desert for so long.*

Sharon imagined this semi-virginal mother, curled on the bare wood floor next to the warm stove. Even the wild unicorn with snow-white body and glacial-blue eyes, dashing over the Alberta winter prairie while breathing hot steam from its nostrils, would fall meekly to the ground before Keturah and place its horned head in the lap of her jeans. The hunter's sword could then drive through it, drawing crimson blood. It was only a young unicorn, a baby, stilled now. Sharon breathed deeply, inhaling mythic fear. Putting down Keturah's letter, she picked up a book from her parents' library, one with a soft black cover and uneven cream pages: *Tales of Rabbi Nachman*. She'd brought it back here one summer after a visit to New York.

"What's in that trunk?" the Canadian customs inspector had asked, looking into the back of her pickup. The trunk held cross-stitched linen tablecloths from her parents' dining room wrapped around an eighteenth-century carved ivory fish with a kimono-clad Japanese goddess astride it. There were also a Russian silver kiddush cup set, etched with dark flowers, and *Rabbi Nachman* and some other books filling the corners.

"Just some old religious things my mother gave me," Sharon answered. The inspector smiled and wrote down *Religious objects from Mum*. The goddess on the back of her large fish was too elaborate to look at every day; Sharon kept her in the trunk under her bed in the cabin and pulled out the sculpture only once in a while. But *Rabbi Nachman* stayed in the pile of magazines and legal journals on the cedar table, exuding his stream of pure faith that melted all prairie winters. The rabbi and his holy son were on the rung of lesser light, but the father was unable to ascend further because present-day enlightenment seemed too sloppy and raw. Of course she was afraid to let Jacob's child lead her up past fear and ridicule. Look inside, she told herself; study the way the branch is connected to the tree and *believe in it.*

*The sky is very black and the stars are so bright. The sukkah has room enough for three of course. Even five!*

Sharon saw she must allow herself to be led by the child up the glowing rungs, branch to branch, into her own elemental nature. *I know why I'm here now*, Keturah wrote in her eleventh-grade handwriting. I have always known, Sharon thought, turning over heavily and sliding the letter under the magazines. Something fluttered; she was borne along, riding on the back of a swimmer with little webbed feet, going fast.

\* \* \*

CELIA'S PREHISTORIAN was as tall and straight, as necessary as a column, and she was a cluster of plump grapes twining around him. He said he adored the concept of Sukkot and connected it to the pacifying of the gods before the long winter sleep: joy before death. Stanley even came downstairs to the cage where Celia kept stacks of paintings and books she hadn't room for in the apartment, and he helped Manley the handyman carry the two-by-fours for the sukkah into the service elevator. Down in the cage, Celia also picked up a water-damaged account of the life of the Baal Shem Tov, wondering whether Sharon had ever read anything of this—a deep look into the truths of nature, which will find one, alone under the trees.

"Marvelous. Manhattan goes primitive," Stanley said now, as they stood in Celia's dining room watching Manley drive in the last nails. The two men had taken turns pounding, Stanley's arm working carefully, searching 101 Central Park West for ancient secrets hovering in the next stratum of consciousness. This was originally Raymond's idea: a real sukkah in their dining room, prefabricated for annual sukkah-partying. The crystal chandelier hung down through a space in the framing. Around it they'd drape ferns and evergreen branches from the florist, and then they'd attach the fruit.

"It's lovely and elemental," Celia agreed, carrying in a basket filled with pomegranates, gourds, Indian corn, and grapes. "I order everything from the Korean fruit store on Columbus Avenue, and I always invite the owner and his wife up for lunch after everything's decorated. They like seeing all their apples and grapes and things hanging from the ceiling of the sukkah."

Manley asked whether they'd be hanging the colored eggs the grandchildren used to make, so she brought him a string of red, purple, yellow and green dyed egg shells she kept packed in a box with cotton wool. Stanley tied knots in the twine and climbed up and down the ladder, sweating as he pulled ferns over the roof. Sophia brought in three heating trays from the kitchen, set up the soups, and sliced roast beef. It was always a buffet, where people served themselves the fruits of Celia's harvest. Watching the artfulness with which Stanley hung a bunch of red and orange Indian corn over the doorway, she felt there was much in life that remained full and richly colored. Each year one lived, one fought and slaughtered the primordial serpent-fish: the Leviathan of old age, with its repulsive smell of bodily decay, breath boiling with complaints, and voracious appetite for young grandchildren. But here it was, killed for another year, the monster's iridescent skin stretched over Celia and Stanley's triumphant heads. *They* went on, beautifully groomed and uncomplaining; *they* sat with their children and grandchildren in principled good cheer and ate warmed slices of the recently vital flesh reserved for the Righteous.

"Doc-tor Ro-sen-bloom!" trilled Sophia, coming from the pantry with a silver tray holding cut crystal dishes filled with red and black caviar. Celia's mother's little Russian silver spoons were arranged in smart rows like her grandfather and his friends serving as the czar's soldiers. "I hope it is what you imagined," said Sophia.

"It's lovely. We'll put it in the place of honor." Celia set the heaps of little eggs in the brilliant light from the chandelier. Inside, the sukkah was a bower of food, a grandmotherly paradise. The Korean fruit-store owner and his wife would be up soon. She could hear the doorbell ringing and Sophia answering Vitali, the Russian painter Celia had met through her work at the Board of Education, and his wife Marina, who was thirty years younger than he—oh, and they'd brought the baby! Her front hallway rang with Russian conversation. The sukkah walls were a wooden lattice you could see through, and there was Stanley, approaching behind the dangling gourds. He came around through the open fourth side that served as a doorway and held her shoulders gently for a moment beneath a hanging pomegranate, giving to her wrinkled cheek an immortal, infinite kiss. The happiest part was that she now fell in love in a new way. Like Sharon, she was mistress of her own shack.

A skilled grandmother possessed a special alchemy, knowing how to turn anything—even an illegitimate grandchild and a daughter living in the bush of British Columbia—into material for bragging. As her arriving guests dipped into the rolls, sliced beef and turkey, and cubes of Persian melon, Celia's mind worked, casting golden spells. The trick was to isolate the purest glimmer of a substance a person could envy. Then, once you knew its proportions and properties you could discover its eternal shape and power, and multiply it in magical geometry.

"Darling, I'm so relieved you're back in one piece." Estelle kissed her and shook Stanley's hand. "We've been looking forward so much to meeting you."

Yedidja folded a slice of turkey into a piece of rye bread. "You two met out there, we understand, in British Columbia. You found each other in a cave in the mountains, yes?"

"No, no," Stanley laughed. "You see, I'm a prehistorian, retired from Columbia, and I *studied* British Columbia."

"So did Celia," said Vitali, who was a dear. "I think she learned a lot."

"About life." Marina, his young wife, put her arm around Celia so the soft weight of the baby hanging from her shoulder in a striped sling swung for a moment against Celia's body. "You learned life's mysteries under those tall trees, of course." Marina laughed meaningfully. The baby's eyes were two fringed crescents, shut tight, purple grapes and red peppers swinging above him.

Marc and Maxine arrived, and they both kissed her under the hanging corn in the sukkah doorway. "Safe and sound!" they exclaimed. "All's well that ends well. You're so *resilient*. After a trip like that, to come home with Delaunay almost finished," Marc added, "*and* build a sukkah for thousands. You must be relieved to be back in civilization."

Actually, civilization seemed a bit too highly colored, a bit laughable after the woods, but Celia had decided to keep this observation for herself and for Stanley, who understood. "Sharon was absolutely wonderful," she declared. "She couldn't have been more solicitous of me. Really darling." The bragging was going well; she could see the gold dust of grandmothers' alchemy floating down on her guests' heads. "And apparently *I* am going to be the proud grandmother of a child who will grow up in a log cabin."

At first she thought it was going over about as well as the log cabin itself had, but then she saw they were merely surprised.

"What?" said Marc. "Sharon's expecting?"

"That's fantastic!" said Marina. Estelle and Yedidja still looked blank.

"A child," Celia continued, "who will know how to paddle a canoe and communicate with the deer. They have a very good school system in Canada too. There are many advantages."

"Is there a—father in this picture?" asked Maxine. Everyone stopped eating for a moment and waited for Celia's reply.

"Yes, of course. You can't very well perform this feat without a father," Celia joked. Stanley was pouring out little cups of wine and handing them to her guests, red circulating, one by one.

"Well, I mean—"

"He's a local land owner, and quite prosperous," Celia said. "Of course he's—involved. They're considering marriage, which I gather is the done thing these days. To consider, I mean." But unlike herself as this sounded, something the naked, defiant centaur would say as she galloped along, it seemed strangely natural. This grandchild was Celia's, and she was claiming it as anyone would, with the Leviathan waiting behind the crest of the next wave. Besides, it wasn't Sharon who had misled her—it was these dear friends, gathered here today beneath her peaceful roof of vegetables.

"People *must* consider before marrying!" exclaimed her former student David's girlfriend Patricia, who had moved in with David while Celia was away in British Columbia. "We're not Neanderthals."

"I do object to that a little," said Stanley. "Neanderthal society must have involved no small amount of consideration for one's immediate family."

"You don't seem too displeased about this little surprise," Estelle observed slyly, omniscient goddess to the centaur, scolding and approving at the same time. "Some people will do *anything* to become a grandmother again."

Celia laughed, delighted her alchemical bragging had worked so well.

"Some people will do anything that everyone else is not doing," remarked Maxine.

"Well, Sharon does end up doing what everyone else does," Marc pointed out. "Just on a different schedule."

"That's true," Celia agreed. "It reminds me of Faigie and Dave. Remember them—from Dad's circle in Brooklyn? They were very involved with fund-raising for the Yiddish theater."

"There were so many people," said Marc, shrugging and sounding like Sharon for a moment: the over-socialized child.

"Anyway, he ended up teaching at Pratt—he was a very gifted sculptor—and for a while they lived in our attic in Brooklyn. He filled the place with enormous plaster castings, modern things, and she wrote very good poetry. Both Faigie and Dave were communists, and they didn't believe in marriage. They lived together very happily in a wonderful old farmhouse on Staten Island and raised two children. When their oldest child, the girl, was about to be married, they decided to get married themselves, partly to regularize her status and that of her own children later on. Raymond and I attended the wedding, as the witnesses and the only guests. Afterwards we all went to eat in a restaurant in Little Italy, and then we went to the movies. Faigie and Dave always liked movies about gangsters."

"But this couple at least *lived* together," Marc argued. "Common-law marriage, I suppose you would call it."

"Most of the time they did," Celia admitted.

"But it isn't political ideology that motivates people these days," Estelle pointed out.

"What exactly is the motivation for this?" Yedidja inquired, his bushy white eyebrows jumping up a little with genuine interest. "It's not my impression that Sharon is a communist. Perhaps she doesn't really like this fellow."

"Yes, although obviously she wants the baby," Estelle added.

"She does love him." Celia laughed a bit nervously. "People seem to think about these matters very rationally now. It becomes hard for them to take a leap of faith or give up one thing for another. They're dazzled by life's possibilities, and they want to create their own structures, do things on their own timetables."

"Well, a baby has a pretty fair timetable, as they'll see," Estelle put in. "Feedings, changings, naps."

"No one bothers with any of that anymore," Maxine told her. "They just schlep it around everywhere."

Marina smiled. "A friend of mine schleps hers through the streets of Brooklyn in a little cart attached to her bicycle."

Celia pictured Sharon weaving through traffic, baby in a flimsy go-cart. "I'll kill her if she does that with my grandchild!"

There was a burst of laughter; yes, she'd been right to utter that *my grandchild*, inserted with the sure intuition of the bragging grandmother. The word curled its fetal magic around her guests: mission accomplished. Everyone looked at her expectantly.

"And now," Celia continued, "it's traditional to say a blessing for sitting in the sukkah, albeit there isn't enough room for everyone to sit."

Her brother Yale cleared his throat. "Yes, we are about to thank God for allowing us to reach this season, when we are commanded to build ourselves a hut and hang the salad from the ceiling."

The guests chuckled politely, but Yedidja objected to Yale's levity. "This moment of the harvest was life or death for our ancestors."

Then, together, the two men—one Sephardic and serious and one Ashkenazi and irreverent—recited the necessary Hebrew blessings for the wine and for the holiday.

Celia and Stanley together, as planned, were the first to shake the lulav and etrog. The long palm spear waved over Stanley's head, and the bulbous etrog rested comfortably in his large hand. He shook them as Celia instructed him in the six directions, north, west, east, south, up, and down. He created anew the unity of the world and the worlds to come: earth and heaven, leaf and fruit, man and woman. Of course the twined leaves of palm, willow, and myrtle made a green phallus with veins running through, and this was held side by side with the yellow womb-fruit. Stanley was the branch and she the glorious citron; he was prehistory and she modern art. The guests were silent, listening to the impressive *shwoo-shwoo* of the branches. He then handed them ceremoniously to Celia, his host and centaur. Yes, she was certain of it now! There would be new figures in the great tapestry of her existence, magnificent scenes unrolling while the centaur galloped ahead.

She held the sacred nature-objects, one in each hand, lifting the etrog in her palm as delicately as if it were the unsupported head of a newborn. "It's the fragrance of the etrog that's the best part," she said, closing her eyes, putting the rippled yellow skin next to her nose and sniffing. She breathed a sweet mysterious sharpness that was both refined and utterly strange, elemental as the Land of Israel itself, with its groves of citron falling to the sea, whitewashed houses and herself awakening in the pulse of adolescence. She took another sniff of the etrog, a long deep one, wishing she could just go on taking this same breath forever.

# XVI

## GREENVILLE, BRITISH COLUMBIA

"Strength! Strength! And we will be strengthened!'—that's what it means," said Zach, bending over and rolling the Torah scroll with his son Itamar. He was all litheness, energy, and strength to everyone, Sharon too, as the scroll they'd now finished reading was rolled back to the beginning. *Again* was in the air. *Again* she'd greeted them, receiving smiles and kisses from all: Dr. Moose Antlers to Katie Applebaum.

"You look wonderful. You're glowing!" said Katie, while Dr. Moose glanced at her belly and stroked his upper lip.

"She does, and she is," he agreed finally, giving his professional opinion of the case before him. "You must have eaten an etrog."

Sharon didn't know what he meant.

"It's an old tradition for creating a sweet and pious offspring," he explained. "The Talmud says that 'the woman who eats an etrog during her pregnancy will have fragrant children.'"

"I'll have to get one in Vancouver," she said. "Though I think they're a bit on the expensive side."

"Well, no one said it was easy to raise a Jewish child," he replied. Then they all became still, almost holding their breaths, as Zack read out *In the beginning*, the creation of the first day.

After the Torah was dressed again in its woven girdle, gold-embroidered blue velvet cover, silver crown and breastplate, and jingling silver pomegranates on top of its staves, the congregation began the *hakafot*. Zack led the way, carrying the Torah, walking in seven circles around the sanctuary. He would create a spiritual membrane around this delicate protoplasm so easily washed away: his congregation. Sharon thought how tradition was a habit, an obsession with someone else's experience—or with your own experience when you were someone else. Following Zach were Tanya and the boys and Jeffrey and his two girls, all singing "*Anenu, anenu, b'yom karenu*: Answer us, answer us on the day we call." Then more people joined the parade and they got livelier, singing "Rejoice and Be Happy on Simchat Torah." Zach paused for a moment next to Sharon, who was standing in front of her seat, and looked down at her, his eyes deep pools of pain as he smiled optimistically at the melancholy of several thousand years and his own life. He waited for her to touch the velvet cover of the Torah, his rolled-up blueprint for her life and all lives to come, his milk and honey for her child and oil to anoint its head, and wine for her own soon-to-be-motherly lips. She knew what all this meant to him. The Torah cover was soft and slightly foreign against her fingers; she brought them to her lips.

Tonight, the end of the story, Moses dying on Mount Nevo, became the beginning of a new cycle: the reappearance of Creation, new water and land, new birds and fish. Under the velvet cover of her own belly skin she felt the child pressing with something sharp, a knee or an elbow, making room for itself. She pressed back with her fingers and the little bone was withdrawn. It was both question and answer, on this day of rejoicing, whose seven circles were always the same and yet were always forming a membrane around a different reality.

Zach and his entourage began to dance, doing a little two-step with the Torah, singing their song. Then unexpectedly Zach was waving a long arm as if in farewell. It turned out he was actually signaling to Tanya to open the heavy front door of the community center. Heads turned and eyebrows were raised, but they all got up and followed him outside in a casual exodus, every last present member of the Greenville Jewish Community. The Torah flowed ahead of them out into the town like a river of wine and oil: fragrant holiness ripened under a hot sun. The autumn night air was sharp against their throats, but they kept singing while heading down the block, first passing the Christ Church and then, after a few more *On three things the world depends*, the supermarket. In the parking lot were some old clients of Sharon's who may or may not have recognized her; they were standing next to a battered pickup truck smoking cigarettes and drinking extra-tall cans of beer. She felt that they smiled with some mirth, though she couldn't quite be sure. Singing *On the Torah, prayers, and good deeds*, they walked up towards the Japanese restaurant and the Greenville Racquet Club, following the bulk of the Torah. Its silver breast plate and crown shone in the streetlights, and the little silver bells hanging from its pomegranates tinkled whenever there was a pause in the singing.

In the darkness the Torah looked like a child wrapped up in a thick blanket with shiny trim; it seemed the shape of all beginnings. The night sky was clouded over and there were few stars, as if rain was gathering over the mountains. Some people smiled and clapped a little as they passed, and some just stared. They were passing the Jehovah's Witnesses now, a long new brick complex, and then the Friendly Burger next door, its parking lot crowded with teenagers. The young girls in jeans reminded Sharon of Keturah. Zach two-stepped along; they stared at him and giggled.

"We must be crazy!" said Bertha, who was walking next to Sharon.

"Their first view of us—it's building community relations," said Gillian.

"Why not?" someone asked.

"—here in our little outpost of Yiddishkeit," said someone else.

I'm from the East, too, one of Sharon's clients had said to her recently, and you know, this is really God's country out here. Sharon and the other Jews felt happy but afraid now, and being afraid made them happier as they two-stepped with their Torah down the sidewalk of the town, towards the dark mountains that rose up in the distance ahead. *Answer us*, they sang quietly in Hebrew. *Answer us on the day we call.*

# ABOUT THE AUTHOR

Leora Freedman is a writer of literary fiction and the author of *The Ivory Pomegranate* and *Parachuting*. Her characters attempt to find meaning in Judaism, relate to the State of Israel, and live as Jews while fully engaged in the wider world. She is the recipient of the Best Short Story Award from *The Southern Humanities Review*; won first place in the Robert Downs fiction contest at the University of Arizona, and was awarded grants from the Henfield Foundation and the Toronto Arts Council. Leora is a citizen of the US, Canada, and Israel. At present, she coordinates an English language program at the University of Toronto, where she is a faculty member. She would like to thank the Toronto Arts Council for a Mid-Career Writer's Grant, which provided support during the writing of this novel.

Visit Leora Freedman on the web at www.leora-freedman.com/ and read her blog at www.jewishshortstoriesonline.com/.